THE
BURNING

D1636222

Bob Mason

BY
ROBERT MASON

THE BURNING
By Robert Mason

*To Dorothy, my skilled proof-reader,
best friend and wife of 51 years.*

All maps by Bruce Fischer

Copyright© 2000 Robert Mason
Second Printing 2004
Third Printing 2009
Fourth Printing 2012

American Traveler Press
5738 North Central Avenue
Phoenix, AZ 85012-1316
800-521-9221

THE BURNING

The Ceremony 1
County Kerry, Ireland 3
Famine 13
The Crossing 21
The Big City 25
The East River 35
Redeemer Church 39
Patrick White 43
Jefferson High School 49
Fort Bliss 53
Sullivan's Island 59
Emma 67
Evacuation 71
Fort McHenry 77
Antietam 79
Libby Prison 83
The Encampment 91
Pea Patch Island 95
Wyoming 99
Martha Jane Canary 109
The Wagon Trip 117
Fort McDowell 121
The Lower Ranch 131
Elisha Reavis 141
Home 151
The Killing 163
The Letter 167
Captain Adna Chaffee 173
Rumors 177
Ultimatum 179
The Burning 185
Nightmares 187
Recovery 195
Despair 203
One More Visit 217
Revival 225
Restitution 237
The Ceremony 239
Epilogue 243

PREFACE

During the author's research on the history of Arizona's Fort McDowell area, he frequently visited the Arizona Historical Foundation on the Arizona State University campus. There, in the late 1980s, he found a map (ca/1904) that showed two house ruins just north of Fort McDowell. One was labeled "White ranch" and the other "Carroll house."

These sites were near his residence and on land he monitors as a Site Steward for the purpose of protecting archaeological locations from vandalism. He found both ruins and noted them for further research.

A phone call initiated by the Historical Foundation led to a meeting with the great-grandson of the Whites, John Micek, and a visit to the site. Micek supplied information that led to the writing of a chapter on the subject, published in the author's 1997 book, *Verde Valley Lore*.

Since then, the death of a family member provided Mr. Micek with more information about the White family. The breadth of the facts provided, the well-known personalities they met and the historical sweep of their lives, prompted the author to compose this portrayal.

CHAPTER 1

THE CEREMONY

October, 1905.

Arizona Territory.

It was a dazzling, crisp day. Willows and cottonwoods along the Verde River were yellow in the afternoon sun. The foothills were glowing with the crimson that Pat and I had watched so many evenings. From this exact spot we had watched the red turn to violet as the color spread up to Four Peaks, dominating the eastern skyline. We loved this place. It was all we had dreamed of for 20 years. It was our Heaven until the burning.

All six children were beside me. They had families of their own by now. It was not easy for them to make the trip but they knew how important it was to me. Josie and James Carroll also came out for the ceremony. What true friends they were through all our good and bad times.

The Army captain folded the American flag that had been presented. As the last sounds of the bugle echoed off Rock Knob across the river, he handed it to me as if to seal the bargain we'd made. That wasn't what filled my chest with emotion—not even what we had received—it was the official declaration that had just been read. A moment of perfection.

This place in time will be etched in my inner self and, I hope, in the hearts of each one of my children. Now they will know that their parents were not wrong, after all. The years of effort were not in vain.

Kate was the first one to speak. "It was worth it, wasn't it, Mother?"

Before I could answer, Josie said, "This is worth more than you can imagine, Kate."

The color guard and the lieutenant walked to their horses and rode away. I didn't want to lose the moment. I gathered the children around me. "My dears, after all this time, it's their way of saying that we weren't wrong. Remember this day. Even though it didn't work out the way we planned, your father and I did this to build something for you."

John asked, "How did you get this place?"

Willie chimed in saying, "We'd like to know more about Father."

Then Veronica asked, "Where were you married?"

From Ned I heard, "You never talk about life at other Army forts."

Kate said, "Tell us again about Ireland."

"Why did you buy this ranch?"

"Why didn't this happen a long time ago?"

"Wait a minute," I protested. "Now is not the time for our life's story. Let's just enjoy today. I promise I'll write it all down later so that you can have it for your children."

These are my memories.

CHAPTER 2

COUNTY KERRY, IRELAND

1845.

"Annie, Annie," I heard my mother calling as I rolled over on my straw mat for just one more minute of sleep. Mother was running toward our hut as she called again, "Annie Dowling, get out here and help right now."

I struggled to my feet and tugged on the only shoes I had, a pair of rough leather slippers with a short piece of twine to hold them around my feet. By the time I was outside my mother was pointing past the scrubby line of bushes that separated our plot of land from our neighbors.

"Quick, get over there and get Spot out of the Doyles' garden. I'll help you turn her back into the pen." I ran the few steps to the Doyles and waved my arms, shouting as loud as my five-year-old voice could muster. Mrs. Doyle was in her yard with a scowl on her face and waving a towel at our beloved cow, the only animal we owned.

With her help we pushed Spot through the hedge and into our patch of potatoes. By then Mother was holding the gate open and the three of us slowly eased her back inside her pen. I was barely awake but had enough sense to wonder how she got out. Sure enough, just then she headed for the back side of the pen and we saw where she had pushed aside the rock walls Father had built.

"We only have five acres t'work so we cin't let 'er use much," he had said as he built her three-sided pen against the house where our playground used to be.

I ran to the break in the fence and stood there while Mother piled the rocks back in place. She finally sighed, "Sometimes I wonder if we did the right thing when we got her. She's gettin' mighty edgy in this small pen."

It was small but it was all we could spare. It used to be a place to play for my two brothers, Willie and Brandon. They were older and now worked in town. When I was four Father had decided that we should get a cow. "But we'll only drink a little uv 'er milk." he said. "Most we'll sell, an' th' butter too t'help with t'other things we need shillin's fer. We kin bring grass in from the river bottom fer 'er t'eat."

So the play yard was gone. When my two best girl friends, Dorah

3

Binchley and Molly Caitlin, came to play we used the lane that went by our hut or sometimes down along the river bank. Dorah lived down the trail and Molly over the next hill and farther away from town.

Mother always told me, "Annie, someday ye'll learn how to read and write and when ye do, write down all about your life in Ireland." Well, I can't tell it all but I'm proud of being Irish and want my children and grandchildren to know what life was like when I was a little girl. Now that I'm 65 years old, it's time to get it done. I'm not even sure I remember exactly how my parents and the others in Ireland talked but I'm going to set it down as best I can.

Since Father wanted a cow he had to find a way to buy it. He and Mother decided that they would both work in the peat bog the next summer. Until then, Father joined the other men in our village of Listowel when they cut peat. He would cut enough for us to use the next winter, then he would stay on and cut more to sell to some of the widows and sick people in town for their fuel supply. He would get enough money to buy some extra food for us to use during the winter.

The Ardagh Bog was a few miles east of Listowel in County Limerick. My parents said it used to be a lake and then a swamp. Somehow things dried up a long time ago and they said the plants turned into peat. I'm still not sure how that happened but when we lived there the bog was the place where everyone went to get their fuel for cooking and to keep warm.

Not many women worked in the bog but the year before, two came from families who didn't have any land. The first few days Father said they were teased but then nothing more was said. So Mother went with him, while I sat under a tree and was told to be quiet. They earned 50 shillings a day. In that one extra month they both cut enough peat to buy our cow.

Spot was the color of mud with a few black and cream places on her shoulders and face. Father sometimes said that if it wasn't for those, we wouldn't be able to see her on the wet, foggy times when it had been raining for days. We lived in County Kerry, I later found out, though I didn't know it then. I never asked and Mother or Father never talked about anything except trying to get food or how to pay our rent every year. They never talked about what was going on in Listowel even though we lived close to the town.

I didn't know that we were near the ocean until many years later when we left. Now I remember that we had a lot of days with nothing but fog and low clouds, and I guess that's why.

4

After Spot was quieted down and scolded, Mother and I apologized to Mrs. Doyle. "Well, I know you dinna mean for 'er to git out, but canna you keep 'er in? She stomped off my carrots and a turnip!"

"Now Bets," Mother said, "sure we dinna want her out and in your garden—but maybe they needed a little thinnin'." She said this with a smile, but Mrs. Doyle was still not happy and she grunted as she strode away.

"Oh, I 'spose 'tall come out even. You kin have Annie help me pick and clean 'em next fall." With that she went through the row of hawthorne that separated our plots of land and my first real recollection of life at Listowel ended.

Maybe I only remember that one so well because Mother told me all about it one day much later when we were so hungry and wishing we had milk to drink. She said then, "Remember the first time Spot broke out of her cote? I came and got you off the floor when you were still asleep. You and Bets Doyle and I got her back. Wish we had her now."

Mother was everything to me then on that little place in Ireland. She was not very big around and shorter than most of the other mothers that lived near us. She had a small face with black eyes that were close together and her hair was long. She always wore it all rolled up on the back of her head. I once asked her why it was so long because it both-ered her when it broke loose.

"Your father wouldna' want me to cut it. He says it makes me pretty."

I remember that her face turned a rosy pink. I didn't know what to call it then but now I must say it was the only time I really saw Mother blush.

Mother had a small nose and ears. Now I would call her a woman with refined features. I remember that her face was smooth and she stood up real straight, as if to make up for her short stature. She explained things to me in proverbs that she had learned from her mother. One of her favorites was, "'Tis the mornin' bird that catches the worm." I heard that one whenever I wanted to sleep later in the morning. Then when I would try to get out of helping with the work she'd say, "Learnin' comes with work."

Other memories of life in Ireland are mostly bad 'cause Mother and Father never had any real money, except that summer when they saved enough to buy Spot. They spent their time trying to make potatoes and barley and wheat grow on our acres.

The ground was rocky—it seemed like there were more rocks than dirt. Even the dirt wasn't very good and since we lived on a hillside, when it rained more of it washed down into the Kavanaugh and Reardon land. Then there would be more rocks showing and my father would have to pick them up and pile them along the sides of our land. Mother helped and just before we left there I had to pick rocks, too.

My father's name was William. He was a lean, shrunken man, even when I was a child. I believe his hair was thin and partly gray even then. His skin was darker than Mother's. It was already getting creases in it from being outside so much. Mother always stood up straight but Father had rounded shoulders. He said it was from stooping over so much while he was picking up rocks. Mother said it was because he worked too hard when he was very young.

Some years we had a good crop of wheat and most years there was some barley. We would nurse those along for that was mostly what we had to use to pay our rent. Father used to say to the whole family, "I dinna' wan' ye to walk on the grain once 'tis planted. Not even 'fore it comes up. Canna' take a chance on packin' th' ground."

Father might try to pull some of the weeds growing in the grain after it was up but he would only do that around the edges, where he wouldn't have to step on any of the stalks.

When the grain was ripe Father and Mother would cut the stalks with a sharp blade that we called a scythe. When stepping around the fields they were careful not to allow any stems of grain to be mashed into the ground. Each head was precious. Only what could be harvested that day was cut. The foggy weather and showers would spoil the grain if it was lying on the ground. They would gather the stalks into little bundles and carry them to the threshing spot near our hut.

It seemed that there was always a wind blowing from where the sun went down every night. They'd put a blanket or cover on the ground on the side of our hut away from the wind. Then they'd hold a little handful of straws and tap the heads gently with a stick. If they were careful no grains would blow away or fall on the ground. If they did it was my job to pick them up and put them back on the cover.

I remember my parents would rub a head of grain between their fingers if they didn't get all of it to shatter by hitting it. When the blanket was covered with grain they would use their hands to scoop it into canvas bags loaned to us by our landlord's middleman. On a good day they might get as many as three full bags.

When I was five, my parents talked about running out of grain to pay Mr. Alter, the man who owned our land. Father said that last year was hard for everybody. First too much rain, then not enough. By the time harvest was ready the rains came again and even though Father and Mother waded through mud and picked up every stalk and head of grain, there wasn't enough.

The way Father told the story sounded bad to my young ears.

"We were just like th' rest. Nobody had enough but the dirty middler wouldna' hear."

"William!" my mother said, "Don' let Annie's ears hear tha' kind o' bad words."

"Well, he's na' good Emma, he coulda' tried harder to make Alter give in. We gave him all the crop we had."

Mother nodded her head. "I'll not forget it. We had to give him half our potato crop so we could keep th' land. With the cold and fog and damp last winter, we near dinna' make it through."

Even though Mr. Alter owned our land, for some reason Mother and Father never blamed him when we had trouble making our rent payments. They did talk bad about Mr. Rahilly, who was our middleman in Listowel. Every village had them—some had several. Usually they were farmers who lost their land a long time ago but somehow figured out how to get the job of enforcing rent payments from those farmers, or cottiers, that were left.

Mr. Alter lived in England. I later found out that most of the land around us had been owned by Englishmen for a long time. Since they were far away they hired men like Mr. Rahilly to see that the grain from the land they owned was shipped to England. They sold it there. Sometimes the middler would take the wheat to nearby watermills where it would be ground into flour. Then they would just send the money.

Mr. Rahilly was the middleman for all the land on our side of Listowel. Mr. Alter's family had been given those acres in 1690 for something they did for the King of England at Boyne. That's just what folks said—I never knew if Boyne was in Ireland or England.

Lots of people said that Mr. Rahilly was honest. Maybe he was and maybe not but everybody said that Mr. Murrough and Mr. Maguire, the other two middlemen in town, had been known to conveniently forget a load or two of grain when it came time to ship it to England. I do remember that all three of the middlers had three rooms in their houses when most of the rest of us had just one. They had stone walls, too, and thatched roofs while we had mud and straw walls with brush and straw for our roofs. I don't know about their floors, for I never saw them, but most of us had dirt floors that had been picked clean of rocks.

We saved every bit of straw each year and gradually built up the floor where we slept. Each year Mother would sweep out the straw that had been ground down to powder. She kept the rest of our room clean down to hard dirt by sweeping it almost every day with a broom made of small twigs. Right after our wheat and barley harvest Father would pick out a few good straws and tie them into a bundle for Mother to use as a broom. They didn't last very long so she would go back to the twigs.

Father and Mother had built our hut years ago and it now needed constant repair. Father plastered the sides with mud and straw and would sometimes stick small twigs in just to make the walls stronger. He would put fresh straw on the roof almost every year to turn the water. Even so, in times of heavy rain we had puddles of water in many places inside. Mother would move the things around to avoid the drips as much as she could.

I once asked my father why we couldn't have more land to raise our grain and potatoes. He snorted with disgust before he replied and I could tell he was trying to think of an answer. "We shoulda' ha'more but I dinna' have the right father, I guess."

When he didn't go further, Mother said, "'Tis a good question William, tell her why you say that."

Father took a big breath and sighed again before trying another answer. "Well, Annie, 'tis 'cause there's na' more land. 'Twas all took up before my father was birthed. 'N my mother and father ha' eight babies and only 10 acres to work. When they died 'twas all they ha' ta' gi' us. Me brothers give me five pounds fer m' share and I left. Had to keep working in th' factory and for other cottiers to earn enough to pay off Rahilly 'n get this land."

"You had to pay him to live on Mr. Alter's land?" I said. "Why?"

"Ah, Annie, thas th' way it is. Ye' gotta work through 'em, or it'll na' git done. As long as Alter gits his due he dinna care. 'Twas do that or work for th' factory or somethin' worse all m' life," Father sighed again and shrugged his shoulders.

Now that I look back, I realize that he never held his shoulders very high. Mother told me later that Father had to work in a factory making harnesses for those richer farmers who owned work horses. He started when he was nine years old to help make money for his large family. He soon did the work of a man but the lifting and 10-hour days six days a week hurt his back and made him a little bent over.

The food his family had was barely enough to get by and not enough to make him grow bigger when he was working so hard already. He worked until he saved enough to move to this land. After that he would help other cottiers pick rocks from their fields and earned a few extra shillings. Finally he and Mother married and rebuilt this hut.

Mother never seemed to get tired—at least she didn't act like it. Even at the worst times she would just take a deep breath and sigh a little and say, "We just have to make the best of it. Get to work and pretty soon the job will be over. At least we have a hut and some don't. We have land and some don't." With the fixing of our meager meals and helping with the farm work, Mother had little spare time.

The only day there was any rest at our house was on Sunday. My parents never missed the mass in Listowel. It was usually at 10 in the morning because Father Donahue served three parishes and we were the middle one. He started at Abbyfeale with eight o'clock mass, then came here and on to Ballyduff at noon.

Mother said he used to ride a donkey between parishes but when I was a little girl he used a horse and small wagon. He was a young priest and very short; not as tall as Father but on the chubby side. He didn't have a lot of hair but he wore it long and curled up on the end. His eyes smiled as he talked—Mother said that was because he had the Lord on his side. I remember that he would tease us children because we were so thin. We didn't think it was unusual because most everyone was thin.

Father Donahue would say, "Every Sunday in Listowel some parish woman brings me a nice basket o' somethin' to eat on th' way to Ballyduff. Then after mass in Ballyduff someone says, 'Father, will ye share our table a' for ye go' t' home?' What's a priest to do? I mustn't offend so I gets m' two big eats fer th' day and it all goes right here!" Then Father Donahue would pat his stomach and chuckle so that we all felt right at ease.

It was alright to work inside the hut on Sunday but there was not that much to do. Our one room was mostly covered with our straw mats and a small table and stools. In one end Mother had a peat stove made of iron and in the corner was a pair of boxes made into what I now call a cabinet, except that we didn't have any doors on it. We would make mud balls and stick them into cracks in the walls. Or we'd sweep the floor to get rid of dust. Those days, Mother tried to teach me little rhymes or simple arithmetic problems.

When I think back on my life in Ireland I mostly remember being hungry and cold. It rained or misted almost every day from fall until the

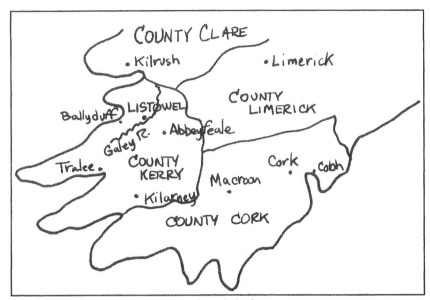

Southwest Ireland BY BRUCE FISCHER

next spring. Sometimes the wind would be so strong that I thought our hut would blow away. Father would again have to repair the roof. Mother would shake her head and say, "'Tis na wonder—we're so close to th' sea. Wind and rain follows the waves, they say." When the sun did come out everyone was outside to enjoy it while we could.

There were a few good times when I played with Dorah and Molly. We would draw lines in the dirt and play hop-scotch. The lane that led from our hut into town wound its way over two little hills. We explored the Galey River that was along one side of our town. Mother said there was once a castle built along the river here. It was just a few piles of rock walls on the other side of the river when we played there. That's where Molly had her accident. As we played "tag" and "sheep-sheep," Molly fell off one of the loose stones and hit her head on another. There was a big gash in her head and blood everywhere. Dorah and I ran for help in the village. The doctor had to make some stitches to close the cut. Molly always had a scar on her forehead and cheek. That was the last time we could play there.

The Galey River always had some water running in it and there were a few places that had a steep bank. We sat there throwing rocks in the water and dreaming about where we would go when we got older. We didn't know what a school was, though Mother had once said to Father,

"I wish Annie cud go t' school. Murraugh's girls go t' Tralee 'n live there four months fer schoolin'."

"Sure, an' Murraughs got shillin' an' we not. Jus' canna do it."

"I know," said Mother, "but if she dinna go now she'll na' do for nothin'.

"Tralee's t' fer away," Father replied. "Thas jus' it, Emma."

Mother came up with another of her proverbs: "Ignorance is a heavy burden, William."

"Learnin' comes through work, you always say Emma."

Since I hardly knew what school was I didn't know to be glad or sad but I did wonder what Mother meant when she said that I 'wouldn't do for nothing' if I didn't go to school.

One day, Molly said, "My mama says there 'tis a place 'cross the water where there's hardly no people. Says y' can have yer own place if you want it. Maybe we'll go there some day."

"Huh!" Dorah said, "Ye'll na' go no place. How'd ye pay fer it?"

Molly came right back at her. "Dad and Mama will take me and my little sister, tha's how. An' maybe pretty soon." The Caitlins did have more acres than we did and it seemed like their land was better. At least there weren't as many rocks.

Until then I had never thought about any country over the water. I'd never seen the big water but sometimes Father Donahue would bring it up in his homily. When I went home that day I asked Mother about another country.

"Yes, dear, 'tis there an' 'tis verra big, they say. Y'know, the water starts jes' a little way from here but we niver had the time ner the way to go t' th' shore. They say it takes a lot of days to git to th' new lands. Yer father and I know a family tha' went over last year. Name was Wilde and they said some day they wud send a letter back to let us know how 'twas. Never heard nothin' so maybe they dinna git there—or it's too fur."

Mother turned back to the pot of potatoes and lifted the lid on the iron pot. "I know this, if I ever git to some other place I'll niver eat another spud. Wish we had shillins so's we cud have somethin' else. They say poverty is no shame but I say it makes fer a hard life." It was one of the few times I heard Mother complain about our steady diet of potatoes or our lack of money.

11

Now, I know that we were no different from most everyone else in Ireland. We had to eat potatoes. That was all we could grow on our small parcel of land that would keep us alive. We had to pay the rent with the grain. Mother fixed potatoes in many ways to make them taste like something else. It was no use—they were still potatoes! Sometimes Mother would bake bread if we could save a few measures of grain to take to the mill along the Galey River.

The potato had been a savior for Ireland. It was about to become our ruination.

CHAPTER 3

FAMINE

Father had talked about how bad things were in 1845 when most of the potato crop spoiled. I was only five then and I don't remember much about it. That year he said there weren't enough potatoes to get through the winter. Father cut extra peat and picked rocks for some big farmers near Abbeyfeale. That earned us enough shillings to buy food to survive.

Some cottiers kept a part of their grain to grind into flour so they would have bread during the winter. When the middlemen found out about it, they threatened to throw them off the land, Father told us. Since most couldn't pay, the middlers just took what they could get and said they would charge us more rent the next year. Father said there had been bad crops before and they always got by just by staying hungry most of the winter.

When I was six years old the crops were growing well in midsummer. The potatoes were the best ever. Little did we know that the beginning of the end for us in Ireland was coming. Before his homily one Sunday morning, Father Donahue read something from the Gardener's Chronicle.

He said, "My friends, I bring ye sad news. Some o' ye may have already heard from th' coast but here is what th' Chronicle says last week:

> We stop the press with great regret to announce that the potato murrain has declared itself in Ireland. The crops around Dublin are suddenly perishing.

"May th' saints preserve us, my family. I fear we will be next and I dinna know wha' can be done. I'm sorry to be a' tellin' ye this but ye should know tha' it's comin'."

Come it did. Within a week, our crop, which had looked so good, started wilting and in another week, started to rot. It's easy for me to remember since that's all my parents talked about. Some said that if they were dug quickly and soaked in peat bog water they could be saved. We tried that but that made them spoil faster. Some said they could be soaked in salt water but we couldn't afford that much salt. Those that tried it said that didn't work either. They said boil them even though they weren't very big and then store them away but when we tried that they just melted away into a smelly mush that tasted sour and couldn't be eaten.

It was happening to every one. They called it the murrain. Some said it was the plague, only in a different form. Everyone had an idea about what caused it. Trains had just started in Ireland and they said maybe it was the streams of smoke from the locomotives. Others said it was from bird droppings and one group of very religious people said it was the 'wrath of God' because not everyone was going to mass every Sunday.

Father said, "It dinna make eny mind wha' it is. 'Tis here an' we canna' stop it. The barley and wheat canna go to Rahilly this year."

"William," Mother asked, "we can't hold it, can we?"

"We jist like all of 'em roun' here. We'll stop him if he tries to git it."

Until those bad years most folks didn't have a choice. But now everybody was without food for the winter unless they used their grain crops. For the next few weeks we harvested our grain and tried to think of a place to hide some of it.

When we saw our neighbors the only talk was about what Rahilly would do. No one talked to him and he said nothing. We later found out that he was waiting to hear back from Mr. Alter after he told him what had happened. Finally, one day he sent boys out to all his farms with the message that each one was to come to Listowel for a meeting. Father said there were 42 cottiers on Mr. Alter's land. The largest one had 11 acres. Some had only three. All had large families so I guess looking back, I'd have to say that we weren't as bad off as some.

Father went to the meeting and so did all the others. When he returned he told us about it. Waiting for him to come back was the first time in my life that I can remember being really scared. I think it was because after Father left Mother said, "Well, na' we'll know if we can stay or if we ha' ta' go."

I'm sure she said it before she thought about me for I started crying and wailed, "Go? Where'd we go?"

"Dinna ye fret. 'Twill be fixed up someway—can't everbody leave. We'll jes' wait n' see when Father gets back."

It was a long wait. Father's face was grim when he returned late in the afternoon. He said Mr. Rahilly was standing on the doorstep of his house and all 42 cottiers gathered round to hear what he had to say. Before he spoke Father said that he coughed and wiped his face several times even though it was one of our usual cool, cloudy days.

Father told us what he said:

"Men, you know why we're here. Last year Mr. Alter wasna' glad

14

'bout things on his land. You dinna' bring in a good crop o' lumpers an' he knows some of you kept back part o' yer grain. I talked fer ye and jes 'cause he's a good un' he says a'right but you send more this year to make up fer it. So now I'm tellin' him 'bout the plague and he heard in the papers there. He says 'tis too bad but you have to send him his grain enyways. You are behind an' he cin't let ye off enymore."

By this time, Father said, there was muttering among the men and finally one yelled out, "How kin we? We'll na' have eny food fer th' winter."

"I dinna know men," Rahilly yelled back. "Thit's yer bizness but Alter's bizness is gittin' rent and if he cin't git it from ye' he'll find somebody else."

When Father told us this, Mother gasped, "You mean he'd throw us off, William?"

"Thas' wha' he did to one las' year when he dinna send anything. Rahilly sez other owners from England are doing it, too. He sez the law is with 'em an' we hiv' to pay up or leave."

All this time I was curled up on my straw mat listening but hardly believing the awful things I was hearing. At six years of age, I couldn't imagine any place else to live. When Father said that last, I started whimpering and Mother spoke sharply to me. "Annie, that's na' helpin'. We must hear wha' Rahilly said and we'll do what we must. But you'll na' add to the sorrow by cryin'."

Father told us what Rahilly said next:

"I dinna like this, men, but I hiv m' orders. A week from nixt Monday is the day ye must bring all the bags uv grain to Listowel an' be checked off. I'll be expectin' ye and all yer grain, na' just part of it. Y'know I hiv ways uv checkin'."

With that, Father said he turned and walked back inside. All the farmers looked at each other with fear in their eyes. Then the fear turned to despair and then anger.

Before anyone left, Father said, a cottier named Donnell said, "My family'll not starve as long as I'm alive. I think we need to get out of here and hiv a meetin' of our own." When two or three other men nodded Father said they all walked the short distance to the edge of town and stopped under a tree near the river on the other side of town.

When they were together Mr. Donnell said, "Last year when we had our bad crop some of the cottiers a' Killarney had a middler tha' did th' same thing Rahilly's a' doin'. They all got t'gether and told him they wudn't send eny grain 'cept what they cud spare an' still git thru the winter. They said, 'If you try t'git more we'll hold it an' you hiv a fight on yer hands'."

When Donnell heard some of the men say 'hear, hear!' or 'yuh!' Father said Donnell acted like he was in charge so he went on. " Them cottiers got t'gether and called 'emselves the 'Levellers', 'cause they aimed to level out th' ground with them 'n the middleman 'n the landlord. By God men, they got by w' it. Their scummy middleman yelled 'n said they was losin' th' land but whin it was done, they sent about half th' grain and had enuf for the winter. Why kin't we do th' same, men?"

Father's face started looking brighter as he was telling us all this. I stopped my crying and Mother said, "But how d' we know we cud d'that? Maybe Rahilly and Alter won't let it happen."

"All I know is Donnell said it worked there. Another cottier north of here said he knew someone from Kilrush. They did th' same thing. If they kin do it we kin, too. All the men said they would save jes' enough fer winter 'n take th' rest Monday next. It'll be a'right, Emma. We kin do it." Father patted my mother on the hand and gave her a small smile. It was the first time I can remember an open show of affection between them. Thinking back on it now, I'm surprised. That first "love pat" came at the darkest time of my young life and when my feelings needed it the most.

The Rahilly cottiers had one more secret meeting later that week. Mr Donnell sent word to all 42 and Father said most were there around Donnell's hut that evening. Donnell did most of the talking and tried to be sure that everyone kept back enough to eat that winter. Father told us that he said:

"Men, y' canna' back down now. Dinna short yerself for winter. We must live an' if we stand tight on this, they kin't come after us all."

After he said this everybody sort of said 'yuh' and it sounded to Father like they were solid. One man said, "Are we goin' to call 'urselves Levellers like them fellas at Killarney?" Donnell replied, "I dinna care wha' we call 'urselves, jes' do it."

Just then a cottier named Finnegan said he heard that there was a big fight between the farmers and the middler up near Kilrush. "Even got the bailiff and his helper into it and they were on the side of the middler. Two men wuz killed. How cin' we stand up agin' that?"

Donnell said, "I heard that and 'tis probably right. Men, we'll na' make it through another winter if we dinna keep back enough t'eat. We got no choice."

The next week on Monday Father delivered four bags of barley and two of wheat. He made three trips to town with a bag balanced on each shoulder. We kept twice that much for our winter food. That and a few turnips that we grew in among the rock walls and Spot's milk would have to do. Without potatoes it was the only thing to do. As Father would arrive at Rahilly's office he would count the bags and give Father credit. When he told Mr. Rahilly that was all, he exclaimed, "All? I know you made more crop than this. You always have 15 or 20 bags." Father said he turned away quickly so Rahilly couldn't see his face and said, "Not this year—'tis all there is." Then he kept walking and didn't look back even though Rahilly yelled at him, "There's more—I know it, Dowling!"

The other cottiers did the same except for two who had relatives in town with a business and gardens. They couldn't bear to tell Rahilly anything but the truth. So they took all their grain and ate from their relatives that winter. When Rahilly added up all the returns he knew that the others had kept most of their grain back. He was afraid for his job and he told Mr. Alter what had happened. We never heard any more about it until the next spring.

My brothers in town still had jobs. Willie was working in a provision store and Brandon was an apprentice blacksmith. During these hard times they worked without any pay just for their board and room.

We were hungry most all winter and Father was sick a lot of the time. We got some of our grain ground at the mill but we had to give them part of it for the grinding. After that, Mother said she would find a way to crack the kernels with rocks and she would have me help her do that. We would sit on the floor and tap each grain between some large rocks. We would hold a shirt around the rocks so we wouldn't lose any of the pieces of grain. It was cold and rainy nearly every day and except for that we just laid on our mats and tried not to move too much. The peat nearly ran out before the sun finally dried up the fields the following spring.

When it came time to plant again Father held back the last of our grain for seed and for several weeks we lived on turnips, milk and greens from the river lands. By selling some of Spot's milk we had enough to buy some coarse flour for bread and porridge. Mother even bought a lamb bone one day late in the winter and for a whole week she cooked that in a pot with everything we ate just to give it some flavor.

17

With no potatoes from the last year Mr. Alter had to buy seed from Northern England and send it to Mr. Rahilly to give out to us. But when Father went in to get our seed potatoes, he returned with a handbill that Mr. Rahilly gave to all the cottiers. None of us could read it but Father told us what Rahilly said it meant. "Mr. Alter sez he knows we dinna give him fair share las' year. He sez we must give him all the grain this year plus some uv our potatoes to make up what we owe. If we dinna do this he will order the bailiff to make us leave."

This time Mother did not say anything but just turned away and shook her head. Father said, "'Tis all we can do, Emma."

That year was a little better and we did give Mr. Alter all the grain. But we kept all our potatoes for it wasn't a big crop. Most of the others did the same and Rahilly never said anything. Father Donahue said that it was the will of God that we suffer through hard times and it would make us better people. That was right after he said, "It is harder for a rich man to get into Heaven than a poor man."

On the way home from mass Mother said, "I wonder if 'tis easier to get into Heaven if you're starvin' than if you're full? If 'tis, all of us are sure to get in!"

That next winter was horrible. It was much colder and we didn't have as many potatoes to eat. When Father went to town the storekeepers told of many people leaving the land. We heard of ships full of farmers going across the water. We got very sick and some days no one could go out to milk Spot. The last of the dried grass we had gathered for Spot's winter feed was gone and we couldn't spare any of the turnips or potatoes. She didn't like those anyway. At last her milk dried up and then a few days later Father sadly told us that we would have to sell her. When he led her away the next day, she could barely walk and the one man in town who might have paid something for her said she was too bad to save for milk. Father had to sell to the butcher for 75 shillings and that was just enough to buy some food for us for the rest of the winter.

We heard of people dying in many places. Some of the families that lived on Alter's land died—mostly young children and older people. We heard of mothers dying in childbirth. Everyone said it was from starving but the doctors always called it dysentery or typhus or pneumonia. It spread so that somebody in most every family was either dead or about to die. Dorah's mother and one sister died and Molly lost a brother and a sister. Dorah almost died and when I saw her in the spring she had bones showing all over her body because she didn't have enough to eat.

Even as sick and cold and hungry as we were there was no missing

18

church each Sunday. One time Father Donahue said, "Almost every mile I travel from Abbeyfeale to here I see a dead body, sometimes more. The famine and sickness is even worse around Ballyduff. Some Sundays only about half the parish can make it to service." In one way we felt better knowing that we were not alone in our misery, but it made our situation seem more hopeless than ever.

With the new season, we all hoped the crop would be good and life could be the same again. But it was not to be. Even now it hurts me to think of it. This time the potatoes never got started well—the murrain again. Not even much grain because the rains never came. By July we knew that we could not live another winter unless some one gave us food. All of Alter's cottiers now called themselves the Levellers for Mr. Donnell had been to their meetings in Killarney. Our Levellers called for a meeting with Mr. Rahilly this time. Father spent a long time that evening telling us about it. They told him they weren't going to have any rent grain this year.

Rahilly said, "I know men, and I dinna' know wha' to do. Wha' can eny uv us do?"

Mr. Donnell spoke for all of us and asked, "Will Mr. Alter send us food for the winter so we kin stay on his land?"

Rahilly answered by saying, "You know he canna do thet. He has to live an' he sez for th' last two years he can't pay his bills neither. But I tell ye, he's a good man an' he dinna wan' ye t' starve. So many 'r leavin' 'n I dinna see how we can live by stayin'. I'll tell him of our meetin' and see what he sez."

For the next month we cut peat and lived on the few carrots and cabbages Mother could grow in the place where Spot had lived. We still mourned her loss and we felt the lack of milk. Father had planted turnip seeds around the rocks again and by late July we had to start on those for there was nothing else and no money as no one in town could afford to buy extra peat.

CHAPTER 4

THE CROSSING

Mr. Rahilly sent word for all cottiers to gather again. We knew this meeting might change our lives but we didn't know how. I can never forget the news Father told us when he got home.

"Men," Rahilly said, "this is the best Mr. Alter can do. As I told ye, he's a good man. He will pay yer passage to the new land in America for every one of ye and yer families. Ye must leave from Cobh in 30 days. Since he is a'payin' yer fare ye must leave your huts and tools jes as they are fer him. For those of ye who want to do this ye must tell me by next Tuesday and ur tickets'll be bought. If ye dinna want to go ye'll hiv t' move out by next spring. Thas' all I hiv to say and may God bless ye." Father said even Mr. Rahilly's voice cracked and he saw tears in his eyes as he turned to go back into his house.

"Great God!" Mother exclaimed.

I said, "Mother, how can we? This is our home!"

Then I broke out crying and ran to my mat, pulling the blanket over my head. Mother started to cry, too, but quickly pulled her sleeve to her eyes and dabbed them dry. She pulled her arms around her as if to pull her thoughts back together and then said calmly to Father, "William, what does this mean? Are we really out of a home?"

Father's chin quivered as I watched from my corner but he heaved a big sigh and cleared his throat so he could speak and said, "Emma, my girl, we dinna hae to. We kin stay fer t'winter. But what'll we eat? There's na' left. We tried—we all tried and God brought us th' blight. Now He's brought us th' drouth an' th' sickness. I'm afraid a' all th' dead I see and last winter it nearly got us."

Mother spoke as if she was talking from afar. "Where's Cobh? I never heard of it."

"It's th' port thas' near Cork 'bout two long day's walk from here. 'Tis th' only place Alter will pay fer us leavin'. Rahilly sez there's a ship comin' in there that'll do th' trip cheaper thin from Dublin."

We all sat still for a minute and I finally asked, "Would Dorah and Molly go?"

Father said, "I dinna know, Annie. We jes' hear of it." Then after another pause he said, "Remember the Wildes? They went to th' new country las' year. They sent a letter back to Kavanagh 'n he jes' got it t'other day. Dinna know the Wildes cud write and Kavanagh cin't read but they got Father Donahue to read it. They sez they hiv plenty to eat and a good room t' stay. 'Tis a good country for them that is able to work. They git the same as 75 shillings a day for pay." Mother and I gasped. That was more than my brothers got for a week of work before the blight came.

Mother said, "God ha' mercy, can it be so good? Do ye think we cud do it too?"

He sat a long time and finally said, "I been thinkin' on it, Emma. The Wilde letter helps me say we go. We dinna ha' a good life here enymore. If Alter will pay for us mebe we kin do better there. Cin't be no worse than this."

The next month was a flurry as we and most of our neighbors said goodbye to Listowel. There was little to pack—some clothes that were worn out and the family Bible and one of my best rag dolls and then we were off with just one bag for all of us. Father Donahue said a special mass for the ones who were going. There were lots of tears at that service.

He told us that many cottiers and their families from Abbeyfeale and Ballyduff were also leaving. Some of the landlords paid for all of their tickets and some only paid a part of it. We had only a short time to say goodbye to my brothers, Willie and Brandon. Thirty-four of Mr. Alter's cottiers did what we did. Not until several years later did we find out what happened to the rest.

We walked with some of our neighbors all the way. We were a pitiful lot—hardly any baggage and our clothes were tattered and worn. As we walked we looked back to see smoke rising in many places around Listowel. We couldn't turn back to see what it was but there was plenty of guessing. Not until much later did we find out the cause.

The Aid Society in town had given everyone some bread before we left. We walked on a cart path to Killarney and on to Macroom. We stopped at every creek and river to get water and all the mothers rationed out bites of bread. Just before reaching Macroom we laid down for the night in a pasture near the Sullane River. We were lucky it was summer and the night was warm enough so that we were alright.

Dorah's family came along and the Caitlins, too, so Mother and I had someone to talk to as we walked. Father hardly said a thing, just trudged along with stooped shoulders and a sad look. After we left Listowel I started getting excited. I suppose I was just too young for that many memories. As bad as events had been, I believed anything would be better. Dorah and I started chattering and found so many new things to see that we acted silly. We were only eight and this was going to be a new adventure. We shared the bread to make it last as long as possible.

On the way we found that some of the cottier groups in other towns called themselves Whiteboys. The ones near Farranfore had fights with their middler and some people had been killed. It didn't surprise us for we were all so desperate that we would do anything to get something to eat. Up around Ennis and Kilrush it was even worse for them. They had three years without crops and more people died there.

By the time we got to Cork, we were hungry and tired. No food was left and many people had blisters on their feet. We found a mission house where nuns had big tubs of soup and cabbage leaves to eat and two slices of bread for each person. It was the most and the best our family had for weeks. I saw the big city of Cork with excitement and, of course, Dorah and Molly and I had big eyes trying to take in everything. Cobh wasn't far after that and even though we were tired, we walked faster for we were anxious to get there before dark. Our ship, the *Good Spirit*, the one named on our tickets, was in the harbor. We knew that we were to get aboard the next morning.

As soon as we got close to the harbor, men started trying to tell us to follow them for a good place to spend the night. Father said to each of them, "I dinna ha' money." There were lots of men there who were called scalpers. They would try to find a person with some money and get them to pay for a place to sleep. They would then take them to a warehouse where they spent the night. While they were sleeping some people had things stolen. They didn't have much value, but for them it was terrible, for those were their only possessions.

Our family just curled up under an awning by a police station and huddled together to keep warm. We found out that the best time to take a ship to America was in the spring, for the weather was better then. We were told that our tickets cost much less since we were going in August. They were also less since we weren't leaving from Dublin or Liverpool. The bigger and better ships sailed from there but Mother said we were in the wrong part of Ireland. "Enyway," she said, "beggars kin't be choosers." We sure were beggars at that point.

The next morning we were taken aboard the *Good Spirit* and by afternoon the ropes were thrown off and the sail put up. Everything was new to us and though exciting, it was frightening, too. Even now, I don't want to talk much about the trip across the ocean. It was not what we thought it would be. Every ship captain had packed his ship with as

23

many passengers as possible. Now that the blight had hit hard for three years out of four, it seemed like all of Ireland was trying to leave.

The ship owners could make more money if they would crowd people on every ship. That meant less space to carry water and food. We thought Listowel was terrible in the winter. The ship was worse except that it wasn't as cold. All of us got seasick the second day out and some stayed that way for the whole 34 days we were at sea. Some were so sick they died. We lost 18 people on our voyage—I never knew how many passengers we had but I know it was at least twice as many as there should have been.

We couldn't cook any food below deck. Sometimes fights broke out among families trying to get to the few places on top where they could fix some food. There wasn't near enough for all on board. Some said the crew was eating well all the way. That didn't make us feel any better.

Dorah and Molly and I tried to play and some days when the waves were not so bad, we wandered around. Most of the time the crew was yelling at us to stay out of the way. Many families were put on the deck and told that it was their place to live and sleep. When the first storm hit during the second week they had to move below and that meant that the rest of us were crowded even more. It was awful. I don't want to tell about that any more.

When we heard people talking that they could see some land ahead some went on deck and watched. Dorah and I did that, but then we were sent back down. We didn't see anything else until the next morning when we were at the dock. There were hundreds of people swarming around with horses, carriages and wagons. Big buildings stretched out on both sides of a big river as far as we could see.

Father was too sick to talk but Mother said, "Annie, here is your new home. William, this'll be a better place. Look at th' people! They look like they have plenty to eat." With that our life in America began.

CHAPTER 5

THE BIG CITY

The confusion here was worse than in Cobh. There were more people and they were yelling at us as we got off the boats. They were trying to sell us something or get us to go with them somewhere. Mother tried to find humor in the grim situation by saying, "They're wastin' their time trying to get us to buy somethin'—we dinna ha' na' money." Father could barely walk.

We had to talk to some men in uniforms about our names and where we started from. Then we wandered around close to the dock and even sat down on the sidewalk while Father gradually got to feeling better. Some nuns began handing out soup and sandwiches. What a stampede that caused! They had enough for most of us. Those who didn't have any family waiting for them, followed Sister O'Day and Sister Noonan to a three-story building where they said we could spend the night.

Dorah Binchley and her father and sister stayed with us. Somehow Molly and her parents went in another direction. I didn't see my other playmate for a long time. The nuns had a convent in this big building and used part of the space to help new Irish people who were arriving with no one to meet them. I can't imagine what we would have done without them, for we had no money. We were starving, sick and would have been lost in such a big city.

Sister Noonan spent time with each family. She was taller than us and very thin with a kindly face. She didn't talk like we did so we thought she must not be Irish. She told us that language should be one of the first things we learned about America. "Try not to speak the way you did in Ireland. Listen to how the other people here say words. If you keep on with the 'dinnas' and 'nivers' the folks will call you 'Shanty Irish' and worse. It will hurt you when you try to get a job."

Sister Noonan had been in New York City for four years, coming there from Galway. She said that was only a little bit north of Listowel. We learned a lot from her in the three days we stayed there but the main thing I remembered was about talking in a new way. Though I was only eight, I made up my mind to do as the Sister said. I started trying to mimic the speech of everyone except my parents and the others who came with us. For a while, I was even imitating the words that immigrants from other countries were using. At that point I didn't know the difference! I must have sounded very funny. Father didn't even try to change but Mother did. It was slow and difficult for her.

At the convent there was a big bulletin board. The nuns had passed the word around New York that they were keeping new arrivals, so that board was used to advertise about places to stay and jobs. Though the nuns never said we had to leave, all the 15 or 16 families who were there knew they were supposed to leave as soon as possible.

The first thing the adults tried to do was find a job. On the second day Father felt better—we all did for we had enough to eat and a clean place to sleep. We had regular beds with a mattress and springs, the first I had ever seen—there was nothing like that on the ship. The bulletin board had several notices about people wanting workers at the docks. Father went there and on the very first day got a job unloading ships. He would receive $1.50 a day.

When Father asked if they would pay him each day, his new boss, Mr. Fitzsimmons, said "no." Father told him we were staying at St. Catherine's Convent and we needed to get out to make room for other immigrants. When Mr. Fitzsimmons heard this he said, "Where y' from Patrick?"

"Listowel, County Kerry," Father answered.

"Saints preserve us, man, I'm from Kilrush in County Clare. We wuz almost neighbors once! Here, Pat, take these two dollars 'n you kin find a room for a week. By thin ye'll hiv yer first pay and ye kin give it back t' me."

When he came back to the convent that first afternoon he was happier than I could ever remember. "At last, Emma, I'm goin' t' have some regular pay. Let's find a place to stay jist as fast es we kin." We looked at the bulletin board, though at that time Father and I couldn't read. Mother knew only a few words.

The sisters helped and showed us how to find the cheaper places that we could afford. They said the Five Points area was the first place where Irish people settled. The Old Brewery rooming house there was the cheapest place to stay but crime had moved in and the streets weren't safe. The sisters said to go on past it a few blocks to the Division and Clinton Streets area.

We did go beyond the Five Points intersection at Park and Worth streets. After looking at two places, we found a three-story brick building at the corner of Ridge and Delancey Streets.

We took the first room they showed us for it was nicer than anything we had seen. It was the cheapest one available in that building—$1.50 a week. That left us only 50 cents for food that first week but we managed to get by with four visits back to St. Catherine's. Our room had two beds, one stuffed chair and a wardrobe, or sort of a portable closet, where we kept the few clothes we had. I had one corner for my bed. It was a long way from the dirt floor and rough mats I slept on in Ireland.

Part of the room was a small kitchen with a table, two chairs and stove. The kitchen had a sink and above it were pipes with hot and

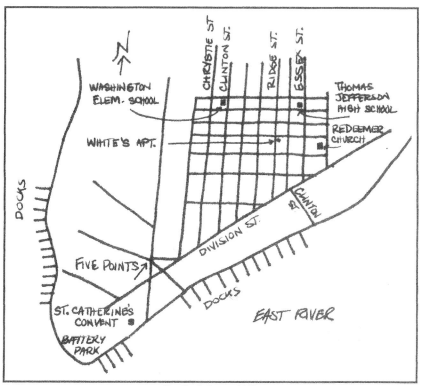

New York City — 1850. BY BRUCE FISCHER

cold water in them. It was the first time any of us had seen such a thing. We didn't always have hot water but it was like a miracle to have water so handy.

There was one water closet for each floor. That was the first experience any of us had with an indoor toilet. It served all six apartments on that floor. We often had to wait a long time for our turn but we still thought it was marvelous.

Father said, "No more thunder mugs! I niver thought we'd someday be this fancy."

27

"Hush, William," said Mother. "At least you could call them rightly 'n say chamber pots."

"Well, what iver y' call 'em, they's messy 'n I'm gonna like this better," Father said.

Mother started inquiring about school for me because she heard that everyone got to attend school without any cost. We thought that was a wonderful thing. She escorted me to Washington Elementary School on Houston and Clinton Streets. It was a fine fall morning with the sun shining and both of us feeling good after a warm breakfast at the convent. The school was only six blocks from where we lived.

The woman in the office was kind and pleasant until Mother told her where we were from and then I got my first real introduction to prejudice in New York. "Oh no, not another mackerel catcher," she said and she shook her head. "That's all we're getting this year! Our whole language will be corrupted before you know it." Then, speaking to Mother, she shook her finger and almost spit at her saying, "You better make sure this one doesn't give us any trouble. Tell her that we don't tolerate any shanty Irish here."

I always admired what Mother did then in the face of that uncivil welcome. She simply smiled and said, "You'll na' ha' trouble w' me Annie. You treat her right and she'll do right by th' school. She's here t' learn— she'll do it th' way you want." After I heard that I stood a little taller. I know that made me want to do better in school just to prove that my mother was right. It was decided to start me in the second grade even though I was a year older than most of the class.

As soon as I was enrolled Mother and I walked back and forth from home to the school until she was sure that I knew the way and wouldn't get lost when I started the next day. Mother then went back to the convent and asked the sisters to help her find some place to work. Sister O'Day took the morning paper and pointed out two or three homes that were advertising for domestic help and that were near our apartment.

Mother and I walked to a home that was closer to the docks and harbor. We went up a narrow flight of steps to a second-floor address and knocked. A black man came to the door—it was the first time either of us had seen a Negro. When we told him our purpose he ushered us into the most beautiful room we had ever seen.

Every part of the walls were covered with red and yellow flowered wallpaper. The lamps were colored glass and the tables all polished and perfect. There was a carpet on the floor and sparkling glass things on the shelves of a big bookcase all along one wall. The black man left and pretty soon the mistress of the house came in to see us. She was a tall, older lady with thin brown hair drawn into a bun on the back of her head. She never did tell us her name or ask us to sit down. She started by saying, "Did you come to ask for work?"

"Yes, we did," Mother replied.

"What can you do?"

Mother started to tell the jobs she was used to doing. "I kin wash 'n sweep 'n cook. T'other things I did was outside 'n I kin see ye ha'ent that here."

The woman interrupted Mother to ask, "Where on earth are you from?"

"Ireland."

The woman said in a bitter voice, "We won't be needing you. You're not only ignorant but I've heard you have allegiance to the Pope, not this country! You can go."

Mother tried not to show it but when we were out on the street I could see the tears in her eyes as I asked, "Why did she hear bad things about the Irish?"

"I dinna know, Annie dear. The sisters said sometimes people here weren't good to the Irish but we jist hiv t' make the best o' it. Mebe 'tis the way we talk different." After this experience I remembered what the Sisters and school woman had said. I was even more determined to learn how to speak "American."

To get to the second place we walked close by where we lived and Mother started to turn in that direction saying, "P'haps 'tis a bad idea fer me t' try n' find work." But after a few steps in that direction she turned around and grimly pointed on up Rivington Street. "Let's try again, Annie, I've got t' work. Mebe they all aren't like th' other woman."

I was enjoying this trip with Mother, for new sights were everywhere I looked. The advertising signs, the people with fancy dresses and hats were scenes I couldn't have imagined just three months ago. Some of the men walked with canes. Then I noticed that some of them even touched the brim of their hats with the head of their canes when they met us.

I said to Mother, "Those men with canes don't act like they are crippled."

Mother laughed before she replied, "No, they're not, notice how fancy their canes are. That's their way of dressing up."

This time we walked up to a third floor address on Rivington just off Chrystie Street. A woman with a baby in her arms opened the door and smiled as she let us in. "Are both of you answering my notice for help?" She said it with a smile that made us know she was just teasing and trying to be friendly. She told us to sit on her sofa which was so soft I almost got lost as I sunk way down in it.

Before this woman asked us any questions she said, "I'll get you both a drink of water—you must be very thirsty after being out on such a hot fall day."

As she went to the kitchen Mother and I looked at each other and laughed for I had said to Mother as she knocked on the door, "I'm thirsty after that long walk."

This friendly lady was younger than Mother, dressed in a beautiful sweater and skirt with jewelry that sparkled as she moved. Her front room was not as fancy as the other one we saw but still elegant with big overstuffed chairs and brass lamps. They sparkled in the afternoon light coming in full windows that looked out on a little park between their apartment building and the corner. After bringing each of us a glass of water, the first thing she said was, "My name is Elizabeth Terrell. My husband is George and this is our baby, little Georgie. Please tell me your names." All this time she was smiling and I could tell that Mother was going to work here and that she would like it.

Before long Mrs. Terrell was showing Mother around the four-room apartment while I tagged along trying not to say anything. I'm sure my eyes were bugging out from staring at the many beautiful things. Mrs. Terrell was telling Mother what she liked to have done and asking if she could come there two days a week to clean and three days a week to take care of Georgie while Mrs. Terrell went to her clubs and did her social work. She never even asked Mother if she wanted to do it and Mother never asked if she could have the job.

Mrs. Terrell was so talkative and so friendly that she just assumed they would get along well and they did. Mother earned 75 cents a day for this work and from then on she and Mrs. Terrell were the best of friends. She started work there the next day.

Later Mother found out that Mr. Terrell was a jeweler and that they had lots of money and another home up in the Catskill Mountains of New York. Mother later told me that there was never any mention of how she talked or that she was looked down on because she was Irish. Mrs. Terrell did tell her that both of them had come from Austria when they were young and that neither of them had gone beyond the sixth grade in school. Mrs. Terrell was always sorry about this and once told Mother that the best thing she did was to get me into school as soon as we got to New York.

Mother worked there for the next five years. By then she was earning $1.50 a day. When Georgie started school, they didn't need Mother for those three days but she continued to clean and wash for them two days each week. With a good recommendation from Mrs. Terrell she found another cleaning job for the other three days. Mrs. Terrell was good to us. She gave Mother some of her old dresses but they weren't always very old. At holidays she gave gifts to both of us and always a special one for St. Patrick's Day.

As I look back on my first school days, I would have to say that they were both good and bad. The good was that most of my teachers were helpful and I was like a sponge, soaking up new things. The bad was that for a long time I was teased and looked down on by many of the other students who weren't Irish. They called me lots of names that were worse than 'shanty Irish.' They would try to make me cry. They would tear my dress or pull on my braided hair.

The first few weeks I would complain to Mother and say I didn't want to go back. She was patient and firm. "Annie, you must go back. Else ye'll niver get t' th' place ye want here. Dinna let 'em get yer dander up—jes mind t' yer studyin' and learn to talk like thim. Jes' remember, th' race is not always t' th' swift but to thim who endure."

She was right but it took a long time and some of the hurts are still there. I think it made me feel more kindly toward the American Indians much later in life. I learned then that just being different than most doesn't make a person inferior. It was a hard way to learn but good for me, I guess.

At first I was behind most girls and boys in second grade so I worked hard to catch up. Soon I was one of the better students in everything but English. This bothered me for I knew that was the thing that I needed most. So between my second and third grade, I asked Mother if I could take a special summer school class for English. There weren't many of those available but Mother found one at the Hamilton Elementary School eight blocks north. After she walked the route with me twice I was ready to do it alone. That lasted eight weeks. At first I found out that most of the other students were there because of discipline problems during the regular year. As soon as the special teacher found out why I was there and that I really wanted to improve my English, she took extra time with me and gave me books to take home.

This teacher, Mrs. Hilty, was the one who helped me the most of all during my elementary school years, even though I only had her for that short time. She patiently helped me get rid of my Irish accent that was so hated by some people those days. She told me about the 'No Irish Need Apply' signs that were all over. I had seen them but didn't realize their significance. She would say, "Annie, it's not right, but that's the way it is and it will take many years before people realize that we Irish are just the same as everyone else. Some good, some bad. Don't forget, it's up to you to decide whether you'll be one of the good ones or the bad ones."

When she talked to me like that, it just made me want to try harder than ever to be one of the really good ones. By the end of the summer Mrs. Hilty had me reading some of the simpler classic books at home and she would insist that I ask her each day for the meanings of words I didn't know.

Mother thought often of my brothers. "Now that we kin afford a stamp fer mail I wish one of us cud write to Willie and Brandon."

"Wen't know how t' do thet 'n they cin't read enyway," Father answered. A few minutes later, as I was studying one of my books, an idea popped into my head.

"I know—Mrs. Hilty will do it. We just tell her what to say." In that way our family all wrote their first letter.

Mrs. Hilty was just as nice about it as I thought she would be. "Why, of course, Annie. I'll be glad to help you. But I'm going to want you to help, too. You have learned enough so that you can do some of the writing." That was the way it happened. Father told Mother and me what he would like to say and then one day Mother took two hours away from her work at Mrs. Terrell's. She walked up to Hamilton School where Mrs. Hilty was finishing up our regular class. Mrs. Hilty wrote out what Mother and Father wanted and then I started to tell her what I was going to say. She grinned at me and said, "Annie, now it's time for you to do the writing. You can go real slow and I will help you."

Mother was all smiles at this. "'Tis just fine if you kin do it Annie. My little girl, writin' on her own—an' only in th' second grade!"

"Almost third grade, Mother!"

"That's right, Mrs. Dowling," said my teacher, "and she will be one of the better students next year, too. She's learning fast and I can tell that she will do just fine." That was the best compliment I'd ever had.

32

Mrs. Hilty made us a copy of our first letter to Willie and Brandon which I've kept. It said:

Dear boys,   *August 1849*

Your father wants to tell you that he has a job on the docks in New York City. He helps unload ships and it is hard work. He says the pay and the food are better here and if you want to come he will help with some money. He sends you his greetings.

Your mother says that they now have enough to eat and that the family is healthier. She is anxious to know how you are getting by. Do you have enough to eat? Have you been sick? Are the crops any better and do you still have your same jobs? She sends her love and wants you to find someone to help you write back here with the news from Listowel.

(Written by your sister Annie's teacher, Mrs. Omar Hilty)

Dear Willie and Brandon,

This is my letter to you. My teacher is helping me spell and get the right words. School is hard work but fun. Not as hard as picking rocks. Haha. I will be in the third grade soon. I like it in New York City. We talk about you and wonder what you are doing. Write to us soon.

Love,
Father, Mother and Annie

We addressed the letter the way Mrs. Hilty said:

William and Brandon Dowling
General Delivery
Listowel, County Kerry
Ireland

Mrs. Hilty told us there was a post office on the way back to our house. The postage was 25 cents for Ireland. Mother almost didn't send the letter. "Oh no! 'Tis enough to buy food fer a day." Then she said, "But Mrs. Hilty was so nice and she did give us the paper and envelope. We want t' hear from th' boys 'n they oughta know what has become o' us." So the letter was mailed with our address on it and Mother ended by saying, "Now we'll jist have t' wait for a ship to sail over and back. It'll take a long time."

Work for Father on the docks was good pay—after two years he got a raise to $2.00 a day and we really celebrated about that. My parents were as happy then as I can remember. With both of them working we stayed right in that same little room even though our weekly rent had gone up to $2.50. As Mother said, "We aren't here much inyway so's why pay fer a fancy place?" They did save enough to buy a sofa at a used furniture store. There was barely enough space for it but what a grand thing it was for me to be able to lay there and nap. I liked it so well that Mother pushed the other two beds together for them and I made my regular bed on the sofa each night.

One of the things that I remember best was our church. We soon found the one nearest our rooming house. It was called Church of Our Redeemer though most of us just said "the church" when we talked about it. Some of the more proper would call it "Redeemer Church" but no one bothered to say the whole name. The church was just two blocks east of where we lived.

Father Higgins was our priest in those years and about half of his sermon each Sunday would be telling about how things were going back in Ireland. He would also introduce each new family as they arrived and came to church for the first time. A lot of the socializing centered around Father Higgins telling where they lived in Ireland. After church all those who knew someone who lived near there would gather around the new people to hear the latest news from the homeland.

There were a few from County Kerry, some from Glencar and Ardfere and Killarney which weren't very far from Listowel. Father even knew a farmer that one of them knew. All the news was bad for the first three years. Then the blight seemed to wear out and the potato crop was almost back to normal again. That year there was a good grain crop, too, and the cottiers finally were able to pay rent to their landlords. By then they said that there were only about half as many working the same acres. Now each family had more to eat and could pay better rent.

Many of the cottiers were working in factories or dead from the disease that followed the blight and starvation. We found out that the smoke we saw as we walked away from Listowel was our huts being burned. The middlers picked up the few tools we left and burned everything. They said it was to get rid of the disease and vermin from all the dying. For the remaining ones, life slowly got back to normal and the number of Irish families arriving in New York slowed.

CHAPTER 6

THE EAST RIVER

Father's back was never good from the hard work he had done all his life. At the docks he spent 12 hours a day unloading things from the boat with only 30 minutes off for lunch. Most of the work involved carrying sacks of coffee, cocoa or sugar from the ship's deck back into warehouses. Some weighed more than 100 pounds. As he did this for weeks at a time, his pains started getting worse.

He was stooped more than ever and hurt so much that he had trouble sleeping. Many nights he would try to stretch his body out straight and couldn't. Most Sundays as soon as church was over he would come back to our room and lay down again. Many of those afternoons Mother and I would walk all the way down to Battery Park. We saw new things and Mother was always trying to explain the meaning to me. Lots of times she wouldn't know about them either but together we would try to guess and would make a game out of it.

There were lots of immigrants trying to get work on the docks for it was one of the better paying jobs for those who didn't know how to read or write. Every time Father or someone else would complain about the work, Mr. Fitzsimmons or another foreman would say, "There's plenty o' men lookin' fer a job here. If ye dinna like it y' kin quit and we'll git someone who'll be stronger." It was no use asking for more pay because the foremen would say they could get new workers for less.

Father never said much about his work. He was too tired and not much for talking anyway. Sometimes he would get a sprained shoulder or ankle. He tried to go right back to work the next day since he wouldn't get his pay if he didn't get there and do his share.

One day he let us know that things were worse than Mother or I had guessed. "Three fellas at work are makin' things hard fer me. They're sayin' I dinna do as much work as they. Now they got the foremen yellin' at me." The way he said it I knew he was worried. Father never brought home troubles to us and seldom talked about what things were like on the docks.

Mother didn't say anything for a while. Then, "Should ye' be thinkin' of another job?"

"What else kin I do?" Father shrugged his shoulders and slumped even deeper into his gloom. " I know nothin' here but th' docks. Most places say y' got t' read or they won't hire Irish."

That was the end of it that night but I heard Mother and Father whispering sometimes and I could tell it was about his pain or the trouble he was having on the job. One night I overheard him whisper something about "them guys that want to get rid o' me."

When I asked Mother about that the next day she just turned away and said, "Oh, Annie, there's always some kind of trouble. Sometimes 'tis not enough for a poor man to do his best." I didn't know then what terrible things would happen. For me, I was too wrapped up in fourth-grade work and in making new friends.

In the middle of my school year I had just arrived home. I heard heavy footsteps on the stairs and down the hall to our door. A knock came. It was the first time anyone had come to the door when I was there by myself. Mother was still working at the Terrells and wasn't home yet.

I asked, "Who's there?"

"'Tis Mr. Horace Fitzsimmons, your father's foreman at th' docks. May I come in?"

I knew his name so I wasn't afraid to open the door. I told him, "Mother or Father aren't here now."

"When will yer Mother be home?"

"In about an hour, Mr. Fitzsimmons." He was the biggest man I'd ever talked to. His hands were huge and his shoulders large but hunched over. His head seemed to be too small for his body and it was pock-marked. There was a sad look on his face and he acted like he didn't want to talk to me.

"I'll be off then, little girl. I'll be back in an hour." He was out of the door and gone so fast I couldn't say any more. He was nervous and didn't look at me when he talked.

When Mother got home I told her what had happened. "I dinna like it Annie, it may be bad news. Mebe yer Father's ill and his boss jes' dinna want t' tell ye."

We heard his footsteps again and a knock on the door. Mother opened it and said, "Mr. Fitzsimmons?"

"Yes, ma'am, I'm William's foreman at the docks."

"Yes, he talks of you," Mother replied. "You kin sit down, Mr. Ftizsimmons."

"No maam, I can't stay. Mrs. Dowling, I dinna know how t' tell ye this but there's been an accident."

"What kind of accident?" Mother asked.

"Well, y' see William was a' carryin' sacks off th' ship 'n he 'n some other men got t' pushin' an' crowdin' each other 'n William fell off the gangplank." When he said this he actually started getting tears in his eyes.

Mother almost shouted, "Then wh' happened?"

"William fell in the water, ma'am, 'n we canna find him. I'm terrible sorry, we jes canna find him yit but we're tryin'." With that Mr. Fitzsimmons put his hands to his head and moved to the door. "I'll be back as soon as I kin tell ye' more."

The next hours and days are just a big black spot in my memory. After Mr. Fitzsimmons left, Mother and I clung to each other and sobbed. She composed herself long before I did. I kept crying, "Why can't they find him? Why aren't they finding him?"

Mother let me sob and kept stroking my hair and saying, "Oh Annie, Annie, I dinna know but they'll do the best they can. Mebe yer Father has caught hold of somethin' an' is a' floatin' down the river 'til someone finds 'im. All we can do is wait."

It was not to be. Mother and I stayed in our room for two days almost paralyzed with fear. Mr. Fitzsimmons did come back the next day but only to tell us at the door that Father had still not been found. "I'll be here again as soon as I know anythin', ma'am." By then we had almost given up hope for we knew Father was not a swimmer.

This time Mother asked him, "How could such a thing happen? William was na' a fighter."

"Ah, Mrs. Dowling, I canna say much. Some of thim men aren't s' nice if'n they thinks somebody ain't carryin' their share uv th' load. But I niver thought Irishmen wud be mean to another Irish. They say 'twas an accident 'n they jes stumbled. I wasna' there. I jes dinna know eny more. The current in East River is strong and we wuz working on the last ship at the end of the dock so poor William jes' went downriver, I'm afraid." Then, after a long pause with his lip quivering, he said, "G'bye ma'am." and ducked down the hall.

The next day he came back to tell us that Father's body had been found in New York Harbor and that the warehouse company would make burial arrangements for us. Mother received the news with a clenched jaw and no tears in her eyes. "Very well," she said with some authority. "Please go to Father Higgins at Redeemer Church and tell him what must be done. Tell him we will be there later today to pray with him."

Never before had Mother been so calm and determined. Now that I think back on it, I would say that she was in a daze but thinking very clearly and deliberately. As soon as she sent Mr. Fitzsimmons on his way to Redeemer Church, she sat me down on the sofa and looked at me straight on. "Annie, this is a bad 'un. We knew yer Father wasna' real well and tha' he maybe couldna' keep up but we dinna know it was this bad. It may be tha' those men he told me about did this on purpose but we canna ever know for sure."

"But Mother, why would anybody hurt Father?" I wailed.

"We dinna know they did, Annie. One thing I do know. There's nothin' to be done about it." Mother sat there for a few minutes then said something that has always stayed with me. "We kin cry and feel sorry fer ourselves but I don't see that we git much help that way. God helps those who helps themself. We can take this as God's will an' make up our minds that we'll be the stronger fer it. We hafta go it alone now, Annie. Kin ye do it w' me?"

She said it so forcefully, even enthusiastically and with a smile, that in spite of my sorrow and confusion I believed her. I nodded my head but couldn't speak.

We went to see Father Higgins and we prayed for forgiveness for all the men that worked with Father and for Mr. Fitzsimmons and for all the Irish in New York. We prayed for ourselves and Father Higgins seemed to be cheered by the new-found strength my mother showed. When it came time to decide on the church service she simply said to him, "You do it in the right way, Father, and we'll be here to give William a proper burial." The warehouse company paid for the burial and even gave Mother the full week's pay Father would have received. I didn't know how these things worked but we thought that was nice. Many years later Mother would tell me that she always thought they did that so we wouldn't make trouble for them.

Both of us were surprised at how many people came to Redeemer Church for the Saturday afternoon funeral. Though Father never said much to others after church services, lots of people knew us and it took a long time for all of them to file past us and tell us how sorry they were.

CHAPTER 7

REDEEMER CHURCH

After Father's death we spent more time in church activities and I was in some of the programs at holiday time. Mother joined a women's group that knitted scarves and mittens for the convent. The sisters were still helping Irish immigrants like they helped us. As Mother said one day after church, "People o' th' same stock are friendly." She was right again.

Each morning before I left for school Mother would brush my long, shiny black hair and make it into braids. Those became my trademark at school. Classes were getting more exciting every year. As I progressed through the grades I found that school was one place where I could do better than most. My effort to use good grammar had stopped any teasing from the others in class and my teachers were using me as an example of what could be done. They'd say, "If a girl from a foreign country can speak properly, you can too."

In the year after Father's death we received a letter from Willie and Brandon. We had never received mail but the man who managed the rooming house brought it up to us as soon as Mother came home. With a pounding heart I opened it and read to her. Mother kept this one all her life. It was printed and the words were spelled just as they are here:

Dere Father an Mother an Annie

We got ur letr and this is writen by mr. Murphy oaner of store wher Brandon works. we r stil here. Brandon wus verry sick for a long tim but is now first rate. I now get payd for my work and sav some. most cottiers gone now but no more famin. same as before famin now. Brandon says he will stay here. I hav girl to marrie nex year for then I will save enuf money. She is Ellen Haggerty. We wil try t have a store like mr. Murphy in Abbyfeale wher she is from. Writ agan.

Love
Willie and Brandon too

(writtin by Joseph Murphy, esq.) County Kerry, Ireland 1851.

Mother had tears in her eyes when I finished. "My boys, oh dear, I'll niver see 'em again. Well, at least they sound alright t' me 'n mebe 'tis fer th' best. They would na' be good in school like you, Annie. Without schoolin' they'd be jis like yer Father—havin' to work hisself to death all day."

"Let's write them again some day, Mother," I said. "This time I can write the letter all by myself."

"'N Willie is gettin' married. I wonder if Ellen Haggerty is part of the Haggerty family that lived north of Listowel. Let's ask 'em next time we write, Annie."

In my fifth grade year, I had a surprise that made school a lot more fun. Dorah Binchley enrolled at Washington School. After we separated at St. Catherine's Convent we had lost each other.

Dorah's father was working as a gardener for the city of New York. Her older sister worked as a cleaner in a big house on 54th Street. She knew how, for she and Dorah had taken care of things since her mother had died in the famine. The Binchleys had a two room flat and it was in a nicer building. That didn't bother me for Mother had convinced me that where we lived didn't matter. Dorah didn't know where Molly Caitlin was.

I began to gain some weight and though I would never be tall, I was at last a healthy person. Mother also shook off most of the effects of our poor nutrition in Ireland. She seemed to have more energy and delighted in my learning process. Some evenings if she wasn't too tired from her cleaning and laundry work, she would have me read out loud and show her how the multiplication tables worked. On weekends we walked around New York City. So many people were moving here that some wooden buildings were being torn down and bigger brick ones were going up. Horses and wagons were everywhere in the streets. Such a hustle!

We were liking America more all the time. When I was starting into my teenage years, Ireland was almost like a bad dream. Every time I'd say something like that to Mother she would come back with, "Annie, don't e'er forget yer homeland. 'Tis who ye' are and allus will be. An' we did have some good years there before the famine." I knew she was right but mostly I remembered being hungry and the cold, rainy foggy days.

When I would mention being poor to Mother she would come right back with another of her proverbs. "Poverty is no shame, Annie." She would say it with the same firmness that my teachers used to emphasize a point in class. Mother's proverbs played a big part in my growing up.

I was 13 years old when one Sunday Father Higgins announced that he was being assigned to another parish on the west side of New York City. He said the new priest would be coming in the next week from South Carolina and that his name was Father Donahue. Mother and I looked at each other when we heard that name. Could it be? Surely not, for he would be coming from Ireland, not South Carolina. After church, Mother asked, "Father Higgins, d'ye by chance know Father Donahue's first name?"

"I believe 'tis Timothy, Mrs. Dowling," the Father replied.

Mother gasped, "That's him—our priest in County Kerry. D'ye 'spose it could be the same one after all these years?"

"I don't know Emma, he came from Ireland but has been in Charleston, South Carolina for some time now. I'm told that others are comin' with him."

All we could do was wait until the next Sunday, but the minute we saw him we knew it was our Father Donahue. We fell into each other's arms. Mother was crying with joy, "Oh Father, I have so much to ask ye."

"Mrs. Dowling!—and little Annie—but ye're not s' little now are ye Annie? Oh, 'tis good to see ye both. We'll talk more after the prayer service tonight."

Father Donahue went back to greeting all the other members of the parish who wanted to meet him. He wasn't as chubby as I remembered him but he seemed even shorter. When I said that to Mother she told me that since I was almost a grown girl now I didn't have to look up to see him so that was the reason.

We sometimes didn't go to prayer service but that Sunday night we did. Of course, Father Donahue couldn't spend all his time with us but Mother had a dozen questions for him. "Ah, Ella, the famine did us all in. The church at Ballyduff went out in 1849. Just not enough people. Some went to Listowel but I fear most dinna go t' chuch anymore. Th' dyin' kept on fer another year. Seemed like all I did was do funerals."

"When did y' come to America, Father?" Mother asked.

"In 1850 'twas. Many of the cottiers around Abbyfeale got t' thinkin' they should come to th' new country. Though they niver suffered quite like you folks, they cud see that 'twasn't goin' t' git much better even when the potatoes came back. They had better land so they had enough t' pay th' fare."

"You mean they had to pay their own ship ticket?" Mother asked.

"Aye, they knew there'd not be enough t' divide for their children 'n they was afraid the murrain would go on. Some heard back from folks like you who came here in '47 and '48. That gave 'em courage to try it. We went to Dublin for we thought we'd get better ships."

"We all came to New York," Mother said, "did you go straight to South Carolina?"

"Aye, we did. We was going to make it for New York but in Dublin there was a tobacco ship that had room for 100 people they said and there was 120 of us. The tickets were less if we would go with them and they said the chances were better there anyway. They packed all of us aboard"

"Our trip was awful, Father. I would never do that again."

"Aye, 'twas a hard trip we had too, and sad to say, we lost some. They called them "coffin ships" for good reason, I guess. Most of the ones from Carolina will be comin' t' church here in the next few weeks," Father Donahue said as he turned to another parishioner.

There were many more questions but those had to wait 'til later. We found out that South Carolina had been hard for them just like it was for us at first in New York. There weren't many jobs in town so both the men and women ended up on tobacco farms. They worked the fields and told us that it was even harder than potatoes and grain. Not as many rocks, though, and the wooden cabins they lived in were better than our huts in Ireland.

Some families kept in touch with the ones that came to New York and many of them decided to come here where the jobs paid more and the women could find work in homes instead of the fields. They sent Father Donahue on the train to New York to find out if this was true. When he returned he had the assignment at our parish.

Chapter 8

PATRICK WHITE

Two Sundays later we met three new families from Abbeyfeale. One was George White and his three boys, Patrick, Tom and Allyn. Mother soon found out that in Ireland the Whites lived along the River Owveg. We lived south of Listowel so our acres were only about 10 miles apart.

While Mr. White and Mother were getting acquainted I was standing in front of three skinny boys and very embarrassed. I didn't know how to begin but I wanted to ask about what South Carolina was like and a lot of other things. They didn't say anything—just stared at me. Finally I blurted out, "What is a tobacco field like and where do you live?"

This strange combination of questions unnerved the two younger boys, Allyn and Tom, so they just shrugged, turned away and wandered off by themselves. Patrick, who was closer to my age, was left standing there with his curly, red hair and the same color spread down over his face.

"Well, 'tis hotter in a tobacco field. 'N we live in New York, not far from here."

By now I was aware of his predicament and I was embarrassed by my questions. Without thinking I asked another: "Why aren't you as tall as your younger brothers?"

By this time he was at a loss for words and moved away to find his brothers without answering. I felt uneasy with myself for I usually knew how to talk to others. This encounter was unsettling.

It was several weeks before I spoke to any of the Whites again. Mother would say "hello" to them at church and we were meeting others from Killorglin or Abbeyfeale every week. I did find myself looking for Patrick and peeking at him out of the corner of my eye. At first I told myself I didn't want to bump into him again for I would probably ask some more dumb questions. After a few weeks of this, Mother said to me as we walked home from church, "Mr. White and his sons are very nice, aren't they?"

Almost before she finished asking the question, I blurted out, "Yes, I guess so, oh, I don't know, maybe, I s'pose." Mother looked at me as I stuttered and noticed that I was blushing and then she knew. I had discovered boys.

Mother began talking about the dances the church sponsored and how the Sunday night prayer services had a young adult Bible class that met in the church basement. She might say, "Would you like to go to these?" or "Would you like a new dress for church?" I'd never had a new dress in my life except the time Mother had made over one that belonged to Dorah Binchley's older sister. Usually Mother would sew them from her old dresses or she would buy them at the bargain store on Second Street.

About halfway through my seventh grade, I started attending Sunday night Bible classes. Our teacher would ask us to take turns reading verses and then we would discuss them. There were a few boys in the group and none of them knew how to read very well. When one of them had to take his turn, we girls would snicker and make fun of him. The worst part was that they couldn't explain what the verses meant.

Most of them still talked with the same Irish accent and their grammar was not good. I was very aware of this because of Mother and Mrs. Hilty. Some of the girls in the group had the same trouble changing over to the American way of speech but a few worked hard at it like I did.

By the end of that school year, I was ready to see what the monthly dances were like. Some of the girls had invited me to come. The church basement was small and the walls were made out of rock with whitewash over them. There were pipes running overhead and some of the tall boys would have to duck to avoid hitting their heads. There were twice as many girls as boys.

I'd never been to a social event before so I was shy and uncomfortable at first. The second one I attended one of the boys, Glen Walsh, asked me to dance. I didn't know how so one of the older girls said they would show me for a few dances. After that they told Glen to ask me again and we tried. I was quivering as I put my arm around his waist and I'm sure I must have been awkward as a newborn calf that first time. I danced with another boy that same evening. When I arrived home, I was chattering to Mother about how much fun it was. I think she knew that a new part of my life was beginning.

One Sunday morning that summer the three White brothers said "hello" to me as we left church. The next Sunday they said "hi" and then the two younger ones quickly walked away. Patrick and I were standing alone outside the church. Patrick grinned and said to me, "I 'spose you have some more questions for me?"

I blushed and stammered, "Not now, I was just glad to see someone from closer to home. When I heard you lived in South Carolina, I thought that was different."

"Yes, 'twas," Patrick said, "but we all like New York better. My Papa has a good job and I like school better here, too."

"Did you go to school in Carolina?"

"Yes," he said, "all three years we were there."

I could tell that he talked more "American" than most. There was only a hint of Irish accent and he stood up straight. For the first time I looked right at him and smiled. Now he was the one who blushed.

In the next few minutes, we had the longest conversation I'd ever had with a boy. I chattered about South Carolina and the White family most of the time that Mother and I walked home from church. As we were getting ready for lunch Mother asked, "You had a nice visit with Patrick White didn't you?" It was my turn to blush and by that time we both realized, even though it wasn't said, that I had a crush on Patrick.

We saw each other at church and he began coming to Bible study and the dances. It was quite a while before he asked me to dance. By that time I'd danced once or twice with most of the boys that attended. Mostly we girls just sat together and giggled over our dreams and guesses about what the boys were like. When Patrick did get enough courage to ask me to dance, I rewarded him with a big smile and accepted with more pleasure than with the others. He wasn't a good dancer but I wasn't either. It didn't make any difference. It wasn't long before I was again asking lots of questions and now he was glad to answer.

I wanted to know about his life in Ireland and he was happy to talk about it. "We lived south of Abbeyfeale and Father had 12 acres. We had a good middler and our land was in the river bottom." Patrick's eyes glowed when he talked about their land. "'Twas some of th' best there. Not many rocks to pick and every year good grain as the river gave us lots of water underneath. Only once when I was very young did we have a big flood and that year there was not much wheat or barley."

He told me about his two brothers. Allyn was the strongest and the one that helped take care of their two cows and horse. Tom had been sickly from having trouble breathing and never worked outside very much. Before the famine all the boys had gone to a church school in Tralee. Patrick went for three years and Tom and Allyn for two.

I wondered how they survived the famine. "Not well, Annie," Patrick said. "But we had grain enough to pay the rent and some years we could keep some to help in the winter. Our problem was getting enough peat for the winter. We were farther from Ardagh Bog than you folks. Sometimes we wouldn't try to keep our second room warm."

"You had two rooms?" I asked.

"Yes, we three boys had our own room. It was really just a small add-on to the main hut. Still 'twas our own."

I didn't want to talk about our ocean trip and twice he had said he didn't want to talk about his. But I asked again just to keep him talking to me. "'Twas terrible, Annie. The *Dauntless* wasn't made to take lots of people and even then they only should have had 100. But they was tryin' to make more money and they cut the rate for us. We came in the winter and got into storms. We were all below decks with no fresh air and everybody sick. Some people went up on deck to heave and was washed over. We lost three that way, one of 'em a child. We did have enough food but the water nearly ran out and some died because of that."

I thought I should tell something about our trip. "We lost eighteen people. It was awful from the sickness and not even a clean, dry place to lie down."

"My mama was one of them that was lost on our ship. She was sick from the time we got on the ship till three days out of Charleston. Just kept gettin' worse. Had to bury her at sea. We never should have gone on that ship."

I could tell that it was not easy to talk about it so I never asked any more. Somehow I felt like I knew him a lot better after he told me all of that.

Patrick's father had an older sister who had lived in New York and moved to Charleston with her husband when the first big textile mills were built there. After he died she stayed on and ran a piece goods store. Mr. White knew that and found out where she lived. She took in her brother's family.

When Patrick heard about some of the bad ways the Irish in New York were treated, he said, "That's nothin'. You should've seen how they talked to us down there in Charleston and on the tobacco farms. Everybody I know is sure glad they came to New York."

Patrick told me that he was enrolled in a seminary school as his Aunt Maude had decided that he should become a priest. Because of that he had read lots of books. After two years Patrick said he wanted out and his father didn't force him to stay. None of them liked what they had down there and they felt that they were imposing on his Aunt Maude. She acted like it, too. So when they heard that Father Donahue was coming here, they took the same train.

Mr. White had found a job driving one of the carriages that provided transportation for the rich people in New York. When Patrick was 15, he started working there after school and on Saturdays helping take care of the horses and mending harnesses.

He and Allyn once got in trouble by taking a horse and carriage out one evening after everything was supposed to be closed. They headed for one of the parks and were acting grown up, they thought. The trouble began when the horse got spooked by some bright, new gaslights on lampposts and the boys couldn't manage him. The animal ran off into some brush along the road and got tangled up in the harness. A policeman and other people had to untangle the mess and of course their father found out about it. Neither one had much freedom for a long time after that.

Patrick said after they moved to New York his father's other sister, Norinda Gath, came to stay with them and help with cooking and laundry for the family. Her husband had died in the first year after they married. It was in the second year of famine, and their farm was above Ballyduff on a rocky slope of Beek's Hill that never did grow good grain and not many potatoes. When the three boys were gone from home, Norinda moved out, too, and went to work in a hospital.

Once they invited Mother and me for Sunday dinner. We all walked together from church up to their apartment. It was larger than ours and on the third floor of a newer building. Each of their two rooms were bigger than our one. We had a happy time. Both Mr. White and his sister talked to me and treated me just like one of the family. As we left Patrick pulled me aside and said softly in my ear, "I'm glad you came today."

A tingle went down my back and I quickly replied, "I'm glad, too. Your family is nice." Then my same blushing came back again but this time I didn't mind. I just kept looking right at Patrick and he also turned a little red and gave me a big smile.

This time I "floated" as I walked home with Mother. At first I didn't say anything for I was quivering so.

Mother could tell and finally asked, "Patrick's a nice boy, isn't he?"

"Oh, he is!" I exclaimed, then realized I was revealing too much. I quickly followed with "Oh well, I guess so." I'm sure Mother wasn't fooled.

CHAPTER 9

JEFFERSON HIGH SCHOOL

I graduated from Washington Elementary with the fourth highest grades in my class of 61. Mother was all smiles as she sat in the second row at the ceremony. That summer she introduced me to the public libraries. There were two within walking distance of our apartment. We went there some Saturdays and most Sunday afternoons. She told me, "Annie, you've shown me that you can learn. Now 'tis time to open your mind to some new things."

Mother had the good sense to ask the librarian what books would be good for me. The librarian showed me how to use their card files and find the books on the shelves. It was a new world for me. Soon I was going there on my own when Mother was busy. I read newspapers and found out about magazines and where they were filed. Although I never got into the really famous classic books, I found adventure and learning in those buildings that helped me a lot as I got older and too busy to spend time reading.

Patrick White was two years ahead of me in school. After finishing eighth grade at Our Lady of Grace school, he went to Thomas Jefferson High School on the corner of Stanton and Essex Streets. That's also where I went. We saw each other in the halls. I sometimes danced and spent time talking with other boys but Patrick was the one I liked the best. He liked me, I could tell, for he always had a big smile when he would see me.

In my second year of high school we took the same history class. I was one year ahead of my class in this course because I had done so much reading. We didn't sit close together since 'D' and 'W' were far apart in the alphabet. He was one row ahead of me and on the other side of the room. I would peek over just to enjoy seeing his rumpled red hair that had to be cut short to keep it from forming ringlets. Sometimes he would turn back to look at me and give me a wink if he thought no one was looking.

Our history class was the last one in the day. Later in the school year, we would walk on Stanton Street together until I had to turn down to where we lived. A few times we would stop to sit on the curb or on one of the low brick walls that most buildings had in front. Patrick would say things like, "I like to hear Mrs. Kingery talk about the West y' know out there past Ohio and Kentucky. All those gold rush men talk like there's no other people there except Indians." Then a little later after I had agreed with him he would say, "Annie, someday I think I could be like those Oregon Trail people or the soldiers that fight the Indians. They say there may be free land someday for anybody that wants it." When he talked I could see his blue eyes shining with excitement.

After several conversations like this, one day I said, "Patrick, you're going to finish high school aren't you?"

"I think so," he answered, "but I can't wait to see the West."

During his last year in high school he had even hinted a few times that he thought I should see the West, too. I wasn't sure—maybe a little afraid. Even so, I found myself studying more about that part of the United States and wondering if Patrick meant that we were to see the West together. He was a dreamer, that I knew. He had big ideas, but in other things, he didn't seem to get excited. I wanted to talk more about us. I was the one who first held his hand while we were walking home one day. He didn't act like he cared but after that I noticed that most of the time when no one was looking he would reach out for mine.

We danced at the senior dance at school and at church. He still worked part time in the livery and usually had some money. He bought me sodas and one glorious Sunday we walked to a park and spent the afternoon watching the ducks and swans on one of the ponds. Couples were being driven around in carriages pulled by beautiful horses.

On the grass, in the shade of a big chestnut tree, he kissed me for the first time. "Patrick, it's broad daylight, what if people see us?"

"I don't care, Annie, if you like it, I think I should do it again." And he did.

We both liked it and for a few glorious minutes we experienced our long-delayed feelings for each other. But after what must have been the fifth intense kiss, I jumped to my feet and pulled myself together as I gasped, "We musn't do this anymore. Someone is watching, I know it! This can't be right, we aren't married and maybe we don't want to be." I said it without thinking and immediately wished I could take it back.

From the little bit Mother and I had talked about boys and marriage, I felt that girls never brought up the subject. It was always the boys who should be the ones who talked about it. Dorah was even more straight-laced. She thought that kissing was only for couples after marriage and that it might be what makes women have babies. In looking back now, I'm amused and a bit ashamed that we were so naive. Perhaps it's just as well for we sure didn't give our parents or our priests any problems.

When Patrick graduated, he immediately joined the United States Army. He told me ahead of time and my first thought was that he didn't like me anymore. I started sobbing. "You'll be so far away, Pat. What will I do without you?"

He gave me one of his big laughs and said, "Annie, you'll finish school and come to see me some day, that's what you'll do—I hope."

"Come to see you? I couldn't do that."

"Well then, I hope you'll write me. Then I'll write back and tell you what 'tis really like out there. They've promised I'll be sent to Texas."

When Pat left I went with his father and sister to the train. Though they were the ones who spent most of the time with him, I was thrilled that I was the last one he hugged. "Don't forget Annie, answer my letters. Maybe give me two for each one of mine. I'll be back for you. I love you." Then he gave me a brief kiss right in front of Mr. White and his sister—and stepped on the train. I was so astonished and delighted by his declaration of love and the public kiss that I was rooted in place and gazing at the train steps where Patrick had disappeared.

"Well," Mr. White said, "Patrick has come to like you hasn't he?"

"I hope so," I said as sincerely as I could. "I like him a lot."

CHAPTER 10

FT. BLISS

Fort Bliss: *This is from a recruiting poster that Pat saved.*

Here is Pat's first letter to me. I've kept it all these years folded up in our family Bible.

Miss Annie Dowling
342 E. Ridge St.
Room 2 C
New York City
New York

Dear Annie,

Please excuse my writing and spelling. I am not as good as you but I will try because I want you to write me soon. All the way on the train I thought of our last kiss and how good you looked to me when we said goodby. I miss you more than anyone there and I have many things to say when we can hold hands agan. I never thougt there was so much diffrince in one country. From Kansas on it was bare and dry. Hardly any trees except on the creeks and rivers. Here tis worse.

Hardly any grass just a lot of rocks. Army life is harder that I thougt. Not the Army part but the sitting around and doing things that dont have anything to do with fighting Indians. The other boys are alright but some don't use good manners or languge. The best man here is James Longstreet. He is the officer in charge. We get along real good. Most are a hard lot but two or three boys and I go fishing in the river Rio Grande when we have time off. Not much else to do except drill and clean baracks and wash dishes. Write soon. Can I say again I love you and miss you?

Patrick White
July 6 1856

Pat's letter was only the second one received at our address so it was a most exciting event when the landlord brought it up one evening. I reddened when I opened it since it was addressed only to me. Mother watched me closely as I read it then as I clutched it to my chest, tears came to my eyes. "Not bad news, is it Annie."

"Oh no, good news Mother. He says again that he loves me. Do you think he really does?"

By now Mother had learned to read almost as well as I so I handed her the letter. As she read it carefully her head nodded evenly and when she finished she looked at me a long time before saying, "Patrick is a good boy, Annie. He's always been honorable to you hasn't he?"

"Oh yes, Mother. Very honorable." Then, seeing a chance to further his cause with Mother, I said, "He did a good bit of learning at school."

My answer took me several days to compose. I knew he would be anxious to get a letter and now that I had his address I wanted to write soon. But I wasn't sure how bold to be.

This was my reply:

Pvt. Patrick White
U.S. Infantry, Eighth Regt.
Ft. Bliss, Texas

Dear Patrick,

Yours of July 6 was most welcome and I thank you for saying I love you. That was the best part. I heard you say it at the train when you left but it was even better when you said it in your letter. It sounds like the army is about like you expected. I wish there were more trees there. No Indian fights yet I hope.

Mother and I are alright and we see your father and brothers at church almost every week. They are alright, too. I don't go to the church dances anymore. You aren't there.(HaHa) School is fine but I miss the walks with you. I got a job in a sewing company last summer and work there now one night a week and on Saturdays. We make dresses and coats. This extra money helps us. I will write again when I have something to say. For now I will say I miss you and please write again soon.

Annie
September 23, 1856

Pat was at Ft. Bliss for almost two years. Since it took about a month for each letter to get to its destination, we only wrote about five letters each year. I didn't keep copies of any of the others. Pat told about Army life and about how the men liked Captain Longstreet. The captain had grown up on a plantation in Georgia and liked to talk about farming. They took a liking to each other. Pat felt that he was one of the few enlisted men that got to know him well. He would later become famous as General Longstreet though he was on the Rebel side.

Pat didn't talk much about the hard work they did but mostly about the barren country around the fort. He did tell proudly about the garden at the fort. He and a group of other men volunteered to start one. The second year they dug a ditch from the Rio Grande River to the garden and raised lots of vegetables. Pat said because he was a farmer in Ireland he knew the work but other farm boys were there, too. For most of these two years his regular Army job was repairing wagons and harnesses for the horses that pulled them.

Some of his letters talked about the soldiers who were complaining about the jobs they had to do. Pat said they called it "housekeeping." These recruits would say that they had joined the Army to fight Indians, not to pick up trash and sweep out the barracks. Pat said they really griped when they had to do the kitchen duties.

Pat's letters always ended with an "I love you" and after a year, I started using that also as my ending. He was acting like I was his only girlfriend and I knew he was my only one but I still wasn't sure how far it might go. Dorah Binchley and I spent hours telling each other our feelings and that helped a lot. Dorah had gone with several boys and now had one that she was real serious about. Except for a few dances and walks with other boys, I really didn't have anyone to compare with Pat.

Mother was always willing to talk about Pat but she waited for me to bring up the subject. Once after I had a long talk with Dorah, I asked Mother, "Is a boy supposed to kiss only one girl before he gets married?"

Mother smiled and answered, "Probably a boy will kiss several girls and then the one he likes the best will be the one he asks to marry him."

After thinking about that for a minute, I said, "Do you suppose Pat is kissing other girls there at Ft. Bliss?"

Mother chuckled and said, "I doubt if there are many girls there. I wouldn't worry about that, dear."

During the summers I worked full time at a factory that had dozens of women hand-stitching clothing. I earned 15 cents an hour. On Sundays after church I would spend the afternoon and evening at a public library. In the evenings I read books checked out from there. I was reading mostly about the Western United States and Army life on the frontier.

My high school graduation was a big occasion for Mother. She knew that Willie and Brandon would probably never go to school. This made her especially proud that I graduated with honors. I completed my time at Jefferson with the sixth-best grade average in our class of 94.

Mother could now afford a nicer place to stay but she put her extra money in the bank where it would earn interest. She would say, "Let the money work for us, Annie, then someday maybe we won't have to work for our money."

In the early summer of 1858 Pat wrote me a short letter to say that in a month he would be getting a leave and coming to New York. When he arrived I soon knew that he was the one for me. He wanted to spend all his time with me and I felt the same way. His red hair was bleached from the sun and his freckled arms and blue eyes seemed more evident than I remembered. He seemed taller and he acted older and more serious.

The second night he was back we walked down to a little park overlooking the East River and talked for a long time about what he had seen on his long trip to and from Ft. Bliss. The more he talked the more excited he became. After a long kiss he said, "I want to stay in the Army 'cause I think I can be sent back to the West and find out more about that land. They will pay me to see it and someday maybe we can find the right place for us."

I looked straight at him and said, "Us, Pat? What do you mean?"

"I'm saying that it should be 'us' from now on. I want to marry you, Annie. Will you?"

Although I'd dreamed about such a moment ever since I knew he was coming back, I still was unprepared and overwhelmed. "I guess so, Pat. Maybe. I think so. Yes! I want to! But is it the right thing to do? Shouldn't you ask my mother? Have you asked your father?"

Pat just let out a burst of high-pitched laughter. He was as nervous as I. "Ah, Annie, we can do all that. First thing I want to know is do you really want to do it? Can you travel with me? Will you be happy with the Army 'til we can someday get land of our own?"

My destiny was sealed with my eager answer, "Yes. I'm your girl and I want to be Mrs. Patrick White no matter what else happens."

My mother and Mr. White were glad to see us marry. It was arranged quickly since Patrick had to report back to duty in a week. It was August of 1858.

Dorah gave a party for me at her house the night before the wedding and invited some of my best friends from high school and one from where I worked. The big surprise was that Molly Caitlin was there. Dorah had asked several of the other families that had come to America with us and finally found her.

The Caitlins had moved to the west side of Manhattan Island where her father had a job with a combination tailor shop and laundry. Her mother worked in a restaurant as waitress and cook. It was wonderful to see her again. Molly had stopped going to school after eighth grade and had a job as a worker in a book binding company. We giggled and teased each other and talked until after midnight, the latest I had ever stayed out.

Father Donahue did the wedding mass and it was a beautiful day for us even though it was raining outside. I asked Dorah to be my maid of honor and Pat's brothers were both best men. Mother bought a new dress for my wedding. She said it was the first new "dress-up dress" she ever had. Pat's father came to get us in one of his company carriages. What a thrill that was to ride from our house to the church in a fancy surrey like that one. Pat wore his Army uniform and was more handsome than ever. It was the happiest and most elegant day of my life. I will never forget it

CHAPTER 11

SULLIVAN'S ISLAND

The first days of our married life were spent at Mr. White's home. He gave his sister money for a week of vacation in the Catskill Mountains, telling her he didn't think the newlyweds would need her cooking or cleaning for a few days. He and his other boys spent most of the days and nights at his livery stable where he arranged cots.

Pat thought that he would be sent back to an Army fort in Nebraska or Kansas but when he reported for assignment three days after our wedding he received a surprise. "Annie, we're not going west for a while. You're going to see South Carolina!"

"South Carolina!" I exclaimed. "You've already been there!"

Pat laughed, "Yes, I have—guess the Army isn't trying to show me new places every time. They need men at a small fort called Fort Moultrie. I'll be in the First Regiment of the Army Artillery. We'll get to the West later."

Two days later we boarded a southbound train. I thought this was luxurious after my disastrous sailing trip. There were 14 other soldiers traveling with us and we soon got acquainted. Four of them also had their wives and by the time we arrived, I knew that one of them would be my best friend at Ft. Moultrie. Josie Carroll was small like I was and loved to talk. She and her husband, James, were from a small town named York, in eastern Pennsylvania. James had just enlisted in the Army so both of them had lots of questions for Pat.

I mostly listened at first and was pleased and proud to hear how well Pat explained what his experience was at Ft. Bliss. I learned a lot about the Army and about Pat. He had learned to speak well at the parochial schools. He also liked to read books. The more he explained things to the Carrolls the more I fell in love with my red-headed Irishman.

When Josie and James found out that we were just married they teased us a lot. They said they would look the other way while we kissed or they would say that they would hold a blanket up over our seats as we traveled during the night so we could cuddle together. Every time they did this I would blush deeply and so would Pat.

We spent lots of time laughing and promised we would find a place to live close to each other in South Carolina. Little did we know how close we would be! When we arrived in Charleston wagons and carriages were waiting to take us to the docks where we boarded boats for Ft. Moultrie. It was just beyond Castle Pinckney and Sumter, two islands in Charleston Harbor. Moultrie was on the end of a banana-shaped island called Sullivan's Island at the mouth of the harbor. The fort was small and on the part of the island closest to the ship channel.

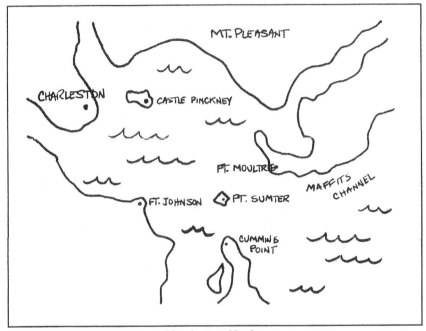

Charleston Harbor

Our quarters were in a barracks building called the Moultrie House. The South Channel beacon light was on the beach nearby. There was one other building like this called the Sullivan House. Each had five double rooms which were assigned to the married soldiers. We were going to be crowded but we were newly married and in love and happy so we looked right past the small room. The Carrolls were in the room right across the hall from us.

Ft. Moultrie had only 85 military personnel, six officers and 79 enlisted men. Our island was sandy and we were told that it was called an off-shore sand bar made by ocean waves. So much of this was new to Josie and I that we were busy exploring for the first month. It was my first experience on a seashore. There were eight married couples and the wives gathered every day or so just to have something to do.

We were amazed at the thousands of tiny sea shells all over the beach.

Some big ones were called sand dollars. We collected them and used them to decorate our window sills. We loved walking the beaches barefooted. On the ocean side of the island there were often huge waves and we learned to walk out in the water until it was up to our knees, then let a wave splash us. Sometimes we would get completely wet or almost knocked off our feet. These were happy times.

The other wives were nice but Josie was special. Though she was about my size, she was heavier. I would complain about how thin I was and she worried about her weight. Josie said she should have been named 'Brown' for her hair, eyes and skin were brown. She told me that her parents were Italian and that's where she got her darker skin. She liked to keep her long hair in braids. I learned to do it for her. Her town background in York, Pennsylvania was much different than mine. That provided a subject for many conversations.

We kept our doors open across the hall during the day so we could talk to each other. After we had walked the outside of the island a few times and exhausted the topics of conversations with the other wives, we started thinking of things to do. We got acquainted with Captain Abner Doubleday, who was the second in command, and asked him if the wives could see the fort. Ten days later he told us that it was arranged.

Captain Doubleday gave us the tour. He made a formal event out of it by starting with coffee and cookies in the officer's mess room at the fort. The kitchen was on one side of this room and beyond that was the enlisted men's mess hall. After visiting with each of us the captain showed us the ammunition storage rooms. We looked at the repair shops and the big guns which were aimed south across the harbor entrance. There were three batteries pointed toward Maffit's Channel and Hog Island. Five batteries faced south towards Cummings Point and east to the sea. I was bold enough to ask, "Captain, do you think any pirates ever sailed into this harbor?" The other women giggled at such a silly question but the captain took it seriously.

He answered, "Mrs. White, we are told that many did, and not too long ago."

We visited the infirmary. This was like a doctor's office with lots of bottles and bandages. Captain Doubleday said that this was an emergency room only. In the event of a serious injury or illness the soldier would be taken to a Charleston hospital.

We saw the rifle slots built into the walls to supplement the big guns. We ended by walking all around the fort on the outside and saw a big ditch that had been dug to slow down any ground attack. It was also interesting to see how the walls were sloped outward to make them extra strong. The strange part was that the wind had blown sand up around the walls. Now they were only about 12 feet above ground and weak in some places. A person could walk up the sloping dunes almost to the top on one corner.

The captain told us this was an old fort. It had been built by William Moultrie during the Revolutionary War. The commanding officer then was Richard Anderson. It was almost a sacred spot for the people from South Carolina because he held fast against the British. Now the commanding officer was his son, Major Robert Anderson.

Captain Doubleday was a well-educated man. He was proud of the fact that Edgar Allen Poe was once at Fort Moultrie as an Army private. Poe wrote a long poem and his famous story, "The Gold Bug," here. This was also where Osceola, the chief of the Seminole Indians, was brought after he was captured just 20 years before we were there. He was a sort of a celebrity for a few weeks but soon became ill and died. His grave and headstone were near the entrance to the fort.

All the wives agreed that we liked Captain Doubleday and that we were glad we got to see the inside of the fort. Many years later I heard this same Captain Abner Doubleday was credited with inventing the game of baseball. We knew someone who would become famous.

James Carroll was assigned as a gunner. They were called 18 pounders because that was how much the cannonballs weighed. The cannon barrels were seven inches across. The fort had 12 of these mounted on big wooden and iron pedestals. James had been reared on a farm near York. He was sturdy—we could tell he had worked hard all his life. He was what my mother would have called raw-boned.

Pat was called an artificer which was a fancy name for someone who does repairs. It was his job to keep the wagons and harnesses repaired. It was much easier than Ft. Bliss, he said, because the Army had only six wagons and 18 horses on the island, not nearly as many as at Bliss. The wagons were used to bring supplies from the docks. He also worked on any other kind of repair that was needed.

On Pat's day off we would sometimes take the boat into Charleston. We visited the library where we both checked out books about the Western United States. The more we read the more we wanted to read. This easy assignment for Pat was a good way for us to begin our lives together. Pat even showed me where he had lived with his father and brothers at his Aunt Maude's house. She was now back in New York City.

I loved Pat, there was no doubt about that. Sometimes his temper would flare up at something that had gone wrong but it was not in anger at me. He was easy to live with and made friends with the other soldiers. We had beach parties on their days off duty and usually included some of the unmarried men also. We even had some dances and by then we both were good at twirling. I was always comparing him with the others and though I might have dreamed of a tall, handsome husband, I was happy with the short, red haired, ordinary-looking one I had.

Josie and I talked about how lazy we were getting. We'd explored the island and part of Charleston and felt that we should be doing something more useful. Mrs. Raines, a school woman from Charleston, came to the fort to speak to the Army wives. Afterward Josie and I asked her if there were any jobs we could do.

"You sure can," she said. "We need a teacher for a school we're opening on the north end of the island. There are about a dozen poor families that have never had a chance to send their children to any kind of a school. Could one of you get it started until we get a full-time teacher?"

Josie and I looked at each other. "How much schooling have you had, Josie?"

"Through high school in York," she said.

"The same for me in New York."

Mrs. Raines laughed, "I like that—York and New York. We should get you both up there and call it the York School."

We looked at each other and almost at the same time said, "Why not?"

An abandoned grocery store was made into a school. Mrs. Raines turned out to be the County School Superintendent. Neither of us could have imagined that we'd be school teachers. When we saw the room, there were some second thoughts. One of the reasons the grocery closed must have been the building's awful condition. Everything about it was sagging. We knew this was for a short time and in spite of what we saw we agreed to try the volunteer job.

Mrs. Raines told us the building would be cleaned and it was. She arranged for a buggy to transport us each morning and afternoon. Different fathers took turns driving the buggy. It was only four miles to the school.

School started in September with 14 children. There were no desks but each child had a chair pulled up to a table. The ages ranged from six to 17. Only one had been inside a school room before. Mrs. Raines spent two hours with us—then we were on our own.

Josie took the arithmetic and penmanship classes. I did English and reading. That was what was taught each day. We had four hours of school—one hour for each of the four subjects. Some children were afraid of being there. Others were angry because their parents forced them to come. Two were just confused—they didn't know why they were there and didn't care.

We didn't have textbooks for each child. Mrs. Raines provided us with five copies of beginning books or workbooks in the four courses. The teacher kept one and the other four were shared by the 14 children as they clustered around four tables.

Josie and I were tired by the end of each day for we had to teach them discipline as well as the subject. By the end of the first two weeks, we loved two-thirds of them and wished the other one-third would leave. Then visits by three parents changed our feeling. It happened that these parents had the four boys that were giving us the most trouble. They must have known it for they apologized for their children's lack of understanding about schooling. The boys were older and hated the idea of being "penned up," as they called it. The parents let us know they appreciated what we were doing and promised that the boys would not disrupt classes again.

Our work was easier then. After three months of effort we both could see that we were making progress. The most satisfying part was the improvement in their reading. I remembered Mrs. Hilty in New York and how much she had helped me. I tried to use some of her techniques, though I wasn't nearly as good as she was. Josie had all the children doing well on their simple arithmetic problems and all but one had learned how to write legibly. Mrs. Raines did find a qualified, full-time teacher and after just two days with her, we were released.

It was all worthwhile when four of the mothers came to school at lunch time on our last day. They spoke to Josie and I and thanked us over and over. One of the women had tears in her eyes as she hugged us goodbye. "Bless you," she said. "Now my little girls will amount to something." She handed each of us a pecan pie she had baked. It was a happy ride home that evening.

Four women from Charleston lived in the post barracks. Two of them did the laundry, ironing and mending for the soldiers, one cleaned and helped the officers' wives and one worked in the infirmary. The two women who did the laundry had just quit their jobs. I asked Josie, "Why don't we apply for those jobs? We could use the money."

"Do you think James and Pat would agree?"

"They didn't argue about school teaching. Let's ask."

They were surprised but didn't mind. The person in charge of these jobs was the quartermaster, Captain John Foster. When we applied for the jobs, he was surprised. "Of course you can do it," he quickly said. "But why do you want to?"

I was the first to respond. "We need the money."

"Need the money? Why do you need money here? Aren't your needs taken care of?" Captain Foster seemed genuinely surprised that we thought we needed more money.

I blurted out, "Captain, we want to start saving money to buy land someday."

"Land? Where?"

It was a concept that the captain couldn't grasp. "Somewhere in the West," I said.

Josie chimed in with, "James and I want some land and we don't care where it is. Besides, we are idle most of the day and we want to do something useful."

Captain Foster held up his hands and told us, "Ladies, the jobs are yours, but you'll have to work at it just like the civilian ladies do. It won't do for anyone to say we're playing favorites."

We found the jobs to be easier than some of the tasks we had already done. We only worked six to eight hours a day and the $2.00 per day wages were welcome. The laundry room was a steamy place, though, and it was summer. A sergeant who was on Captain Foster's staff was our supervisor. He and a private would scavenge drift wood and pile it next to the laundry building.

It was our job to carry wash water to the big cast iron kettles and build a fire under them to heat the water. When the water was boiling we would drop the clothes in along with chips from the lye soap made by the local farmers. We stirred and moved the clothes around with a long stick and after 10 minutes of this we used the same stick to dip clothing out into cool rinse water.

If some of the items were badly soiled we would put them into a smaller tub of hot water and scrub them on a washboard before rinsing. Then they would be hung on outside clothes lines. Pat would say that if he saw them on the line by noon, he would know that we were on schedule and that our day's work was half done.

The clothes lines were inside the fort's walls and we felt we didn't get a quick job of drying since we missed a lot of the ocean breezes. But maybe we got less salt spray in them and that was an advantage. When they were dry, it was time to starch the dress shirts. The collars and cuffs got two starch applications.

Most things had to be ironed. Some of the officers even wanted their underwear ironed and we made a few jokes among the wives about that. There were three of the officers who had their wives with them on the island. They each had a house one half-mile away from our barracks. Though they were polite, they were older than the rest of us and clearly felt superior. Except on the two or three occasions when a party was planned for the entire fort, we weren't together.

Weeks became months and soon we had been on that little island almost two years. I surprised Pat one evening by telling him that we were to have a baby. The quartermaster was also the officer in charge of the infirmary. When Captain Foster found that I was with child, he insisted that Pat take a day off and accompany me to Charleston to see a doctor there. The Captain also sat in with the nurse in charge of the infirmary when all my information was recorded at the post. He assured me that I would be well cared for. His courtesy made me feel much better.

Josie Carroll was a big help to me. She was excited about the child, especially since she and James desperately wanted children but had none. With the time drawing near, Josie and I spent more time together, knitting and sewing for the event to come. I worked at the laundry until just two weeks before I was due. Then Josie recruited another enlisted man's wife to take my place at the laundry. I was anxious to have a family but I knew I'd miss the $2 a day that I was saving. We also saved $4 a month from Pat's wages. Our nest egg was building.

Chapter 12

EMMA

The first week of November, I had a bad cold and first thought my pains were from coughing too hard. Soon I began to have contractions and since it took almost an hour to get to Charleston, the infirmary nurse ordered a wagon with a mattress laid in the bottom. Sure enough, by the time we rattled over the sandy, shell-packed road to the docks and took a boat across the harbor, my baby was ready. From then on things went fast.

Our little girl was born early the next morning and Pat was able to come in and sit with me about an hour later. We named her Emma. That was my mother's name and both of us thought it sounded good for both a child and an adult. She had black hair that they said was long for a baby. The first day she was sleeping most of the time. All I wanted to do was look at her. She was beautiful.

Pat came in on the boat each night to see us and Josie came with him twice. We were happy and chattered about all the things we would be doing when Emma and I returned home. We were to go home on the fifth day after her birth but I noticed that she was coughing every time the nurses brought her in for a feeding. I wasn't concerned for I knew she had probably picked up her cold from me.

The doctor came in to see me on the day I thought we would be released.

"I've sent a message to Fort Moultrie that your husband shouldn't come in for you today. Your baby needs close attention and some medication for a day or two. We'll give her a dose of paregoric every four hours and get her congestion cleared."

I asked for some too, but they said I was far enough along so that I would get better on my own.

The next day was Monday and Emma was about the same. The doctor sent word to Pat to wait until Tuesday to come for me. Monday evening I heard a scream from down the hall toward the nursery and then the sound of people running and talking in low voices. I was able to be up on my feet by then so I started down the hall to see what was happening. A nurse saw me coming and ran to me. Her face was ashen. "Mrs. White you must go back to your room! The doctor will be there soon."

"Why?" I said, "Why does the doctor need to see me this evening?"

"Just go back—please!" she said in a loud voice.

As I returned to my bed, fear gripped me. What could be wrong that involved me? Could Emma be worse? Why wouldn't they let me go down there to join the group? I felt that something was wrong but I couldn't imagine what it was. As my thoughts tumbled around with no good reasons emerging, my doctor and a minister walked in the room and closed the door. "Mrs. White," he said with the greatest sadness in his voice, "I don't know how to tell you this, but something terrible has occurred."

I gasped, "Did something happen to my Pat?"

"No, Mrs. White, it's your baby. Her cough got worse this afternoon and the nurse gave her a double dose of medicine. I'm afraid the medicine got mixed up and she...she...your baby..." The doctor's voice choked and he turned away. The minister looked directly in my eyes and said in a low voice, "I'm sorry to tell you this, Mrs.White, but your little girl is dead."

My only recollection of that moment is a terrible scream that went on and on. I can't remember it ending. I only remember thinking that the noise of the scream caused the walls and roof to tumble in on me, crushing my life into oblivion. The next memory is of a darkened room with Pat and Josie sitting by my bed and the same minister in a chair nearby. There was a blanket hung over the window, allowing only a sliver of light to penetrate the gloom. Josie saw me blink my eyes and clutched my hand. "Annie, oh my dear Annie, we're here with you now."

As I heard her soothing voice I focused on Pat's face and the tears came in a torrent. "Oh, Pat, I've lost her. I'm sorry, I'm sorry. Oh what have I done?"

Pat stood over me and kissed my forehead as he said, "Annie, you didn't do a thing wrong. 'Tis not your fault and you needn't blame yourself. But I've screamed my lungs out at that doctor and nurse who did this beastly thing."

The minister cleared his throat and stood. "Mrs. White, it has been determined that a nurse gave your little girl a double dose of the wrong medicine yesterday evening. The paregoric bottle is dark and has a black label on it. Close beside it on the shelf was a bottle of laudanum. That bottle was also dark colored and had a purple label on it. The light in the room wasn't good and she picked the wrong bottle. She gave your baby the laudanum which is used as a sedative. It was just too much for her. The nurse has already been discharged."

With this, the minister took a deep breath and said, "I suggest we all join in a prayer." He started by saying, "Dear Lord and Savior, receive the soul of our dearly beloved, Emma White...," I must have fainted for I never heard the rest of what he said. I didn't see him again.

This time when I awakened, there was more light in the room and Josie was the only one with me. "Annie, dear, please drink this water. Pat is making arrangements and I'm going to stay right here with you until you feel like going back to the fort." I only shook my head back and forth as I tried to comprehend what had happened. It is still just a hazy shroud of desolation in my mind. A day later a brief service was held at the hospital. Pat later told me that I was allowed to hold my dead baby and that I attended a burial service in a Charleston cemetery but, like a nightmare, those events have been erased from my mind.

Back at Moultrie people expressed their regret and followed up by saying, "God will punish that nurse for the evil thing she did." Pat and I never thought such a thing but we heard it so much that we were hardly surprised when Captain Foster told Josie three weeks later that the poor woman's body was found washed up on a beach on Sullivan Island. The papers said that it was a suicide.

Josie took some time off from the laundry to spend with me. I loved her for it. She seemed to know that I didn't want to talk about the tragedy so we remembered our girlhood days. Josie would tell about growing up in Pennsylvania. I think she even made up some funny events just trying to make me laugh. I didn't have anything very funny to tell her but together we would find some things to smile about. Slowly, I became able to face the world again. I adored Josie for the time and effort she devoted to me at this crucial time of my life. I needed someone near me and she was there.

Pat was quiet, even moody. He sat many hours by himself on the barracks steps late at night. Though he was never much for using tobacco, he now took up smoking a pipe.

"Just to give me something to do with my hands," he'd say.

Some days he would say only a few words. Often he would be staring out into the ocean with a blank look on his face. He walked the beach, which was unusual for him. When Josie and I did that early in our time on Sullivan's Island, he would stay home and read. But now he wanted time alone.

After about three weeks, Pat held me in his arms one night and said, "Annie, it's time we got on with our life. I've done a lot of thinking and 'tis not right to be sad forever. I've been that way too much and I'm going to change. Do you think it's alright t' try and forget?"

I knew what he meant and after thinking about the right answer, I finally whispered, "Mother used to say 'We can't undo what's done.' I think we must let her go and do the things we did before." That conversation seemed to turn the page for the next chapter of our life.

Chapter 13

EVACUATION

1860.

I went back to work with Josie in the laundry and things were almost like before. One thing had changed, though. The papers were filled with stories about how the folks who lived up north were trying to make the plantation owners get rid of their slaves. Every time there was a story about opening up more lands in the west, there was another argument about whether the homesteaders could or could not have slaves. President Buchanan was on the side of the anti-slavery people or at least that's the way it sounded in the Charleston newspaper. The editor of the paper and the reporters were saying that they weren't going to let someone in Washington, D.C. tell them what South Carolina and the new territories had to do.

Pat and James Carroll said that the talk around the fort was that something big was about to happen. Some of the officers had said that they were either going to get a lot more guns and ammunition or we were going to have to leave. An officer and a small group of soldiers from Ft. Sumter, the island one mile away, came to our fort one day. They spent the entire day talking to Major Robert Anderson, the commanding officer of our fort. There were lots of rumors after that.

On December 20th the South Carolina government voted to leave the United States. This was big news in the papers the next day. When Pat came home that evening and told me, my first response was, "How can they do that?"

He just shrugged and replied, "Nobody knows but they did. I guess it means they won't let anybody from Washington tell them what to do. They probably won't pay them any taxes. The talk is that some other states down here will do the same. There may be hard feelings."

It was worse than that. On Christmas morning Major Anderson and Captain Doubleday called a post roll call inside the walls. Major Anderson said that all soldiers and their families were to be evacuated to Ft. Sumter the following day. The families were to wait there until a ship arrived to take us back to a northern port. It was stunning news and none of us were prepared. It also brought the possibility of serious conflict closer. We suddenly realized that there might be fighting and that casualties were possible. It was not a usual Christmas Day as we packed our few belongings.

Pat said that the Army was afraid that the South Carolina hotbloods would try to take over Fort Moultrie, Castle Pinckney, Ft. Sumter and Fort Johnson. None of these posts had many soldiers nor were they well prepared for a fight. At this time we had only 77 soldiers and an eight-man brass band. All of Moultrie's guns were pointed to the harbor and the sea. It was now felt that the attack would come by land. It had been decided that Ft. Sumter, isolated on the little island, would be the easiest to defend.

The soldiers set fire to the gun carriages before they left. We saw the sight from Fort Sumter.   NATIONAL PARK SERVICE

Right after that announcement there was quite a stir among the soldiers. The ones from the southern states got together and said they weren't going to Sumter but were going to join their own state's militia.

Pat and a lot of the men from the northern states were amazed. They never thought of the men from the south as being any different but apparently the southerners felt that they were. Six of the men and one officer resigned from the Army that day, leaving on a boat for Charleston.

For a month we marked time in makeshift quarters in Ft. Sumter. There was little to do except worry. We weren't even able to move about since construction and strengthening of the fort was underway day and night. Finally a merchant ship arrived but there were no supplies for the soldiers. The ship had been dispatched to return the wives and children to New York. We left Sumter on February 3, 1861. This ocean trip was serene by comparison to my first one. We had no sea sickness and the crowded conditions were nothing like those on the *Good Spirit*.

We arrived in New York five days later during the night. A big snowstorm was in progress. Josie departed for her Pennsylvania home with a

Fort Sumter

tearful goodbye and promises to keep in touch. I was allowed to spend the early morning hours on board the ship. After daylight when I thought some of the sidewalks would be shoveled, I started walking home, carrying all my possessions in one small suitcase and a bag made from carpeting with a handle sewn into it. It was only about 20 blocks through a city beautiful with a clean layer of snow but oh, how cold it was. A few shops were opening so every few blocks I would step in and get warm before proceeding.

Our rooming house was a welcome sight. I knew our door would be unlocked—it always was. Without trying to unpack, I found a few pieces of bread and an apple and lay down for my first good sleep for a week. Of course I startled Mother when she returned home from work. We had written her about the rumblings of discontent in South Carolina but none of us could have imagined this happening.

At first Mother thought my coming home must have something to do with my grief over losing little Emma. When she found the real reason she seemed relieved that it was due to something beyond our control. "Well," she said, "I'm glad you came back. 'Tis much better for you to be here than all by yourself." Although I missed Josie and Pat, she was right. This was the place for me right then.

After two days, I knew I should return to work. There were many jobs now for New York had grown even more and some people were talking about the danger of a war. The factories were busy piling warehouses full of goods and new office buildings were going up. I visited two laundries since that was the work I knew best. Both of them were smelly, steamy places and the people who worked there were unfriendly. I looked for something else.

The best place was in a fabric factory where there were dozens of women at sewing machines making all kinds of clothes. It looked like pleasant work and the pay was $2 a day. I had seen sewing machines when I worked during high school, but had no experience with them. I soon learned the work. Mother insisted that I keep all of my pay since she was getting by on her own. So our savings grew and I was proud that I was contributing.

In March I got a letter from Pat saying that the Army was sending more soldiers and supplies to reinforce the garrison at Ft. Sumter. He said the Army thought they had to keep the Charleston harbor under the control of the North to keep supplies from getting in to the secessionists by ship.

Pat also said they had received the news that Fort Bliss and all the other Texas forts were surrendered to the Confederates. As soon as Jeff Davis was elected President of the South, the Texans had swarmed in with big numbers and overwhelmed every garrison without a shot being fired.

The day after President Lincoln was sworn in, he declared that he would send more supplies and that the Union would not abandon Fort Sumter. The New York papers were talking as if there would be a war if any other states split off.

Then April 12th came and the papers were full of the story that Ft. Sumter was being fired on by the states that had seceded from the rest of the country. You can imagine how anxious I was. I believed that hundreds of shells were bursting right inside that poor little fort and that I might never see Pat again. It was a terrible few days. On the way home from work on the 15th, I saw the headlines in the papers saying that Major Anderson, the commander of Ft. Sumter, had surrendered. All soldiers were safe and would be sent back to the North. I ran the last three blocks to get home and tell Mother the wonderful news. What a relief that my Pat was alright!

The next thing we heard was a letter from Pat which read:

Dear Annie

I am in Maryland at Fort McHenry where most of us from Sumter have been sent. We are going to be a part of a new bunch, the 2nd Maryland Infantry and guarding the Baltimore

74

harbor now. We feel bad that we got run out of Sumter but the extra supplies and ammunition never got through. We would have been out of everything in a few more days so we are lucky to get away. We did lose one man as we left. He was trying to blow up the shells and big guns. I knew him pretty well but don't think you did. He was a good man.

They say we will be here a while so maybe you can live down here. I will find out how it is and write you soon. I miss you.

Love, Pat
May 2, 1861

CHAPTER 14

FORT McHENRY

I knew where Baltimore was for we had passed through there on our train ride to Ft. Moultrie. Every day I looked anxiously for another letter. Though I was glad to have a place to stay with Mother and was earning good money, I wanted to be with Pat.

The next letter came in June and told me that he had found a rooming house that took in Army wives. He gave me an address and said I should ask for Mrs. Lohaus. It didn't take me long to get ready. Mother walked with me to the station. As I boarded she said firmly, "I'll miss you, Annie, but this is what you should be doin'. Give Pat all the support y' can." Then with a big hug she sent me on my way.

Just as Pat said, Mrs. Lohaus was expecting me; she just wasn't sure when. "Oh yes, Mr. White paid your first week's rent but we just didn't know when the week would start." She was a big, hearty German woman with a booming laugh and happy to be taking care of Army wives. She said, "It's my way of helping with the war. There's some here in Baltimore that is 'secesh' but not me. I say we all stay together. I'm glad the Army is here to keep us in the Union."

There were five double rooms in her big house. Each one was rented to two Army wives. Most of us got along real well but there were two wives that thought they were better than any of the rest of us. Their husbands were sergeants and they never stopped letting us know about it. They didn't work but all the rest of us found jobs.

I couldn't stay in that room all day with nothing to do. Since I had sewing experience in the factory in New York, I had no trouble finding a similar job in Baltimore. All the places were hiring anyone they could and the demand for clothing for the Army kept every factory busy. When they found out that I knew how to operate the machines, I soon was made a supervisor on the assembly line. I still used a machine but I was also supposed to see that all the pieces kept moving at the proper speed. It was the first time I'd been in charge of anything and there were some tough times as I tried to make women do things they didn't want to do. I was earning $3 a day and saving half of it.

Every other week the men at Fort McHenry got two days off. It wasn't always on weekends but could be any day of the week. At those times they would come in to the city and Mrs. Lohaus would rent the couple her best room so they could be by themselves. Sometimes two or three of the husbands would end up on leave at the same time. Usually the extra one or two could get a hotel room for $2. We tried not to spend that kind of money when Mrs. Lohaus only charged $1 for her extra room. Each of us paid $2 a week for our room.

Beulah Swinter was my roommate. She was big and strong but not very intelligent. I was not used to being around someone so large— almost fat. She would say, "I've always liked to eat an' I don't aim to stop now."

Pat never liked his McHenry assignment. I think it was because they were kept inside the fort walls just about all the time. There were no horses or wagons involved with this place so he didn't have a chance to work at the jobs he liked best. The soldiers drilled and practiced maneuvers every day. The Army felt that an invasion could take place at any time with ships from the South so everyone had to stay on watch and be ready for battle. It was a tense time.

We looked forward to our days together. Much of our time was spent walking around the city of Baltimore. The best part were the parks close to downtown. The rest was a newer, smaller and rougher version of New York. Most of the buildings were still wooden. The city was built to be close around the harbor. Only a mile or so away, the farms began.

Since we were north of Washington, D.C., it seemed odd that so many from Maryland were in sympathy with the South. You would think that anything north of the capitol would stay with the North. Pat and Mrs. Lohaus said it was due to the slavery issue and that many Maryland farmers had slaves. I could see both sides. I worked with a lot of women who were very outspoken in their beliefs. Some would say they were going to quit the job they had since the clothes and uniforms we made were going to the northern Army. They would say things like, "We want to take our government from Annapolis, not Washington."

I tried to stay out of the arguments. Since I wasn't sure what was right, I listened and kept on working.

CHAPTER 15

ANTIETAM

The time with Pat nearby ended too soon. In May of 1862, the 2nd Maryland Infantry was moved out of Ft. McHenry and assigned to General Ambrose Burnside. The papers said every able man was needed on the battle lines. The threat of an invasion by sea was less, the papers said.

The 2nd Maryland was at New Berne, North Carolina and then with McClellan on the Virginia Peninsula. I heard from Pat perhaps once a month. The letters were short and written hurridly. They didn't give me many details—I suppose he wasn't supposed to do that. But I longed for more. Most of these letters were lost but I kept one that talked about Clark's Mountain:

My dear Annie

How I miss you. This war is getting worse and I have seen too much killing. When the boys get injured there isn't much the doctors can do to help. It is worse than I thought it would be. We are now at Clark's Mountain and just got a break. One of our boys found a secret message from Jeb Stuart and it helped us trick them. The officers crowed that we almost got whipped but instead we did it to them. We even captured Stuart's fancy feathered hat. Ha! Ha!

I have had a bad cold and some dysentery but now am better. A lot of the boys are sick. More sick than wounded. I'm glad you are making clothes there. We need more. I will be careful.

Love, Pat
August 1862

The Baltimore papers reported every battle. Since both armies were so close we were all worried. Some people thought that Lee would come right on in and take Washington and then come at Baltimore. It never happened but it was too close for comfort. Right after Clark's Mountain the papers were full of news about a big battle near Manassas Junction. Most people called it Bull Run and it was on the same ground where the armies fought right after Ft. Sumter. It sounded bad for the Union boys again.

The papers then talked about General Burnside's troops against General Longstreet in another big fight. I knew Pat was with Burnside so I worried all the time. I thought it was ironic that he was fighting against an army led by Longstreet, someone he once knew and liked at Ft. Bliss. After it was all over, the papers called it the battle of Antietam since most of it was along a creek by that name that ran into the Potomac River. It was close to Sharpsburg, Maryland.

I had a hard time during the next weeks. Several of the women where I worked heard that their husbands had been killed at Antietam. Others found out they had family who were wounded and then a few days later they would be told they were dead. I was terrified for I never had been so close to so many deaths, even as a little girl in Ireland. Just as then, there seemed to be nothing that could be done about it. I spent extra evenings saying prayers at the little church I attended. At other sad times I went to funeral masses with some of the wives.

I will never forget the next important date for me. It was October 25th, 1862. I was in my room with Beulah, when a knock came at the door. When I opened it a Union captain stood there with a very grim look on his face. When I saw this all I could do was scream, "Oh no! No! It's Pat isn't it?" Beulah came to the door and put her arm around me and asked the crucial question, "What is it, sir?"

"Mrs. White, it is my duty to tell you that your husband, Patrick White, was taken prisoner at Antietam. We are informed that he is injured but not severely and that he is being held at Libby Prison in Richmond, Virginia."

The news that he was prisoner was so much more welcome than what I had feared that I gained my senses and asked, "Is there any other news about him?"

"No ma'am, we are lucky to have this much. Usually they don't tell us right off where they take prisoners but this time they did."

Remembering my manners, I asked, "Won't you come in and have a cup of tea with us?"

"No thank you ma'am, I must be on my way. I have several more notices to give yet this evening. I'm afraid Antietam was a bad one for us."

As the captain left I thought of one more thing I had to know. "Can I write to him?"

"Yes, ma'am, but I'd wait until he writes you so you'll have the right address. Also, they say the Rebels censor all your letters hard so be careful what you say. Good evening, ma'am."

Beulah and I weren't close friends but we fell into each other's arms as the door closed. "Annie, the message could have been much worse, you know."

"I know. For a few seconds I thought everything was lost. Maybe Pat's safer now than he was."

There was hope for another reason. By now I knew that I was with child again. This time the doctor said that I was due in about February. The pain of losing Emma was still with me and this news brought it back again with bad dreams and moody spells that didn't make me very easy to live with. Beulah was patient and tried to be helpful during the few "awake" hours we spent together. Now I longed for a letter from Pat so I could share the news.

The next days dragged by as I hoped and prayed to hear something. My whole being was pointed to that event. I felt sick all the time even though I really wasn't sick. It was just worry. I knew Richmond wasn't very far south of here and for some reason that made me feel better than if he was way down in the Carolinas or Georgia.

CHAPTER 16

LIBBY PRISON

By the end of November, I was beginning to wonder if Pat was injured worse than the captain said. Then the letter came. Beulah and I walked home from work together and saw the letter on the desk at the rooming house hallway. I couldn't wait to walk up to our room and raced to a chair to read it. She was thoughtful enough to stand across the room but stay close by. I've kept that letter in the Bible:

Dear Annie,

Well, they got me and I'm sorry about that. We had a hard fight at the creek but just after noon we finally got across a stone bridge and were on the edge of Sharpsburg when the boys of General XXXXXXXXXXX(censored) came upstream and captured about 80 of us. They came up on our side and had us cut off before our officers even saw them. The officers told us to give up. In the gunfire I got a ball through my lower leg and it broke a bone. The small one the doctor says. It is getting better.

XXXXXXXXXXXX They mostly have officers here but they found out I was a repairman and wanted me here. I will be alright, Annie, but don't know how long it will be. I wish we could be together. I love you.

Pat
November 1862
Libby Warehouse, XXXXXXXXX Richmond, Virginia

When I finished reading this I clasped it to my chest and burst into tears. "Is it bad news, Annie?" Beulah asked.

Through my tears I sobbed, "Oh, it's good news, Beulah, he says he loves me!" Then we both realized the silliness of that answer and dissolved into each other's arms, crying and laughing at the same time. Beulah was a farm girl from Delaware with very little schooling but she was good-hearted and just what I needed in this anxious time.

She said to me, "Do y' think they'll treat him alright there in Libby?"

"I don't know, Beulah. Our family priest used to say, 'We must live right and pray to God that others will do what's right, also.' I suppose I'll have to remember that as long as he's there."

I lost no time answering Pat's letter. I had so much to tell him and wanted to send my love to him a dozen times. I told the news of the baby to come, news from Mother and from his father since both of them now wrote me about once every month. I talked about work, about Beulah and about the last letters from Josie.

Pat was allowed a letter only every three or four weeks. After I had spent a lot of one letter telling about the war reports in the newspapers, Pat answered the next time saying that almost all the letter was blackened out. Then I remembered that I shouldn't use any of the precious space talking about things like that.

Pat told me that most of his time was spent repairing wagons and harnesses. He did this even before his broken leg healed. After he was there about five months, he wrote that the cast was off and his leg was alright again. He also said only one other prisoner was an enlisted man there. This man had medical training and they wanted all of their own medical men in the front lines. I was surprised that they didn't censor that out but I guess it didn't make any difference to them if someone else knew.

Pat didn't mind the work because that is what he knew best next to farming. He would hint about sickness and not having enough to eat and I could tell that life wasn't very pleasant. He did say once they slept on the floor and that there wasn't any furniture. The papers talked about some prisoners getting swapped between the armies but Pat never said anything about it and I didn't want to bring it up in my letters. The months went by slowly and I was lonesome but kept busy at the factory and saving money every week.

Right after the start of another year, I was getting so big they wouldn't let me work anymore. I wasn't feeling well and was glad to have some time to sew new things for the baby. This time the birth was easier. Mrs. Lohaus knew of a good midwife. I told her all about our trouble with Emma so we were both very careful about how this little girl was cared for. The midwife was a Negro, Sadie Brown. She was a wonder. No matter what came along, she wouldn't get excited or upset. She just took everything in stride and took the best care of me that I could have hoped.

Mrs. Lohaus gave me a separate room. Sadie stayed there with me for six days. My girl was a big baby and healthy right from the start. I named her Katherine but Beulah and Sadie and I called her Kate.

Now I couldn't work but I was getting Pat's pay while he was a prisoner so that was enough. Our savings could stay in the bank. Beulah stayed close and helped me care for her. By now Dorah Binchley was married and still living in New York. She had my address and wrote me every month. Getting her letters was a treat and I had a lot to tell her when I answered.

Josie Carroll also kept in touch. James was still in the Army but was sent to a post in Tennessee. She was with her parents near York, Pennsylvania. They still had no children. She was happy to hear about Kate and talked about us getting together again.

Mother wrote me of the draft riots in New York City that summer. Many Northerners didn't want to fight the South. Some of the protests got violent and took place not far from where Mother lived.

I didn't get much information from Pat's letters. He told me more about prison life when we got together again and I can remember some of it. He said there were lice and fleas everywhere all the time he was there. They had only an open hole in the ground floor for a privy and it was never cleaned. Flies and awful smells were present always but worse in the summertime. At first the floors and walls were washed every few weeks but after the first year, nothing was done and the food got worse.

The warehouse was built as a tobacco building and was on the James River. Their mail came and went on boats that carried a flag of truce that both sides honored. This boat also brought in packages of presents and food for the officers that were imprisoned there. Somehow they allowed the officers to tell their families they could do this. Pat said he wrote me this, too, but it got censored out for I never knew I could. This has been one of the things I'm the most sorry about, for all that time Pat thought that I just didn't bother to send him anything. He did say that lots of times the Rebel guards would break open the packages and take most of the good things that were sent. Other times the packages would get through and he would see the officers sharing candy or clothes. There was a Brigadier General Joseph Hayes, in charge of distributing mail and packages to the officers.

When I got a letter from him in October of 1863, I realized that he had been there a year. He was talking about Kate like she was the first one for us. It seemed to me that he had put Emma's death out of his mind as if it had never happened. I tried to but couldn't. I was still bitter toward the nurse, the doctors, the Charleston hospital and even my God for allowing this to take place. Pat seemed to be able to forget it as if there was nothing we could or should do about it.

One time I poured all these feelings into a letter to Mother. Two weeks later I received a wonderful letter from Father Donahue, our dear priest from Ireland who had married us in Redeemer Church in New York. I wish I had kept it. Father Donahue said all the right things to cause me to forgive the people in Charleston and to let go of my grief for little Emma. I can't remember the exact words he used but they were just what I needed. I felt much better from then on. That was just another way that Mother helped me in her own quiet way

Pat was involved in another activity about that time that couldn't be talked about in his letters—or anywhere else. I didn't learn about it until much later. Pat was the only one in the entire prison who was regularly allowed outside the walls. Their security was so tight that the prisoners weren't even allowed to look out the windows. Two men were shot and killed just this way.

Pat worked across the street in the wagon repair shed. That was the only reason he was sent to Libby. Because of this work, two of the officers found a way to talk to him alone late one evening. A Colonel Rose and Lieutenant Brady got Pat aside and asked if he would be willing to cooperate in an effort to escape the prison. Pat said he would and they allowed him to join in the building of a tunnel. They had found that the bricks of a fireplace in one end of the dark prison basement could be loosened and removed. Beyond that was dirt and they proposed to dig a tunnel to freedom. They wanted Pat to help them because when he left the prison to work across the street he could pace off the exact distance to a dirt alley where the officers hoped their tunnel would surface.

One of the officers knew that when his hand was opened wide it was exactly 12 inches. Using this as a guide, they measured Pat's step. They had him practice dozens of times so that he would get his stride exactly two and a half feet with every step. Pat knew that the measurement was critical.

For three months they extended this passage, spreading the dirt over the floors in a way that wouldn't be noticed. They used tin cans, their pockets and even an old spittoon to carry out the dirt. The tunnel was only about 18 inches wide and not much higher. It was decided not to make it any larger since there was no wood to shore up the sides. Any larger and the officers were afraid it would collapse. The air was foul in the shaft which was 60 feet long.

The conditions in the prison by this time were unbearable. Over 1,000 prisoners in a place fit for no more than 300. The officers were

Libby Prison: *Pat never wanted to look at this picture. I saved it from an old calendar about the Civil War.*

getting desperate and work on the tunnel was furious. Pat was proud that he was trusted to keep the secret and to be involved in the work.

On February 8, 1864, the escape was made. Pat and 103 officers got out before the alarm was sounded. Pat was one of the last to leave. By then, scuffles were breaking out as prisoners who were not in on the tunnel work tried to break into the escape line. The noise finally alerted the guards and stopped the break-out. Some were recaptured right away but about half, including Pat, made it back to Union lines.

I knew none of this until the middle of March when a letter arrived from Pat. He was in a field hospital in southern Maryland. He told me the good news that he was out and that the Army was reassigning him to a new outfit. He said he was still weak but gaining with better food and would write when he knew where he would be.

My prayers had been answered. Pat was safe again and I had a rosy-cheeked, healthy little girl to keep me company. In early March a knock on the door made my joy complete. Pat stood there in a new uniform with a big smile on his face. As we flew into each other's arms I felt how thin he was.

He had nearly been recaptured three times as he worked his way north. One officer, Captain Henry Sanders, traveled with him the first week. They'd cover themselves with brush and leaves at daylight and stay as quiet as possible all day. At night they moved through fields, avoiding all roads and buildings. They had almost no food and drank from creeks. After the first week they separated, thinking it would be safer that way.

One day when Pat was by himself, he realized that he had bedded down near a slave cabin. By now, he was starved and decided he must take a chance that they would give him food and not betray him.

It was a lucky choice for they gave him all the hominy and sweet potatoes he could eat and even some fat pork to take with him the next day. He said that was what saved him. When he saw soldiers on patrol, he watched for nearly all of one day to be sure they were Union soldiers. Then he called to them from a long way off and walked out of hiding with his hands up to be sure they wouldn't shoot him by mistake.

As we lay in each other's arms one night, Pat said, "I feel like I've been to Hell and back. An' you're my Heaven, Annie."

Our two weeks together were blissful. We had so much to tell and plans to make. Pat was to be assigned to the 5th Maryland Infantry division and stationed at Fort Stevens. This group was now considered a part of the Army of the Potomac and would be used for the defense of Washington. I liked this—it sounded safer! We still talked a lot about the West. We were agreed that our destiny was there. That and caring for our baby, Kate, were our two objectives.

Josie Carroll wrote to tell us how grateful she was for Pat's escape from Libby Prison. She had just heard of the death of an officer in Libby Prison who was a good friend of hers from her high school in York. She also told me that James was being sent to a Kansas fort and if he stayed long enough she was going to move there. In those war days the Army wouldn't pay for a wife to go to a camp.

When Pat returned to duty he was feeling much better and had gained a few pounds. I teased him by telling him that when we were together all the time, I'd fatten him just like the pigs he wanted to raise some day on our farm. Fort Stevens wasn't far away and if there were no battles he would be able to get two-day passes to come see me every month or so. His job at Stevens called for him to make wagons. Most of the parts were supplied but Pat sometimes made changes and improvements.

The next year sped by as my attention was on Kate and on Pat's work at Ft. Stevens. There was one scare when General Jubal Early pushed up to within sight of the fort but reinforcements were sent and Early backed away. The threat of Pat's being in combat again had passed.

Since I wasn't working we weren't adding to our savings but we could live on his salary. He said he didn't need any money; he did not use tobacco now and felt no need to buy any of the goods available for sale near the Army forts. I agreed with Mother when she said in one of her letters to me, "You have a good man there, Annie." I repeated that compliment to Pat the night I told him that another babe was on the way.

On a sparkling spring day, the glorious peace was declared at Appomattox. Baltimore erupted with fireworks and crowds cheering in the streets. General Grant allowed the defeated troops to surrender with honor. President Lincoln said the right things about not being cruel to Southerners. Still, it was a time of unrest as the two sides learned how to be at peace with one another. Pat was hoping that he would now be assigned to the West.

Late in 1865 he arrived in Baltimore with news. "Annie, it's not west for us yet. We're being sent back to South Carolina."

"Where in South Carolina?"

"Orangeburg, Annie, it's going to be a main place for the wagons that will supply the state from the Charleston port."

It wasn't what we would have chosen but the Army made the choice for us. It was to be Pat's third stay in that state.

CHAPTER 17

THE ENCAMPMENT

Spring 1866.

My morning sickness was wearing me down. Our quarters here were dreadful. The barracks buildings were being thrown together when we arrived. Pat said it was green lumber and would warp and shrink.

The unmarried men lived in tents since the Army expected this camp to last only a short time. The whole thing had a temporary feeling about it. There weren't any of the usual Army services—we were expected to use those in Orangeburg.

Camp Orangeburg was a main junction point on the railroads in the state. It wasn't a Civil War fort—just a good place to have a supply depot as the North tried to help rebuild the South after the war. There was a lot to be done. Crews were repairing the railroad tracks and the roads just to get transportation going again. Some of the towns and plantations were burned out. Other places had missed the devastation of the war.

Wagon teams left here for Charleston to meet the supply ships and then fanned out over the state delivering supplies to the small Army posts that had been established to maintain order. We had three large warehouses at Orangeburg that were used to store material.

We soon found that many of the local people didn't think the Army was there to help them rebuild. They talked about us as if we were an army of occupation and thought we were there to keep them subdued. I learned this before Pat did as I went shopping in the town. When the clerk at the dry goods store found out that I was an Army wife, she said, "We don't need any of you down here. You tore up our country but we can get back on our own. Just because Lee gave up, don't think the rest of us have."

When I told this to Pat, he reminded me that we musn't get involved in the politics of why we were here. "That's for the big shots to decide, Annie. We just need to get along as best we can and do our job."

It was different for us—no more beaches to walk, no sea shells to find. We were in piney woods without a view of anything past a hundred yards. The land was flat and sandy, the weather was humid and hot.

Pat had more work than ever since wagons were used to haul food and supplies to all the small towns in South Carolina. The North was sending down lots of food, small farm tools and equipment on the railroad to help people build things. The only way to distribute them was with horses or mules pulling wagons. Some of the iron parts were being shipped in and Pat made the rest of the wagon right at our camp. Pat said a lot of the drivers were inexperienced and damaged the wagons more than they should. He was the only one at the camp who could keep the wagon fleet in working condition. The last few months he did have a helper.

The best thing about this time in South Carolina was the flowers. It may have been the joy about the war being over or maybe people had more time to care for gardens. It seemed as if flowers were everywhere. Dense woods grew close to the barracks at this camp and they popped into a stunning scene of pink and white.

In September of 1866, our son, John, was born. This delivery was long and difficult. The Orangeburg hospital was small and not fully rebuilt since the war. It would have been worse than the one in Charleston when little Emma was born. For this reason, I used a midwife that was said to be the best on that side of town. She was a Negro named Wilda. I only saw her twice before John came but she assured me that she could help. She did as much as she could. After the birth, Wilda became one of my best friends while we were there. She helped me for the first week after John was born and then came to visit every week until we left. I could talk to her easier than the officer's wives and the white women that I met in town.

Wilda told me of the hardships they had during the war. All of her family had been slaves on tobacco and cotton plantations. She had shown an aptitude for nursing and had been doing that and domestic work for plantation owners since she was 12 years old. She was about 25 years old and had four children, all of them sired by different "bosses," as she called them. When I acted surprised at this she just shrugged it off. "They's all do it, Annie. They says it's one of th' privileges they gets fer bein' slave owners. I 'spect they'll not have s' many chances now that we is free."

Many in South Carolina were still "fighting" the Civil War. It was a tedious time. All of us in the Army were instructed to be especially courteous to Southerners. We were supposed to avoid giving them any reason to further dislike Northerners. It was hard to smile and turn away when we were called "damn Yankees" but that's what we had to do. I had to smile to think that a lot of other northern folks were finding out what it was like to be scorned like we Irish once were.

There were twelve wives living in the married quarters barracks. We joined together twice a week to make clothing and bedding for the poor whites. We also gave them to some blacks who had just been freed from slavery and could not find good jobs. I didn't make any close friends here. One wife never got along with any of us. She was Cecelia Taylor, who was from Tennessee. She fancied herself as a southern belle though her husband was a private just like Pat. She tried to be a part of the Northerners when it came to winning the war but then a Southerner when it came to putting on airs and pretending to be above doing any work. When the wives were organizing the work sessions, Cecelia said, "I'm not going to do sewing work for those that aren't willing to help themselves."

Several of us said things like, "But these folks are suffering from the war and haven't had a chance to recover yet."

Cecelia fired back, "It's not worth my time to work for trash!"

When she saw how shocked the rest of us were she softened a little. She did attend the Tuesday and Thursday meetings but she never did much except to complain and move pieces of fabric just to look like she was working.

One of the black laundry women left her job to go north with her husband. After discussing it with Pat, I decided to apply for the job. This was a way to again save money for our farm. Close to that same time, one of the older wives mentioned one day that she wished she had children to care for. She and her husband had none, yet she was a happy person who wanted more to do. John was five months old and Kate was two.

I applied to the assistant post commander, who was Captain George Rittler. He couldn't imagine a white woman in the South wanting to do this but when I explained our reasons he finally said, "I don't see why not." For the next year I worked four days a week at this job and by the time we left South Carolina I was making $2.00 a day. All of it went into the savings account.

Pat was becoming known as an expert wagon man. He could make all the easy parts of a wagon and also knew how to form the wooden wheel spokes and rims. If he was supplied with the right iron rails, he could make them into rims and shrink them onto the wheels. He was good at making wooden wheel bearings and well-balanced yokes and wagon tongues. He also knew how to put an entire wagon together without using nails. These wagons usually held together better and as Pat told me, "If we're in the field sometime, we might not have nails. 'Twould be good to know how to do it that way."

Before we left Pat was promoted to Private, First Class. This was in recognition of his re-enlistment and also because of his wheelwright skills. He now made $15 dollars per month. We celebrated that evening!

At a post party held as a farewell to the 18 men being transferred, Captain Rittler said to me, "We'll miss your Pat. He is the envy of all here at the camp and even in the other posts around the state. They all want to have wagons made by him."

When I repeated this to Pat, he just commented, "Maybe they're just saying that because there isn't much competition." I could tell that he was proud of what the captain said.

CHAPTER 18

PEA PATCH ISLAND

Pat's next assignment was with the 5th Maryland Infantry at Fort Delaware. It was located on an island in the Delaware River just before it gets to the Atlantic Ocean. Many of his companions were being mustered out but Pat re-enlisted for another term. The Army promised him that his family would be sent with him wherever he was transferred. Some of the men from his old company that fought at Antietam were sent to Ft. Delaware with him.

He told me that the town where we'd live was called Delaware City. When he reported for duty some of the men started calling him "Paddy." I heard that name used for men named Patrick but until now it hadn't been applied to my Pat. From then on at Ft. Delaware, that was his name. It even carried over to our later posts but to me and our close friends it was still Pat.

By this time I was with child again and it was decided that I would go live with Mother until Pat got settled at the new post. Mother's health was worse now. She had stopped working nearly one year before as she had trouble breathing. Her letters hadn't told me much but Dorah Binchley wrote to express her concern.

Our time together was precious. She recalled our hard times in Ireland. That helped me write the first part of this story. We talked about Father and our first explorations around New York City. The only subject we avoided was the ocean trip and the one time it was mentioned we agreed that we both still wanted to forget it.

Mother's life was much better in New York than in Ireland. The jobs were easy compared to what she'd known there. Though her circle of friends didn't extend beyond Redeemer Church, she had many there and her modest needs were well supplied.

She was her usual tender self as my time to deliver came near. After my good experience with the midwives, Sadie in Baltimore and Wilda at Camp Orangeburg, I asked Mother if she knew of a good one here. I also knew this would save us money.

She found one that was from County Limerick. Kathleen had come to New York just one year after we did. She was like a second mother to me for those weeks. The birth was easier and simple right in Mother's apartment. There were no complications.

95

Our baby girl was small but healthy and so bald that everyone laughed when they saw her. How could one have long black hair and another one, none? Pat couldn't be with us but in his last letter he told me to name the child. I had a favorite rag doll in Ireland that I called Sally so that's what I chose.

Mother seemed to feel better after Sally's birth. She bustled around and babied me in the little apartment that had been our haven when we arrived nearly twenty years before. By now it was one of the most run-down buildings in that part of town but to Mother it was home and she wanted to stay there. The old lime-green walls had now been painted a cream color and Mother had purchased what she called "new" furniture. It really was used but it didn't matter, it was new to her and she was proud that she had saved enough to be able to buy it.

By the time Sally was a month old I could see that the four of us should not stay longer with Mother. There were too many of us for the space. Kate was now almost six and needed to begin school. Mother, bless her heart, acted like she wanted us to stay but I could tell that all of us were too much for her.

Pat found a two-room apartment. It was a hectic stay, for our children were active. Delaware City was a small town but the fort was immense. Pat told me that it was the largest Army fort in the country. It was five-sided, of brick and log construction and located on Pea Patch Island in the Delaware River.

We found out that the name of the island came from the early days of barge traffic on the river. Once a barge load of chick-peas, a favorite crop of the colonists, ran into the rocks at the upper end of a small sand bar. The peas spilled and the island became covered with pea vines. By the time the fort was built the vines had collected enough sand to make the island more than a mile long and it covered about 70 acres.

I found Fort Delaware to be the most interesting Army fort of those I saw. Pat was told that there were 25 million bricks used to build the huge pentagon-shape walls. They were 32 feet high.

There was also a moat, a channel of water, that was about 30 feet wide all the way around the outside. This moat was connected with the river on each end so the water was always moving through. It was never attacked during the Civil War and I could see why. The fort was considered such a safe place that the Union Army brought a lot of the Rebel prisoners-of-war here.

It was rebuilt to take care of 1,000 prisoners but they said that by August of 1864 there were 12,500 Rebels here. By the end of the war

2,700 prisoners had died within these walls. So it wasn't just Libby Prison and others like it in the South where the conditions were bad. In fact, some of the people said Ft. Delaware was called "the Libby of the North."

Fort Delaware: *This came from a magazine that told about the Union Army prisons.* W. EMERSON WILSON

I asked a lot of questions while we were there because I found the stories to be exciting. We were learning. I tried to tell some of them to Kate and Johnny but they were probably too young to remember much of them.

Pat did not like the duty there since there were no horses or wagons on the island. Everything came and left by boat. He should not have been sent to such a post but we were finding out that the Army has strange ways. So he fussed and fumed as he worked as a repair and maintenance man.

We were at Ft. Delaware less than a year when Pat told me that the Army was asking for volunteers for several Army posts in the Western United States. "I can take my choice, I think, for they need wagon men out there." This was what we'd dreamed about. He hated his "monkey work," as he called it. The decision was easy.

We had saved about $900 by then and it was earning one and one half percent interest in an Army savings account. Even though our expenses had increased because of our children, we were proud of what we had accomplished so far.

A telegram came from Dorah telling me that Mother was dead. Pat was able to get a three-day pass and went to New York with Kate and me. John and Sally stayed in Delaware City with one of our neighbors. The funeral mass at Redeemer Church was simple just as she would have chosen. More attended than I expected. Mother had made a lot of friends. The doctors told me that Mother died of tuberculosis.

When Father died it was Mother who saved me from a valley of despair. Now I had only Pat and though he tried, he didn't quite know the right words. It was Kate, with her playful, happy ways that gave me hope for the future without Mother. Really, it should be said that all of the children were mostly well behaved, considering all the moving around we had done.

Just two months later, we received word that we were going to Fort Russell, near Cheyenne, Wyoming. Pat had asked to go to some Arizona post but Wyoming was his second choice. He would be in the 8th Infantry Regiment. I was grateful for the way the timing worked. If we had already been there it would have been too far to return for Mother's funeral.

CHAPTER 19

WYOMING

1869.

My memories center on a long train ride. Pat and I and our three children were finally headed west. I can almost see and smell the smoke drifting back into the car. We had to leave the windows open for it was too hot otherwise. This was new country for me. Kate was old enough to be interested in what we were seeing. John was running up and down the aisles and getting in the way of the porter and other passengers. Pat or I had to hold little Sally except for the times when we laid her on the floor where she slept on a blanket.

The different scenery fascinated me. Pat didn't comment on it but I chattered about everything. The trip to Cheyenne took three days and two nights. We slept sitting up or huddled on the seats. By the time we reached Chicago and had a three hour stay in the railroad depot, we were dirty, tired and wondering if we were doing the right thing. There were smoky factories along the track and we didn't see anything but warehouses and business places. There was nothing as nice as the New York City parks.

The Army gave us some food money for the trip. We had only two large and two small suitcases and half of those were clothes for the children. We knew there would be hardships but we were comforted by the knowledge that our Army savings account was intact and growing.

On this trip Pat told me more about Libby Prison which I related earlier in this journal. He also opened up a bit about Antietam. Until now, he didn't want to talk about it. The sickness in the Army must have been awful. There wasn't much that could be done. Dysentery and cholera killed many of the soldiers in his regiment.

He was captured on the second day of battle. The 2nd Maryland Infantry was sent to take and cross a stone-arched bridge over Antietam Creek. On the first attempt they had to fall back because so many men were killed. They then re-grouped and added more troops and fought their way across.

Pat said that he came very close to being killed several times. He would see men on either side drop from being shot or blown up by shrapnel from the big guns the Rebels had on the hills beyond the creek.

His company was a part of General Rodman's regiment. After crossing the bridge, they followed the creek downstream, attacking on the Rebel's right flank and moving steadily ahead. Then the Rebels broke through back to the creek and came up to recapture the stone bridge. That cut off the escape and didn't allow any more reinforcements. About 80 men were surrounded. The only hope was to retreat over the creek but the steep banks and heavy fire from three sides made that hopeless. The officers called for all to surrender.

" 'Twas a bad time, Annie," Pat finally said. "We could see dead and wounded all around us and our officers knew that if we didn't throw down our guns, we would all be dead in a few minutes. I thought I was going to die, anyway."

After a long pause, he then said, "At Libby Prison, there were some times I have to confess that I wished I were dead. It was that horrible."

I didn't know what to say so I just squeezed his hand as we looked out the train window.

Then he said, "Now that it's all over, I feel that whatever happens to me can't be all that bad. With a pretty little wife and three fine wee ones, I'm finally going to the land of my dreams." Pat wasn't one for telling his feelings so this made me happy all over.

After Chicago the trip became more desolate and the time went more slowly. The tracks weren't always smooth and there wasn't much to interest the children. It was still exciting for me and now Pat began to study the land and comment on whch parts looked good for farming. Omaha was a pretty city for there were hills all along the river. The tracks went close by where some of the wagon trains had started for Oregon and California. The train conductor told us about it before we got there. This conductor reminded both of us of Captain Abner Doubleday who was so good to us at Fort Moultrie.

We had only a 45 minute stop, just time enough to walk around on the train platform. Pat noticed how the buildings were all wooden. I remember him saying, "Some day they'll tear these down and put up buildings that are as high as those four-story brick ones in New York."

By now the children were getting wild and Sally had a terrible cold, probably from sleeping on the floor and being around so many different people. We could hardly wait for the trip to end.

We followed the Platte River most of the way now. It was like no river either of us had seen. It was mostly just rows of trees along big stretches of sand. We learned that the trees were called cottonwood. Sometimes we would see a bit of shallow water. The conductor told us that in the spring there was usually lots of water, but this was September.

Pat said, "They call this a river?"

A watch and jewelry salesman sitting near us turned and said, "The Creator made this ol' Earth in just six days. I don't think he's had the time yet to make up His mind where he wants to put the Platte River."

Another traveler heard this and chimed in. "You know what they say, the Platte is too thick to drink and too thin to plow!"

At last, Cheyenne came into view and it wasn't impressive. We were used to the Eastern cities with their smokestacks and bustle everywhere. Cheyenne was only five blocks square and filled with wooden shacks that looked like they had just been built. The tallest buildings were two stories high. Horses and wagons were parked along the dirt streets and the wind was blowing dust in our eyes as we got off the train. Cows, pigs and goats were wandering the streets. There were two blocks of stores that had board sidewalks and the rest was dirt. We started to exercise our stiff legs.

Kate and John started running before we could get our bags off the platform. They started across the dusty street just as a stagecoach came rushing down the street. The driver was swinging his whip and yelling at the team as he tried to hurry them along. John was in front of Kate and looking away from the wagon. To my horror, he ran in front of it and was struck by one of the big horses. The first one knocked him down and the other one stepped on him as he lay in the street between the wheels. The wagon passed right over him. Kate rushed to her brother laying crumpled in the dust. I screamed from the railroad platform as I saw the accident happen. Pat and I got to him just as other men arrived to help.

John wasn't moving. A large blue bruise on the side of his head was already swelling. Blood was running from his nose. Someone shouted, "Quick, go get Doc Appleby." I felt faint and sat down in the dusty road as I held Sally tightly. Pat put his coat under John's head and tried to gently shake him back to life. I sat there stunned at this awful turn of events. What were we to do? Is this place so dangerous that a child can't cross the street? Then I realized that John didn't look both ways as he had been taught to do. We couldn't blame the driver. With that small comfort, I sat there and prayed. Kate sat numbly beside me.

In a few minutes the doctor arrived. By then John was groaning and moving his legs. The doctor put some smelling salts under John's nose and he opened his eyes and coughed. As men started to carry John to the doctor's office, he yelled in pain. They put him down again and the doctor looked at one of his arms. It had been broken.

From then on, things happened so fast I can barely remember. John was in the doctor's office on a table. The doctor kept us out of the room and we could do nothing except pace the floor of the waiting room. John had a cast on his arm when we next saw him and the doctor said that he must stay in his office for the night because of the huge bruise on his head. Pat started acting almost like he did after our baby Emma's death. He raved and yelled at the stagecoach driver when the accident happened and kept telling everyone what an evil man he was. I tried to quiet him. Then when he did calm down, he said nothing—just stared at the wall. Finally, he insisted that he had to report to Fort Russell that same day so the doctor arranged for Kate, Sally and me to stay in the nearby hotel.

What a hotel! The rooms were smaller than we had in the convent during our first night in New York. It was a one-story building. Dust from the streets covered everything and there was a privy in the backyard. Our water was from a hand pump outside the building. We had a pitcher that we were to fill. One rickety bed, a sofa and a small table— that was all. I had to pay $1 for the night and 50 cents for us to eat at a family-style table with a group of rough looking men. I let Kate hold Sally while I ate and then we changed off so she could eat. We must have looked a sight. The men were nice enough though, when they heard of our troubles.

I found out from them that the stagecoach drivers almost always whipped their teams to a run as they arrived at the edge of the town. They wanted to cause as much commotion as they could. If they arrived at their stop in a cloud of dust maybe they would stir up more interest in riding the coach. The men said this was their way of showing off.

Sally was more sick than we realized. By morning she was coughing constantly and had a high fever. Pat came in to get us and the doctor said John could leave. Pat had our bags settled in the quarters for married enlisted men. When the doctor saw Sally he said "You can take one but leave the other so she can be treated with steam and poultices." I was reluctant to do this but he insisted. We left Sally and rode an Army wagon out to Russell. John was hurting too much to be excited, but in spite of our problems, I wanted to see where we would live.

Fort Russell was three miles outside Cheyenne and looked as temporary as the town. The soldier's barracks had cots along both sides of the center space. There was only one building for married families. It was close to the Cheyenne and Northern Railroad tracks and next to the carpenter's shop. This one had two-room living quarters. They called them apartments but they were nothing like the apartments we knew from New York City. These were drab—made from rough lumber that was poorly sawed and nailed together in a sloppy manner. The floor had splinters in it and on the sunny day we arrived there, I could see light coming through around some of the window frames.

"Oh Pat," I said, "how will we ever manage here?"

"It won't be so bad, Annie. We can fix up the big room for all three children and make our bedroom in the smaller room. That can be our living room, too."

"Maybe we can be mostly outside," I replied, trying to make the best of it.

After we unpacked what few things we had, I headed back to town to see about Sally. She was a little better since the doctor had given her something to make her sleep. His wife was tending her. It was then that we got our first example of Western hospitality. Pat told me that I should find out what the doctor's bill was for taking care of John and Sally. When I asked about it, Dr. Appleby said, "Right now Mrs. White, it's nothing."

When I expressed my surprise, he said, "You folks have come a long way and I can see that you're off to a tough start in Wyoming. We'll talk later about the bill. It won't be much 'cause we appreciate the Army being here to protect us from the savages."

Pat and I didn't necessarily agree about the "savages" but at that point I wasn't going to argue since we had so little money with us. The doctor said, "Leave Sally here one more day and then I think she'll be well enough to get by just fine."

That's the way it worked out. We brought Sally out to the fort the next day. By then she was her usual happy self. John didn't let his cast slow him down. In a few days he was getting along so well we hardly knew he was injured.

There were enough families at Camp Russell to make it possible to have Army transportation to and from school. Most of the children were from officers' families. Each morning and evening a wagon enclosed with canvas took children from the camp to the school on the west edge of Cheyenne.

One day Pat asked an officer why there were only two enlisted men with families. The lieutenant replied, "Some say if the Army wanted their men to have wives, they would issue them one." I could tell that didn't apply to officers. There were five officers' wives at Russell.

The land around the fort was barren. Even the natural vegetation was sparse. After the Army started using the land, they quickly chewed up all the sage and grass. The soil particles were fine and the least breeze kicked up clouds of dust. When the cavalry did their practicing, there was dust everywhere. Sometimes, when it was windy and especially dry, the lieutenants would take their mounted troops away from the compound so that the dust wouldn't bother the rest of the people at camp.

The year before we arrived 2,000 trees had been planted along the two gravel roads and officers' row. Most of them were cottonwood and aspen. Already half of them were dead but we were glad for those that survived.

The parade grounds here were different than either of us had seen. They were in the shape of a diamond with the water tower and guard house at one corner. The house of the commanding officer, Colonel John King, was at the other.

Fort Russell: *There weren't any hills but a soldier drew this as if he was on a hill just west of the fort. Our barracks were in the right background behind the water tower.* COLONEL GERALD ADAMS, (HET.)

The water tank was unusual. It was a tall, wooden one with shingles over the sides. A steam engine pumped water from the creek into this storage tank. A water wagon drew from it and delivered to barrels that were behind each house and barracks. The fort was new. We could tell that from the green lumber. It had been built in a hurry to protect the railroad men when the tracks were laid about three years ago.

Pat threw himself into his new western Army life with the 8th

Infantry. It was what he'd dreamed about ever since Fort Bliss 13 years ago. We now had $1000 in a bank savings account in New York. We were determined that it would keep growing every month until we could have our own land. Even with his promotion, Pat's job was still a wheelwright—a person who made and repaired wagons. There were more than 100 wagons here in constant use, he said. Most of them were pulled by mules, some with horses. Since Cheyenne was on the railroad, it was a major depot and transfer point for 14 forts. In this part of the country, wagons were the way people and merchandise moved across the great distances where there were no trains. Only the Army and large ranchers owned horses.

The land was rough and rocky. Every trail passed over ravines and rugged terrain that mangled wagon wheels and shook the wagon boxes. They needed regular attention and that was Pat's job. After each patrol there would be extra work to do. In between times, he was making new wagon parts and building new wagons.

One part he couldn't make on his own was the metal that was used for the wheel rims. The rough bars were shipped in. Pat would heat the metal and mold it to fit the wooden wheels he'd made, then "shrink" the rims on. It was the most exacting part of the wagon-building process and as he worked at it he got better. The officers were saying that he built a better wagon than the ones that were factory-made in the East. When he heard that, Pat said it was his proudest day. I was proud, too, for my red-headed Irishman was respected among his comrades of all rank.

He used metal to plate the axle and for the kingpin that held the box and axle and wagon tongue together. He could make almost all the metal parts by heating and shaping the pieces like a blacksmith. Most of the emigrant wagons were lighter for they usually had to last for only one trip. The Army wagons had to be more sturdy for they got constant, hard use.

As soon as John's arm was healing well, I became restless for something else to do. The job of laundress was open and I got it since I told them I'd had previous experience. The job paid $2.00 for eight hours of work. One of the younger wives without children volunteered to watch Kate, Sally and John for 50 cents a day. With Kate in school most of the time while I was at my job, that worked out fine. I was mighty proud of myself for this would mean another $1.50 a day into our savings account. We were also able to save some from Pat's Army pay.

The first two years in our post near Cheyenne were full of new experiences. We went to band concerts and theater performances right on the post. The P. T. Barnum circus even came to Cheyenne for a weekend in early 1872 and that was another "first" for us. The officers allowed most of us at the camp to take one day off to see it. The children loved the animals. We were also on the Chatauqua lecture circuit.

Pat asked Captain Henry why there was so much outside entertainment in this camp that was so far from civilization. The captain said, "Because we're right on the main line of the railroad and also because the Army wants to support its troops that are on the frontier."

This was my first experience at an Army cavalry post. It was an impressive sight to see the troop stand at "retreat" on the parade grounds at five in the afternoon. The bugle calls and the formations thrilled me. The "tattoo" and "taps" later on nearly always sent a quiver of pride through me and I tried to teach the children to feel the same way. I think it made them more patriotic.

A new officer came to the post with the name of Captain Brady. Pat didn't think much about it until he was introduced at roll call the next morning. His name was George Keyports Brady, the lieutenant who had been one of the organizers of the escape from Libby Prison. Pat made it a point to speak to him a day later. Captain Brady remembered their hard times together and was very friendly. Pat said it was the longest talk he'd had with an officer since his time with Captain Longstreet at Fort Bliss.

The Army patrols were going farther away from the fort as they searched for bands of Indians. The Army policy was to constantly harrass the Indians. The theory was that this would keep them from building up their food stocks in the summertime as they traditionally did. If this could be accomplished, then the Indians couldn't survive the winter season.

One scouting trip took the Cavalry to the Black Hills in Dakota Territory. Since it was to be a long patrol, they asked Pat to go along. Lots of supply wagons were needed for such an extended trip and they knew that many would get damaged. Having a good wheelwright along might make the difference between success and failure of the patrol. Pat smiled and swelled up a little as he told us this the night before the troops left.

They were gone five-and-a-half weeks. The time passed slowly for us for there was danger lurking in every canyon. The officers assured the families that the men were well armed and would easily be able to subdue any Indians they found. We still worried. There were only six other wives at Fort Russell and for some reason we were never close. You would have thought that we would cling together for support but the other enlisted man's wife was younger than I, and five were officers' wives and didn't want to mix with us.

When Pat's patrol returned, he had stories to tell about the jobs he did. Lots of wagons needed fixing and one was completely destroyed when the mules pulling it slipped on a narrow trail in the Black Hills. It fell into a steep canyon and took the men half a day to bring the salvaged supplies back up the hill. The mules had to be put away and only a few parts could be saved from the wagon.

In the Black Hills they met with a patrol out of Fort Lincoln, in Dakota Territory that was under the command of Major Marcus Reno. Pat said he was a short, rumpled man with eyes set back into his head. He looked to Pat like a small version of President Grant.

During their scouting around the hills, they saw Indians every few days but they never put up a fight. If the troops found any camps or stores of food they would take or destroy them to make it harder for the Indians to survive. Only once did they fear for their lives. The entire company of 65 men and 12 wagons were passing through a canyon when they spotted Indians on both ridges above them. Pat said there were about 75 warriors just watching. He could see that some of them had guns. Captain Harker ordered the company to keep on marching and not to shoot unless the Indians fired first. Nothing happened but Pat said it gave everyone a spooky feeling to be surrounded like that.

CHAPTER 20

MARTHA JANE CANARY

The last week out, Pat's patrol was joined by a detachment of 37 soldiers from Goose Creek, Wyoming, not far from Sheridan. They had been sent to get field experience in the Black Hills and to provide replacements for some of the Russell troops. One of the drivers in this patrol was a woman named Martha Jane Canary. Pat said she was tall, sort of rough-looking and had short hair that was tucked in under her Army hat.

The men from Russell wouldn't have noticed that she was a woman but the Goose Creek troops didn't take long to talk about her. They said she could swear better than most of them and that she was a crack shot with a rifle. Most of the men called her "Calamity Jane" instead of Martha.

I first knew her as Martha for that's how she introduced herself when we met at the laundry one day soon after the patrol was back. She came in to do her own clothes. "I can tell you're from the East," she greeted me loudly.

"Yes," I replied, "but I'm liking the West more all the time." I told her who I was and she remembered Pat as the man who fixed the wagons.

"He sure knows how to make 'em roll again. The one I was drivin' threw a rim and he had it going in less than two hours. Don't know how he tightened them rims up so fast."

I asked Pat about this that evening.

"Everyone does it, Annie. When the wooden wheels shrink, the iron rims get loose. We drive wedges under the rims and that works for awhile. Or we soak the wheel overnight—that'll make it swell back to tight again."

"Does that always work?" I asked.

"Until the wheel gets too dry or if some of the spokes get broken. We keep extra wheels around because so many get mangled in the rough country."

I saw Martha Jane only at a distance until we met at the laundry. There was a lot of talk about her in camp but Pat and I tried to stay out of it, for as far as we could see she did her job as a driver and didn't cause trouble. Pat said she also had scouted for one of Fort Russell's patrols one time south of here and did a good job at that, too.

Pat went out on one more patrol that fall. This time they went toward Ft. Fetterman in north-central Wyoming. Captain Brady, the officer he knew at Libby Prison, led this expedition. Their job was to escort a small party of officers and their families back to Fort Russell where they would provide replacements. On their return they entered some sharp canyons where Indians had prepared an ambush.

While most of the soldiers dug in and engaged the hostiles, Pat was ordered to take the five loaded wagons on ahead. The officers hoped this would allow the women and children to escape. The only quick route was over a 35-foot high cliff. Every wagon was loaded with household goods and families. The women and children got out and slid down the rocky hill but one woman was eight months with child and had to stay in her wagon as it was lowered.

Pat had participated in this sort of a tactic before but never under this kind of life-and-death situation. He tied the young woman to the inside of the wagon and they lowered it slowly down the steep bank. Mules and troops were holding the ropes tight at the top of the cliff. Pat gave the order, "Lower away." Inch by inch the huge wagon creaked its way down the slope. The families already at the bottom were too frightened to speak. Pat was on the crest giving the orders. Once the wagon seemed ready to tip but quick action by two of the rope teams kept it upright.

As it finally reached the bottom safely, Pat said he looked up for the first time in five minutes and looked right at an Indian standing on a rock not more than 20 feet away. He was holding a gun. Pat said he yelled loud enough to be heard two miles away. The Indian seemed more afraid than Pat and turned to run away. None of the soldiers fired at him for they knew that he could have killed them as they were intent on the lowering of the wagon. They were thankful that this Indian was probably from a different band than the ones involved in the ambush a few miles away.

After the wagon train had moved on they were joined by the rest of the patrol. They had successfully driven the Indians from the canyon and Pat witnessed the joyful reunion. When they returned Pat told me proudly of his important part in the escape. I think he was more proud of how he handled that incident than of his many jobs of wagon building and repair. Captain Brady told Pat he was putting him in for a special commendation but nothing came of it.

During November and December of 1872, there was a bad flu

epidemic at Fort Russell. Cheyenne had it, too, but it was worse at the fort for the men were out in all kinds of rough weather. The Army kept the patrols going for they wanted to starve the Indians that winter. One of the officers asked me to work part of my day in the hospital. A woman from Cheyenne came to spell me in the laundry.

On the days Martha Jane Canary wasn't out on patrol or assigned to some other job, she would come to the hospital and help. I know she didn't get paid much by the Army and she didn't get paid anything for doing this. But she wanted to pitch in and during these times we got well acquainted.

There wasn't a lot we could do for the soldiers although the one doctor there tried many remedies. One that seemed to help was some kind of smelly ointment with hot cloths over it. We'd leave that on for a while and then alternate with a cool compress. Other things we tried were epsom salts and cream of tartar. We had some deaths and lots of men were laid up for weeks.

Martha told me of her life in Missouri and Montana and the hard times she had with her parents. It sounded like when she left home she wasn't leaving much. She said that her mother was a free spirit and known for her outrageous behavior. "Guess I came by it natcherly," she said. Martha was a big-boned woman with a buxom figure on the top half. Maybe that's what appealed to the men.

Martha talked rougher than any woman I'd known before and I heard nasty stories about her but as far as I was concerned, she was easy to visit with and a hard worker. I must say, she surprised me the first time I saw her roll her own cigarette and smoke it. That was the time when I said I liked her last name.

"I do, too," she said. "My folks spelled it with 2 n's but I decided I'd rather it sounded like a bird than a place where they cans things."

The hospital became short of help and I started working full time. Two different wives helped take care of our three children during my working hours. We had an outbreak of diptheria and whooping cough that caused us to work longer. I liked the work and three months later, when the hospital matron left, I was asked to take that job. The pay was $3 a day which made me real proud of myself. Now I was in charge of the two civilian nurses. I still worked with patients but had more desk work. That was good for I already knew that I was with child again. I didn't tell anyone for a while because I wanted to keep the job.

Three wives were about to have babies and each of them came to me to talk about it. Maybe it was because I already had three children and was a supervisor at the hospital. We were between doctors at the camp so the two officers' wives, Mrs. Mills and Mrs. Henry, decided to go to Doc Appleby in town. They asked me to go with them. I was surprised but arranged to go. Doc didn't seem to mind that I was along and when they had their babies each of them asked me to assist in the delivery.

The doctor only charged $15 for two visits and the delivery but when the enlisted man's wife, Mrs. Farnham, was ready to deliver, she asked if I would be her midwife. When I told her she should go to the doctor, she said they couldn't afford it. She told me that she and her husband had decided that I knew as much about birthing a baby as Doc Appleby did. That was a stretch but it all turned out alright and the word got around camp that I was good help for all three of them.

I kept working until three weeks before our next child was born. This birth was easier and blessed us with another little boy. When he was one week old we arranged for the priest in Cheyenne to baptize him. The priest asked if we had someone to "stand up for him" as a Godparent. Our choice was easy. With us at the altar in a new buckskin jacket was my hospital helper, Martha Canary. When the priest asked for the baby's name, she was given the honor of speaking it. "Edward Patrick White," she said in her strong mule driver's voice. She was proud to do it and we were happy to consider her our good friend.

As we later found out, Martha had held several part-time jobs with the Army as a scout, bullwhacker and courier. We didn't know it then, but when she arrived at Fort Russell there was quite a stir. Some of the men had heard of her and the officers thought it wasn't good for her to be there. She had a reputation as a trouble-maker. At other Army posts and at some of the frontier towns she had been known to get rip-roaring drunk and the word was that she was an "easy mark" for any romantic conquest.

One trooper said to Pat one day, "She's a take off-er." Pat was not up on all the slang some of the men used so he innocently asked what that meant. "Hah, you don't know? It means it doesn't take much of an offer and she'll take off fer the brush and take off 'er pants."

There were several stories about how she got her nickname of Calamity Jane. I never asked her about any of them for I didn't want to embarrass her and I was too self-conscious. Some said that wherever she went bad things happened. Others said that she was a loose woman and they were sometimes called "Janes" in those days.

There was a story going around that she once tried to start her own "hog ranch." That's what the soldiers called the places where the camp followers were. It was really just a house of ill repute, I guess. I didn't like to think about such things but Pat said they were near most of the Army posts.

In early 1874, a company of the 8th Infantry arrived with Lieutenant John Summerhayes in charge. He had a new bride and for a while they were the main conversation in camp. Lt. Summerhayes was an engineer by training and was put in charge of the wagon supply train operations in and out of Russell. Because of that, he was soon acquainted with Pat.

In May of that year, Lt. Summerhayes was asked to lead a patrol to the Spotted Tail Agency where the Indians had made threats of breaking out of their reservation. This took them into the northwest corner of Nebraska. It was planned as a three-week trip but that depended on how the Indians responded.

When the lieutenant's bride of four months heard this she was very distressed. The lieutenant had found her a competent "striker," who did the cooking, cleaning and house care, but he was a bit of a radical on religion. Mrs. Summerhayes did not feel comfortable being with him all day by herself. She made inquiry at the post laundry and at the hospital for a woman to spend the days with her. They suggested my name and word was sent to me that I should call on her.

Lt. Summerhayes called at our barracks and escorted little Edward and me to their home on officers' row. His wife was a small person, very pretty and dressed in the finest daytime clothing I'd seen since I was in the East. She put me at ease when Lt. Summerhayes left and asked, "How long have you been here, Mrs. White?"

As I responded to each of her questions, I was pleased and impressed that she called me Mrs. White. She treated me with respect just as Mrs. Terrell treated Mother so long ago in New York. She knew that I'd worked in both the laundry and the hospital, and asked, "Now that you have a new baby, will you be wanting to go back to one of those jobs?"

"Perhaps in a month or two but if you want me to stay with you during the day until the lieutenant comes back, I will. I can always go back there at that time."

"Yes, I know you can, Mrs. White. The officers in charge of both of those jobs told me that you are an excellent worker. Mrs. Mills and Mrs. Henry say you were a great help to them when they had their babies."

"Thank you, Mrs. Summerhayes. That's good to hear."

"I would like you to be with me while John is gone," she said. "When are your children at school?"

"They leave at 7:30 in the morning and return on the wagon at 3:00."

"That will be just fine," Mrs. Summerhayes said. "If you will come over as they leave and stay until 3:00, I will plan for my striker, Adams, to be here during those same hours."

The lieutenant and his patrol were gone for five weeks. My time with Martha Summerhayes was exciting and pleasant in every way. She was well educated. Some of the times I was there she would be busy with her own activities outside the house and I would walk home for a few hours to do my own housework. She only wanted me there to avoid being alone with Adams. She told me that he was probably not harmful but he sometimes got wound up lecturing her on spiritualism and religious beliefs. When he did that, she felt frightened.

After the first week, she insisted that I call her Martha. I wasn't prepared for that informality with an officer's wife and sometimes forgot. When I did she would smile and say, "Now Annie, you don't want me calling you Mrs. White all the time, do you? Remember, when it's just the two of us, I'm Martha."

When Martha learned that I'd been a supervisor in a clothing factory, she asked if I'd do mending and dress-making for her. I spent many hours at her house from then on, even when she was away with the other officer's wives. Adams didn't bother me and I liked doing things for her. When Lt. Summerhayes returned, she apparently told him how pleased she was with the arrangement for he came over and gave me $100. That was more than we had agreed on but he insisted that it was fair for all I'd done. It was a change for me and didn't interfere with the family things all that much.

Although she was from an upper-class Eastern family, she wasn't snooty. She once said that she thought Cheyenne was an amusing but unattractive frontier town. Then she remarked that cows, pigs and saloons seemed to be the main features of the place. That was the only complaining I heard from her. With Martha our conversations got outside the familiar boxes used by Pat and me. She opened new spaces for me — ones I'd only touched with my summer library reading during high school. Even though we knew each other for only a short time, she allowed me to become her close friend. As I think back, that was not an easy thing for an officer's wife to do with an enlisted man's wife. I thought it strange that my two closest friends at Fort Russell were both named Martha.

Soon after Lt. Summerhayes returned, Pat received word that the 8th Infantry Regiment was being transferred to Fort McDowell in Arizona.

We heard that there were some serious problems with the Indians and the Arizona detachment needed reinforcements. When the news got out some of the others who had been there told Pat about the good land along the river that was near McDowell. They said, "If you want land in the west, Pat, that's the place to get it. It's deep and when you put water on it, anything will grow."

All of Company C was going. There was more good news. Pat was promoted to corporal. The report by Captain Brady about his good work out on patrol must have done it. People around the camp also knew that he was one of the best wagon makers. I'd say this was one of the happiest days we had. Pat was being recognized again and we were going to a place where we might have our own land.

Pat was excited. Our transfer was about all he could talk about in the evenings when we were together. I hadn't started working again at the hospital. Now that we were leaving, I had more time

Martha Jane Canary: *This was taken in Cheyenne. Martha gave it to us when we left.*   MONTANA HISTORICAL FOUNDATION

around the house. John was running everywhere but if we could keep him away from the horses there wasn't much else that could give him a problem. Kate was old enough to watch Sally. By now, we were calling Edward by a nickname, Ned, and he was in his basket all the time.

In the evenings Pat would go over our savings account statement. We

115

had just over $1300 now. That seemed like a big figure to us. It was more than either of our parents had saved in their lifetimes. Dreams of our own land were getting closer.

The day before Company C was to leave, Martha Jane came to our barracks with two new buckskin jackets over her arm. "Here Annie, I want you and Pat to have these."

I was bewildered. "Why, Martha?"

"You've been the best friends I ever had. You honored me when I stood up with you fer little Ned. He's too young fer a jacket but I got these two fer you so's you can remember me."

"We'll always remember you, Martha," I said as I hugged her tightly. My eyes were misty and my voice so choked, I couldn't say more. She was known as a crusty woman but she looked a little teary-eyed, too, as she turned to walk away. I never saw her again even though we heard a lot more about Calamity Jane as the years went on.

Pat and I objected to all the bad things people said about Martha. The fact that she was a crack shot and called many a man's bluff gave her a reputation as a show-off. We think she used this skill to let the men know that she could meet them on their own ground. She did a lot of good things for people that we will never forget.

When Pat came home that evening I showed him the beautiful jackets. Later he said, "I'm going to go by Doc Appleby's place in the morning and give him my buckskin. He never charged us for what he did for John and Sally those first days we were here."

"Do you really want to do that?"

"Yep, it's too fancy for me. I don't think Martha would mind if she knew why."

That's what we did and I was proud of Pat for honoring the debt we owed.

CHAPTER 21

THE WAGON TRIP

The ride from Fort Russell to McDowell was the worst travel experience since we were married. We had one small wagon all to ourselves because of our four children. There was one seat set on springs. It held three people, really only two if it was Pat and I. We took turns sitting on the floor and on our belongings that were wrapped in canvas for protection. At least our wagon was covered. Only the two of us with families were equipped that way. We said that we must have looked like the '49ers on the Oregon Trail. The men slept in tents or on the ground in the open just as they did when out on patrol.

This was my first experience with Dutch ovens. The ovens were the standard issue for cooking in the field. Biscuits, bread and other pastries were made in them. They were also used for other cooking. They were like the cooking pots I used except that these were made of stronger metal.

The first part of our trip wasn't too bad for we went south along the east side of the Rocky Mountains. The land was mostly level except for a few creeks and washes. It was summer, the grass was good and flowers were blooming. The older children walked alongside the wagon part of the time.

As we got into New Mexico Territory, we joined the Santa Fe Trail and for the next week the road was dusty but easy to follow. Four mules pulled each wagon. During this stretch of trail, they got gassy. Pat just laughed about it. He said they were usually that way on the trail and it was a common sound as the patrols moved along. Now we were right behind them in the wagon and with the children there, it was not only irritating but really disgusting to me.

Our wagon didn't have a brake. On each downhill slope the front end would bump against the mules' back ends and spook them. Pat complained that he would never rig a harness that way. At Santa Fe he found some good harness straps and got the lead team fastened to the front of the wagon tongue. That took care of the problem.

We tried to make about 25 or 30 miles every day. The troops were used to doing more when they were mounted, but with the supply wagons and our two families we slowed down a bit. This still meant travel from daylight to late afternoon and little time for rest stops. We only washed clothes twice, once in a creek and at Santa Fe. The cooking had to be done after stopping at night or at breakfast. The officer in charge, Captain Howard Collins, wouldn't take the time to build fires for cooking at midday. We even kept rolling on Sundays and some of us were upset about that. It was hard to be a faithful Catholic out here.

Each day Captain Collins sent scouts out ahead to pick out a place for our midday stop. The afternoon scout was important since we wanted a site with fresh water. Only once during our trip through northern New Mexico did we have to get by with a dry camp. The other wife said to me one night, "The men just keep on doing what they always do, but for us women it's twice as hard out on the trail." She was right.

After Santa Fe, the weather turned hot and the roads were rocky and rough. The mules kicked up dust and it seemed like the wagons would shake to pieces. I didn't understand how it could be rocky and dusty at the same time, but it was. We were crusted with dirt from head to foot. Then Kate got sick. It was the dysentery and soon it was something like the whooping cough.

Kate was 11 years old and usually the one I depended upon to help with the other children. She laid in the wagon, groaning, as I fretted about her. At the same time, I was trying to keep the others out of trouble. We were dirty, tired and short-tempered. Then little Ned got the whooping cough, too.

This was one of the few times Pat and I got mad at each other in front of the children. There wasn't any place to go—they had to hear us. It was all about why we couldn't stop along the Rio Grande River to rest a few days. That was the only stream of any size that we had seen for days, and with Kate so sick I feared for her life. We were all exhausted.

I shouted at him, "If we can't stop here, we're all going to be sick!"

"I've told you a dozen times, we can't stop anywhere by ourselves!" Pat yelled back. "This company has its orders and I'm not going to ask the captain to stop the whole wagon train. He'd think I'm crazy."

"Well, we are going to be crazy if Kate doesn't get better."

We went on like that for a few minutes, then Pat put his arm around me and said, "I know how hard it is. 'Tis bad on everyone but worse now that you have two that are sick."

We rode on in silence for a few more miles until I felt like answering with a smile and a forgiving comment. We were both riding in the seat mounted on the front of the wagon. After a few hours of that our backs would give out and we'd have to stretch out alongside Kate and Ned. Pat drove the mules most of the way but sometimes I'd spell him a bit.

The other wife told me that sheep's milk was good for the whooping cough. The next day after she said that we passed by a Navajo herder with a large band of sheep. I begged Pat to stop and try to get us some. John and I drove the wagon on while Pat borrowed a mule. He took an empty can and rode to the herder. After much sign language, he persuaded him to let him milk a ewe. When he caught up with our caravan, I almost didn't give the milk to the children for it looked so dirty. I decided I had to try it and gave them a few sips every two hours. I don't know if that helped or not, but they got a little better after that.

It seemed that we would never get to our destination. The only good thing was that we had plenty of food and the soldiers had lots of guns and ammunition so we weren't worried too much about the Indians. We avoided going through any deep canyons where we could be ambushed. We also were careful to keep two sentries posted all night around the camps. The Little Colorado was dangerous, with quicksand in many places and a shifting current. The men scouted up and down for a couple of hours before deciding on the best place to cross.

We saw five warriors with headresses soon after we crossed the Little Colorado. They were on horseback, watching from a ridge about a half-mile ahead of us. Captain Collins said to just keep moving, and by the time we got even with them they turned away. We never saw them again.

We expected it to be hot in July—and it was. As our wagon caravan moved south and down off the rim in Northern Arizona we felt the first waves of desert heat. We passed Stoneman's Lake and down the rocky trail into the Verde River Valley. Surprisingly, as we progressed along, the shade and the air movement kept us comfortable. I believe the low humidity was the big difference. In South Carolina we felt the heat more than we did now. That probably helped in our later decision to make this our home.

After nearly a month on the trail we crossed the Verde River and made our way for Fort Whipple. This was the Army headquarters for Arizona in those days. Kate was nearly well but still weak. We rested there two nights while the officers made their reports and got instructions for duty at McDowell. What a relief it was to sleep on a real cot and have walls around us again. I spent the day doing laundry and mending clothes for my family. Kate was able to help, and the minor colds the rest of us had were not bad enough to worry about.

We took the wagon road to Wickenburg and stopped for the night on the Hassayampa River. This route had been used by the Army for about 10 years, so it was in better condition than many we had been using.

Our second stop overnight was at Cave Creek. This was the best water we found since long ago in Colorado. We were now on a trail cut by General Stoneman which made the trip from Wickenburg to McDowell easier than going down to Phoenix and back. The last day we took the short cut southeast to McDowell. The last 12 miles were downhill into the Verde River Valley. We mostly followed a dry creek bed in the desert that the soldiers called a "wash."

Even though we'd seen a lot of mountains, the view of the mountains to the east was thrilling to us. The mountains were named with an old Spanish or Aztec name that looked funny to us, so everyone just called them the "Mad as Hell" mountains.

Pat and I liked what we saw. This land was called a desert but it was not like any of the deserts we had read about in school. There was more vegetation than in Wyoming or Colorado or the other parts of the long trail we had followed to get here. Pat said it must be that the soil was better. That was mostly true, but we also found out later there were two rainy seasons that helped make the growth possible.

CHAPTER 22

FORT McDOWELL

We reached the west bank of the Verde and turned south to our new home. We saw irrigation ditches bringing water to fields of grain and hay. After all we had seen in the last month this was like finding an oasis in the desert. The Stoneman Road took us through the irrigated land and into the parade grounds of the fort, where the cavalry did their training.

We were anxious to find out where we would live. The married soldiers' quarters were in one-story adobe buildings on the east side of the post.

Fort McDowell: *An Army photographer took this postcard picture looking east towards the river. Our quarters can barely be seen in the background.* ARIZONA STATE UNIVERSITY ARCHIVES

We were given a double space because of our children. This gave us four rooms. Even though the floors were hard-packed dirt, they were worn smooth and when a little water was spread over them every few days, they were almost dust-free. Even the officers' homes had dirt floors, but I later found out that they were covered with canvas. I had a good chuckle out of what we used for brooms. They were twigs tied with string—just like my mother had used in Ireland so many years before.

Oh, how happy we were to unload our trunks and little bit of cookware from that wagon! The children were anxious to explore our new post. The main point of interest was a flag pole and large sundial that was located in the exact center of the parade grounds. We found out that the children in camp used that for a playground when the troops were not drilling.

By the time we arrived the cavalry troops had roofs on their barracks. This wasn't always the case. During the first few years they lived in tents, since the barracks walls were all that was finished. The men had been pulled off construction to build irrigation ditches and clear the land for the post farms. They did that because of the epidemic of scurvy the first year. There were no fresh fruits or vegetables. When the task took longer than expected, civilians were hired to finish the job. The soldiers completed the buildings, then went back on patrol. By the time we got there a discharged officer, Captain William Hancock, was leasing the farm land from the Army. He was also the post trader and ran a store located at the northeast corner of the parade grounds.

Captain Corliss was the commander of the post. There was only one company of soldiers in camp when we got there. The other two were out on a long patrol into the mountains to the east. About 10 days after we arrived, they returned with big stories about destroying several Apache camps, and the battles that took place. One soldier had been killed and buried in the mountains. Three troopers came back with injuries but only one was serious. This brought home to all of us how close to danger we were.

There was lots of building going on. Since the soldiers were needed out in the field on patrol, the Army had hired civilians from Maryville and Phoenix to work on construction and repairing. The first roofs were layers of brush with mud and straw put over them to absorb the rain. When they built them this way, it was thought that any rain that fell would be so light that the mud and straw would soak up the moisture. That didn't work. We were told that the rain could come down as hard as it does anywhere and the water would go right on through and make everything a mess. The tin roofs we had on our quarters had been put on the previous year.

Pat's job here was like it was at Russell except that he did more harness and saddle repair. I didn't think bridles and harness would need work, but in the rocks and snarly vegetation they encountered on patrol, pieces were getting torn and lost all the time. After the 23rd Infantry pulled out, Pat was the only wheelwright, so he was busy. As patrols crossed the river, the land to the east was rougher than just about anyplace in the west. Wagon tongues, wheels and axles broke often.

There was a page out of the Army and Navy Journal pinned on a bulletin board when we arrived. It was written by a soldier from McDowell:

> To show how bad things are here, we have not been paid for three months. We get mail maybe once a month. Economy rules and in the end makes double the expense. Wagons are falling to pieces, mules and horses unshod. Six deserters last month alone.
>
> We have one-tenth of our roster in the hospital from scurvy. No fresh fruit or vegetables.

H.T. June 1874

There were only three trails out of McDowell: the one we took coming in from Fort Whipple, the one to Phoenix and the one built seven years ago to old Fort Reno in the Mazatzal Mountains. If the patrols wanted to go any other place, they followed faint Indian paths or "bushwhacked" through the thorny brush and rocks. Sometimes they had to "whack" a lot of it. The only way to supply the long patrols was with wagons, since the pack horses and mules couldn't carry all the food and ammunition that was needed.

The air was drier than in Wyoming and the wheels would shrink in the desert air. When the patrol was away from McDowell and a wheel would throw a rim, the soldiers would sometimes just tie it on with rawhide or rope to get it back here. Other times they would use wedges like they did in Wyoming. Wagons were used on the Stoneman Trail to Ft. Whipple for supplies, or to Phoenix, then to Maricopa Wells where they met the train that brought in mail and material from California.

The first month here there was a shooting just a few feet away from our barracks. A Private Ward was drinking too much liquor and tried to force his way into the room of Marie, one of the camp laundresses. She called for help to the Wordens, who lived next door. When Mr. Worden told Ward to leave, the private fired at him. Mr. Worden then shot back and killed Ward. What an introduction to Arizona!

Pat got to see the patrol reports and sometimes he would bring one home to show me. In December, Captain Sanford took a patrol up the west bank of the Verde. There were 42 cavalrymen on this trip. They followed a creek 25 miles northwest and near Mount Humboldt they surprised a band of 11 Indians. The soldiers were able to surround the hostiles, and in a three-hour gun battle, killed every one of them. Privates

Joseph Darragh and James Howell were also killed. Pat was good friends with Darragh, who was from our part of Ireland. Pedro, a Mexican guide, was injured severely in the leg. Captain Sanford, in his report, commended all the men for their bravery. He was highly critical of the Remington revolvers the men carried. Many became clogged and if it had not been for their dependable rifles, they would not have been successful in their mission.

In February, Captain Sanford scouted in the Superstition Mountains. He had a patrol of 51 men with him this time. When he got into the area around "Weaver's Needle," he said that it was the roughest country he had ever seen in this territory. The horses wore out all their shoes and became exhausted and footsore. After only five days out, they had to return to McDowell with nothing to show for their trouble.

The soldiers loved their horses. They would do almost anything to keep them in good condition, for it was the only way they could cover the territory and keep the Indians on the run. They had a saying at McDowell: "In the Arizona cavalry, a good horse can't be replaced but a good man can."

McDowell wasn't as well built as Ft. Whipple—not even as good as Russell. There was a trader's store, hospital, bakery and laundry. Water was pumped from the river into a large tank. Every few months the "settlings" in this tank had to be cleaned. There was so much silt in the river that it was cloudy. The soldiers used this silt as a sort of fertilizer on the post gardens and I must say, the vegetables really did get big when they got plenty of water.

The soldiers built ramadas in front of the barracks. These were really just sunshades made out of mesquite posts with brush crossed back and forth over the top. It surprised all of us how much cooler it was to sit there. Even on the hot afternoons we could feel a breeze. We would also go to one of the two irrigation ditches that flowed just above the post. That water was warmer than the river but it was nearby. Sometimes we'd just dangle our feet in there to cool off.

Insects and flies were everywhere. The horses attracted them, I suppose. Although everyone talked about rattlesnakes, we saw only a few. Scorpions were more common. Before we dressed, we had to shake out every piece of clothing. Even then, we were bitten several times. The bites made us sore for a few days, but nothing serious.

Ants were worse. They were everywhere. We put the legs of our cots in tin cans filled with water so the ants couldn't crawl up into our beds. Sometimes a sheet would touch the floor and they would find their way up to bite us in our sleep.

We often slept outside because of the heat. Never in our travels had we been able to see so many stars. The starlight was so bright we could see to move around with no difficulty—-even when the moon was not out. At full-moon times, the reflection off the granite and gravel was dazzling. For the first time, the children became interested in the constellations. My library reading in New York helped me identify Orion, the Pleiades and the Big Dipper. We made up stories about how they got their names and searched for them as the seasons rolled on.

Kate was good about taking the children to the river during the hot days. Along the west bank of the Verde there were big mesquite and cottonwood trees. In some places the land sloped into the river so gradually that it was almost like a beach, except that it wasn't sandy. It was either gravely or like clay, and the soil stayed moist. Kate would lay the baby in the shade and let the two other children play in the shallow back waters of the river. There were still some beaver dams in channels along the west bank and these made part of the current slow. As I think back on it, I'm surprised that we weren't worried about the kids playing there but all the families did it and it was the best place to stay cool.

We were amazed to see so many birds along the river. There were more than in South Carolina or Delaware. We saw many kinds of hummingbirds. There were birds that none of us had seen before. The brightest one of all was a tiny thing not much larger than a wren. It was grey with a bright crimson breast. Big herons and bald eagles stalked the river banks looking for fish. It was a peaceful spot to observe all kinds of wildlife.

Pat was busy with his work. His pay was now $19 a month. Because he was usually needed at the post, he wasn't put out on patrols. He was busier here than any place we were sent. There were normally two patrols a month, but that changed during the second year we were at McDowell. The hostiles were not so dangerous and most of the trips were to follow up on some incident of horse stealing or other raiding.

He made many new wagons. Iron wagon parts were shipped on the train from California to Maricopa Wells, then brought here by wagon. Some of the wooden parts came from the cottonwood trees that grew along the Verde River. The flat lumber for the wagon boxes came in from a mill in Prescott. In the few years before we got here, the military road to Camp Reno was so rough that half of McDowell's wagons had been ruined or burned by the Indians. Pat was sent here to rebuild their wagon inventory.

One patrol into the Mazatzals and the Sierra Ancha Mountains was especially hard on the wagons. Lieutenant Cleave took 110 men on a trip that lasted 31 days. For a trip like this, they took many supply wagons on the old McDowell-Reno road. They thought it was a successful trip for they killed 33 Indians and captured 16, bringing them back to McDowell. They were later shipped to San Carlos to be confined at the reservation there. The men were bragging about destroying fields of corn the Indians were growing along Tonto Creek. No soldiers were lost on this patrol, but eight of the 17 wagons they took with them were abandoned or brought back in pieces on the other wagons. Pat didn't have to bring me the patrol reports now. They were posted on the board at the sutler's store. I tried to read them all just to keep up on what was happening.

I started working in the post laundry. With the extra troops in camp, another laundress was needed and we wanted the money it would add to our savings. Kate was a responsible girl and could take care of Sally and Ned. By now, John was old enough to help with a lot of the chores.

The laundry building we used was a miserable excuse for shelter. The work here was harder than at Moultrie and Russell. We had to make our own soap. There were no ranchers or farmers nearby to make it for us. I'd use wood ashes and get fat from William Hancock, the post trader. Four days of the week I washed and ironed and one day a week I made soap. After Mr. Hancock did a lot of butchering I might make soap for two days just to get ahead.

The officers' wives said that my starching and ironing were better than they had been getting. In most Army camps civilian women worked in the laundry. Some were good and some were not. I prided myself on doing as good a job for the soldiers as I did for my family.

There were five officers who had families here. They had a total of six children among them and they played together with our family and the two children of the Egans, who lived next to us in the other married men's quarters. Amanda Egan and I became good friends. Her husband, Robert, was also a corporal. He was in Company C with Pat. Their two boys, Ernie and Tad, were 10 and 12 years old. The Egans were from Ohio.

They pronounced their last name with the emphasis on the "gan" part. He said it was a holdover from the Welsh or Celtic origins of his family. The first time we heard that, Pat and I thought they were being a little "stuck-up," but after while it became common and we thought nothing of it.

126

Robert Egan had been with the Army for 15 years and was in both the Antietam and Gettysburg battles. It was at Gettysburg that he was shot in the left shoulder. He still had a limit on the way he could move that joint. Corporal Egan was nearly a foot taller than my Pat. He had sandy hair, bright blue eyes and was a well-built man with callused hands. We could tell that he knew hard work.

The two men didn't know each other at Antietam but spent a lot of time talking about the battle. Robert would ask Pat a lot of questions about Libby Prison, since he had heard so much about it. I liked these conversations because I learned new things that Pat hadn't told me.

Amanda was taller than I was, with red hair. With my black hair and darker skin, the sun didn't bother me, but Amanda had freckles on her face and arms and had to be careful. Amanda had come from parents with a lot of farm land in eastern Ohio. They had nice family things in their quarters.

Whenever we had a few spare minutes in the late afternoons we would sit under the ramada and talk. We watched the sun turn the mountains a purplish red, then lavender. We would pick out shapes on the hills and watch them change as the sun set lower in the sky. The best times were when clouds dimpled the mountains with patterns.

We told each other about our lives before McDowell. Amanda was eager to hear about Ireland, since she thought that sounded so romantic. When I got through telling her about the famine and sickness, she didn't think it was romantic at all. She had good stories about her parents and their pioneering from the east into Ohio.

Robert was a platoon leader in Company C. He was gone from the post almost half of the first year we were at McDowell. The Army was hot on the trail of the Indians and Company C did a lot of the hard patrols. Sometimes he was in fierce battles. During that first year five soldiers were killed during the fighting. I was glad my Pat wasn't out on patrol.

This was the first place I heard the saying, "The only good Indian is a dead Indian." I was shocked to hear it come out like that. Pat and the Egans said it was common among the Army men that were in battles with them. It didn't seem right, for there were many Pima, Yavapai and Maricopa Indians that were good scouts for the Army then. We knew stories of how different tribes had befriended the first settlers, helping them learn how to live with the uncertain climate in the west.

Geronimo and his followers had just escaped from the reservation at San Carlos and they spread terror over the southeast part of Arizona

Territory. The men said that it could happen here if we weren't careful. The Indians at San Carlos had been unhappy ever since they were forced to move there from Fort Verde, which was upriver from here. Even though we had friendly Indians around camp, the word was that the Tonto Apaches were ruthless and had to be starved out.

Pat didn't tell me a lot about what the men said of their battles. Pat wasn't much for conversation unless it was about farming or wagon making. Robert liked to talk about his life in Cleveland before his Civil War duty. That's when Pat would remember that he had work to do at the "shop," as he called his wagon repair area. But once, when he began to compliment Pat on his skill at making wagons, the conversations took on a new tone.

Bob said, "You should see how Pat puts those wagons together. Most wheelwrights just bore a hole for the bolts, but Pat knows how to burn the right holes in the frame.

Amanda asked, "How does he burn holes in the frame?'

Pat puffed up a bit and explained, "I make the hole with a red hot iron that is just a little smaller than the bolt I'm going to use. I hammer the bolt through and then there's no chance for water or sand to get around the bolt and cause it to rust or wear out."

"Not many men know how or take the time to do that. He also does a beautiful job of making those mortise joints. Not many nails in the wagons Pat makes," Robert exclaimed as he slapped Pat on the shoulder in a way that Pat clearly appreciated.

The first year was busy as we adjusted to our new home. Pat talked about striking out on our own, but his enlistment term with the Army had two more years to go. In the meantime, we were building our savings account. We now had almost $2000. We thought we were wealthy for we had never known anyone who had saved this much money.

The desert fascinated all of us. Quail would walk right up through the barracks area. They weren't afraid for the soldiers never shot at them. Only one officer, Captain Wilson, the post doctor, had a shotgun and when he hunted quail he went away from the post. The quail had plenty of natural enemies, though. Owls, hawks, eagles, bobcats and coyotes were after them.

The most unusual plant was the saguaro cactus. Some of them were huge. They were new to us. We were told by Captain Hancock at the sutler's store that this area was the only place where they grew. Sometimes the children would pick out saguaros that had a shape like a person. When they found one that was really different, they'd insist that we walk out to see it.

The ocotillo, or coachwhip, was another strange plant. The soldiers called it the devil's candlestick. To build a fence, they would cut off the stems and stick them in the ground close together. If they'd water the stems they could sometimes get them to start growing. There were lots of ragged looking fences like that around the camp.

Our first springtime was a surprise. We had heard of the cactus blossoms, but had no idea that they were so brilliant. From late March until the end of May something was in bloom. They were more vivid than the flowers we had seen in the east. Amanda and I took the children for walks into the desert on Sunday afternoons to see them.

The wildlife was new to us. There were more animals here than any place we had been. I believe it was because of the river. Animals had to come in to the river for water. We had never seen a ringtail cat before but they were as common as raccoon in the east.

There were more coyotes than in Wyoming. At night we heard the animal sounds from the river. We could hear the rabbits cry out as bobcats, coyotes or mountain lions caught them. Strange birds called roadrunners were favorites of the children. They had curious habits and we were told that this was one of the few places in the United States where they lived. We all thought they were cute until we heard that they ate baby quail, and then we didn't like them as much.

We cooked and kept warm in the winter with a cast-iron wood stove. There was plenty of mesquite wood along the river, so fuel was never a problem. How to get healthy food was a puzzle, though. Most of what we ate were canned foods with not much variety. The post farm still didn't supply enough vegetables. Butchering time and the fresh meat it provided was one of our highlights.

When Kate was 12 years old she started staying with other children down by the river when their mothers couldn't be there. It was known around the camp that she was good with their care. Lt. Henry Kearney and his wife, Elizabeth, had two girls who were three and five years old. Elizabeth was never very friendly to me but one day she asked if Kate could stay with her girls while they went to a big party at Maryville.

Maryville was a town down by the Salt River, about seven miles from here. They were hosting a holiday dance party. Kate did stay with their girls and they got along fine. The Kearneys paid her 50 cents for the evening. That became her regular charge. It was a thrill for her to finally have some money to call her own. There weren't any other young girls at the post who were available for this work.

Each week, Kate would have one or two sitting jobs with the Kearneys, the Wilsons or the Corliss children. When they weren't going to parties on the post or at Maryville, the officers and their wives would get together and play games or have picnics along the river. Kate liked the Wilsons the best. They had two babies, ages one and three.

The enlisted men would say, "Grace Wilson is as common as an old shoe." They meant it in a most complimentary way. She was a tiny person who was as friendly as she was small. Her bright blue eyes twinkled as she talked. She had been a dancer in Virginia before they were married.

During the days, Kate was busy caring for our children for I was spending six or seven hours in the laundry. In the evenings I would do seamstress work for the officers' wives. We had good kerosene lamps issued to us. Pat got an extra one for us because of my work.

Even though they were living in the middle of the desert, when parties were held, the officers' wives wanted to look just as nice as the Eastern ladies. Each one had frilly dresses that needed lots of starch and ironing. They all said that I was an expert with my fluting iron that I used for the ruffles of their gowns. Some wanted fancy dresses made and I knew how to do that. It gave us some more money for the savings account.

CHAPTER 23

THE LOWER RANCH

Benjamin Velasco, a man who was from the country of Chile, had some dairy cattle that he pastured east of the river. He sold milk and butter to Maryville and Ft. McDowell. The Army didn't mind him using their land across the river as long as the animals stayed below the camp. They didn't want the cattle polluting the river above where they drew water for our use.

We had been in Arizona a little more than a year when Pat found that Mr. Velasco wanted to sell his cows and move to Phoenix. Pat thought this was a way to get started on our own even before his time with the Army was finished.

We bought all seven of his cows and one bull, paying $100 each. It seemed like a lot, but Pat and I figured that we could get our money back in just one year. It did work out that way. We used the pasture land that Velasco had been using. The grass and hay they grazed on was free. Our family provided the work. Velasco had been irrigating some of the bottom land. His ditch was still there but the heading was washed out when he left, and we didn't get much use out of it.

Soon after buying the stock we had a bill from Doc Wilson. He was really Captain Lawrence N. Wilson but everyone called him "Sawbones" or Doc. The first time Pat needed him was when a mountain lion tried to kill one of our yearling calves. He jumped on her neck and made four deep claw marks. The cow must have been tough, for the lion went away and didn't do any more damage. Doc said, "I never thought I'd be sewing up cows when I was studying medicine. But then I didn't think I'd be out here on the edge of civilization, either!"

We worried about the animals after that but didn't have any more trouble with the lions until much later. One of the cows did get her leg tangled up in some of our new barbed wire. When that happened, Pat said, "We shouldn't have used that new-fangled stuff. It's too hard on the animals." This time the cuts weren't as deep as with the lion, but there were many more of them. The poor thing had spent the night tangled up and kept kicking until her whole leg was bleeding. Doc spent three hours working on that cow. It cost us $5, but he kept the leg from getting infected. If the wound wasn't closed up quick the screwworms would get in and make a real mess.

Howard and Betsey Rollins, our neighbors to the east, had been the first in our part of Arizona to use barbed wire for their beef cattle corral. It was just invented, they said. We all had a laugh after hearing Howard call it "bob wa-er." Pat said, "You can tell he's a Southerner."

It was much better than the smooth, plain wire we used before. The cows wouldn't push against it so it would last longer. Though it was more expensive per rod, we only needed three strands where we had to use four or five before. When we bought the wire it cost us $35 for enough to fence in a corral about an acre in size. That was the biggest expense we had except for buying the cows.

We built the corral to keep the cattle in at night, when the danger from predators was the worst. It was among the big mesquite trees, and for most of the way we nailed the wire to them. We'd let the cows out to graze after the morning milking. They would come back to the corral in the evening, for they'd want to be milked, and that's when we gave each of them a handful of grain.

Pat usually got away from his duties in time to walk the mile and a half to the corrals and do the milking. Kate and John helped and I did, too, after I got off my job in the laundry.

In late 1875, just as we were well settled with our lower ranch, I was with child again. This time I was not at all happy about it. My faith had taught me to be thankful for children and that each one was a blessing. This time, however, I was bothered worse with morning sickness and I was put out with both myself and Pat for allowing this to happen.

We were busy with the Verde ranch. We had chores to do morning and night and we were building our herd. My laundry job was tiring, but it was bringing in money that we could save toward our purchase of farmland. Kate had all she could do with caring for Ned and Sally, and she was earning money with her sitting jobs. How were we to handle all this?

As I think back on it, I have to admit that I was quarrelsome with Pat and the family during this time. I thought we were working too hard. The pain of another birth and the bother of caring for a newborn weighed me down. I couldn't see how we were going to keep up with the ranch, Pat's work and my laundry work and still care for our children.

Much to my surprise it was someone I didn't know well who straightened me out. Two children were hacking with bad colds and Sally had a cough that turned into the croup. She seemed to get sick easier than the others. I wondered if it was because we let her get so sick while sleeping on the floor of the train on the way to Cheyenne. I took her to Doc Wilson's office in the post hospital and he seemed concerned about her breathing and fever. He said as I was leaving, "Give her this medicine every hour. When Mrs. Wilson and I are out on our evening walk, I'll stop by your house and look in on her again."

After they came by to see her that evening, Pat and I visited with both of them before they walked on. Mrs. Wilson asked me, "How far along are you with your baby?"

''I'm five months now. I wish it were 50 months, though. I don't know how we can manage when we already have four. It makes me tired just thinking about it."

Mrs. Wilson laid her hand on my shoulder and said, "Annie dear, of course you're tired. But I'm a believer that your children are your legacy. That's how you live on after you and Pat are gone. That's your statement to the world of what you accomplished. That's your Heaven, Annie."

"Grace," Doc Wilson said, "you're getting awfully philosophical. Maybe that doesn't fit with Pat and Annie's idea of religion."

"That's alright, Mrs. Wilson," I said. "In fact, that's a good thought. I like that way of looking at it. Thank you."

With that, they were off again on their walk. Pat never said a thing and I thought a long time on that before I spoke. Then I said, "That's the best reason I ever heard for having lots of children."

Pat replied in a way that surprised me. He said, "It's also a good reason to raise 'em right so that we can be proud of 'em while we're here and others will be proud after we're gone."

I never had a chance, or had the nerve, to bring up that conversation with Grace Wilson again. I wish that I had, for her thought that evening helped me a lot from that time on.

Our post was rocked one day in January of 1876 by the shooting of Private Charles Harris. Private Harris was trying to steal melons from the farm one evening. That wasn't so unusual. Many soldiers were known to have helped themselves-midnight requisitions, the men called them. This time two Mexican employees of John Smith, the new farm operator, saw him and told him to stop and return to camp.

Private Harris yelled back some cuss words to them and raised his Army rifle like he was going to shoot the farm workers. They both drew their pistols and each worker hit Harris before he could fire. There was some argument about whether he really meant to fire on the farm workers or was just trying to scare them.

The Army investigation asked John Smith why he let his farm workers carry pistols. John reminded them of the continued Indian problem and the need to be able to kill any coyotes or big cats they might see. After an investigation, his workers were let off since it was ruled to be in self-defense. Private Harris was badly wounded and in the hospital here all summer. Then he was transferred to Ft. Whipple and discharged.

In February of 1876, Captain Sherman had 24 men out in search of four horses stolen by Indians from the new Phoenix settlement. He went up the west bank of the Verde, then northwest to Cave Creek for his first night's camp. After following Cave Creek to its headwaters in the springs area, he found the renegades. There were Indians around them on the ridges and they were shouting insults at the troops. Captain Sherman's report said, "I did not deem it prudent to divide the command and pursue them since they were not bunched up together." The Indians escaped, the patrol never saw any of the stolen horses, and on the third day marched back down the west bank of the Verde to McDowell.

Pat and I were learning to love this place. Most mornings one of us would comment on the sunrise over the mountains to the east. We'd find a reason to remark about the beauty of the morning. Our wake-up calls were stitched together by the many species of birds. One would sing and hand off to another. Then they'd compete with others for our attention. They seasoned our early hours.

Our barracks were above the tree line along the river, so we had a clear view to all of the mountains. They were like an inspiration to us and made us feel better about starting another day. During the winter time we could see the river, since the leaves were off the willows and cottonwoods. We were up early to do the morning milking before hurrying off to the rest of our work.

Each spring and fall, when the sunrise would be right over the Four Peaks mountain, I played a game with the older children. We would mark a place on the mountain where the sun rose. Then every few days we would note how much it moved from the last place. This was my way of teaching them about the seasons and the sun moving north and south in the skies.

We were happy with our good fortune to be able to be in a desert, but with a river running right by the fort. Pat and the Egans would talk for hours about how the soil here was fertile because it had washed down from the mountains west of us. The land had pieces of granite on top but underneath it was deep with very few large rocks. The Egans said it looked almost as good as their Ohio land—it just needed water to make things grow.

That first year, our little dairy herd grew to 10 milk cows, as we kept the female calves. Instead of hauling the milk in buckets, we now put it into five-gallon milk cans. We would put the containers in a fenced-in place we built in the edge of the river. It was in the shade of a big mesquite tree and this kept the milk from spoiling. While the milk was cooling in the river, the cream rose to the top and I'd skim that off to make butter.

We didn't think much about it when Benjamin Velasco left his butter churn at the lower ranch as we bought his dairy cows. Then we found out that John Smith, the new post trader, would pay 50 cents a pound for butter. The butter he got from the outside was often spoiled. Churning increased the chores but helped our income. John Smith paid us 40 cents a gallon for milk. The children looked forward to a trip to the sutler's store. John would often give them a lemon drop or a piece of horehound candy.

We hauled milk to Smith once a day, using one of our yearling steers to pull the cart. It was a half-wagon that Pat rebuilt from a wrecked one. He made sure that an officer gave him approval to take the salvaged portions for his own use. Not until months later did we know that Lieutenant Kearney learned of this and made a fuss about it to Captain Corliss.

When our bull calves were about a year old, we would sell them to Smith. He butchered the animals for meat to sell to the Army. The money we got from those sales was enough to buy a little bit of grain for the cows while they were in milk. We never bought any more milk cows, we just raised our own. Pat had been told that he should change bulls every few years to bring in some new blood so he would swap bulls with Charles Whitlow or Thomas Shortell down at Maryville. Sometimes one or the other would pay $10 or $20 if one of the animals was better.

We added chickens at the lower ranch, as we began to call our farmstead south of the post. Although we knew we didn't own it, the officers at McDowell (except for Kearney, we found out) were glad to have us do the work and supply the post with milk and eggs. We only had about 75 chickens but that was enough to produce 25 to 30 eggs a day. We got 50 cents a dozen for them. They were fresh and that was a big advantage since the only eggs they had before had came a long way and were sometimes spoiled.

Our chicken project didn't go very well at first. The coyotes and owls loved them. We started to let them run loose along the river bank and just bring them in at night like we did the cattle. The first year we lost a lot of them, even during the day time. We also found out that they would lay their eggs just about anywhere. The children and I were looking up and down the banks of the river each evening. Then we noticed that roadrunners and ravens were breaking the eggs open and eating them. We realized that they would have to be penned.

Buying chicken wire was another big expense This wire cost us $25 for just the sides, and we spent another $10 for enough to cover the top to keep out eagles and great horned owls. We figured out a way to use smaller trees for most of the posts for our chicken pen.

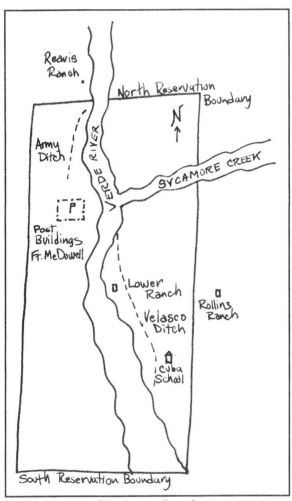

The Lower Ranch

In early April of 1876, Captain Ross took a patrol of 30 men on a trip all the way around Four Peaks. There had been some raiding and the officers thought they could find some "rancherias." That was the name they gave to the camp sites where Indians stayed and tried to grow crops. Usually, they were near a spring and in a part of the mountains where they wouldn't be discovered. The troops ran into strong winds and a severe snowstorm at the higher eleva tions. Two mules fell off steep, rocky trails and had to be destroyed.

His report said that everywhere the troops went they saw smoke signals warning other bands of Indians that the soldiers were

136

moving that way. They found four rancherias but all were abandoned because of these warnings. One day, they were in the saddle 20 hours pursuing the hostiles but could not corner them. They covered an estimated 200 miles in four days. The captain was critical of the Pima scouts that were on the mission. He said they were careless in exposing themselves to the Apaches at several times, allowing them to send the warning signals. Captain Ross said future patrols in the Four Peaks area must travel only at night.

Pat spent all of his free time at the ranch and the children helped every day. Kate was now 13 and John, 10. They knew this work was important, so they willingly did it to help the family. I say "willingly" now. As I write that, I can think back to a few times when it wasn't so voluntary. Like all young children, there were lots of times when they begged off to play. Most of the time, though, they pitched in as we expected.

Ned will remember the time I washed his mouth out with soap. We had all been to the lower ranch milking and taking care of the chickens. After we got back to our barracks, he complained about the chores he had to do. He was arguing and trying to sound "grown up" when he spouted off a few cuss words. That brought out the soap. He cried after I did it and let me know that I wouldn't do that to John or Patrick. Then I knew that was where he heard the words.

"No," I said, "but I sure would paddle John and I'd let your father know that it was wrong to say those words!" That was the last time I heard any of them try that around me. I think I may have taught them all a lesson with that one "soaping."

For four months each winter there was now a school for them to attend. It was called the Cuba School and was on the east bank of the Verde below our ranch. The classes were only for five hours, including lunch. Kate, John and Sally attended here for two years.

At first, the building had a dirt floor. Then John Smith married the only school teacher in the new village of Phoenix. This prompted John to pay for a wood floor to be put in the school house. He also paid to have the inside and outside of the structure whitewashed. John said, "It's time that children here have the same advantages that Tempe and Phoenix children have."

One winter there were seven children, and the next year they had nine. Except for Carlos Monroy, a rancher's son, the children were from McDowell. All eight grades were in the same room. They bragged about how fancy the school was with the new floor. Later, blackboards were installed along one end of the building.

My laundry building was getting in terrible shape. Working there was worse than being outside, for the roof kept dripping dust and debris over the clothes we were trying to clean. It was not much more than a brush shelter when it started. The soldiers tried to plaster mud over the brush and call it adobe. When the last company of soldiers came to the post, another laundress was added. She was a civilian who lived on the post. That is when the soldiers built a room alongside for her. It wasn't constructed any better.

I tried to keep Grace Wilson's philosphy in mind during the last few weeks before our fifth child was born at the post hospital. It helped me to remember that each child would be a gift that Pat and I were making to future generations.

We called our new little boy William, for my father. The other children soon made it Willie. He was a cheerful baby. Sally and Ned tried to show him off to the neighboring familes along non-com row, as we called our barracks then. I only took four weeks off from my laundry work and the milking.

Kate and John were now able to do most of the milk handling and all of the work with the chickens. Kate was the one I depended on most to get things done. She was a big girl—already taller than I was, and stronger. She made John do his work properly, too. I could count on them to take good care of the chores and the three younger children when I was at the laundry. Amanda Egan would sometimes look in on them to be sure things were going alright.

Amanda never worked at McDowell, and neither she or Bob seemed to be concerned about building up their savings. With Pat and I, the earning and saving of money occupied a lot of our conversation together.

In May of 1876, an Inspector General came to check on the entire post. One of the worst things he saw was the laundry. He showed me what he wrote in his report:

> The laundress work area is in an almost uninhabit-
> able condition. In case of rain the roofs leak badly and
> are very poorly constructed. The rain having damaged
> the adobe walls considerably, the weight of earth on the
> roof makes it very dangerous.

Two months after that, the word came down from the command in San Francisco that a new laundry was to be built.

The big job of hunting down Indians in the mountains was nearly finished. We were glad the killing was over. As it turned out, it wasn't, but we thought so. Until he left Arizona in early 1875, General Crook's policy was to pursue the Indians and destroy their food supplies so they would have to come in and surrender.

When they were starved out, they would send a messenger in to McDowell to ask for food. The Indian would show up east of the river waving a white piece of cloth to show that he was peaceful. This happened many times in the three years we had been there. An officer would meet with the messenger, feed him and give him presents and some food to take back to his tribe. Our scouts, who could speak some Apache language, told them if they would be peaceful to the whites and the Army, they could come in to the fort every two weeks for food rations.

We had several good scouts here that had lived among the Indians and had their respect, even though at times they had fought against each other. The chief scout was Al Sieber. He was a tall, dark man with a big, drooping mustache and a noticeable limp. He got his injury at the battle of Gettysburg. Sieber's right-hand man was Tom Horn, who was good looking and much younger. He was a favorite of the camp children. He later got in trouble up in Wyoming, we heard.

There weren't any farmers around except John Smith, who took up the lease on the post farms after Captain Hancock. He raised grain and a few vegetables. The only other folks who raised livestock were the Rollins family who claimed land just east of the military reservation boundary. They ran their beef cattle and hogs in the open country and their stock sometimes mixed in with our dairy herd.

We got along fine with them, for they were hard workers and always treated us fairly. Howard Rollins was maybe 55 years old, but his wife, Betsey, was much younger. Howard's first wife died many years ago in Tennessee. Howard and Betsey hadn't been married long when we knew them. They sold their cattle and hogs to John Smith. He would butcher them and sell the meat to the Army.

After we had owned our livestock for about a year, the Rollins invited us to visit them one Sunday. We all went over after we finished with the morning milking. Pat could have borrowed one of the Army wagons, but it was such a nice day that we walked. They lived east of our corrals about 1 mile. They had built an adobe house and covered the roof with mesquite branches, brush and grass.

The Rollins were a happy couple. Howard was a tall man who reminded me of President Lincoln with his beard and hollow cheeks.

His hands were huge and scarred, with big veins and knuckles. I could tell that he had done lots of hard labor.

Howard came to Arizona Territory in the late 1860s and prospected in the Prescott area. That's where he met Betsey. He never struck it rich, but found enough to come down to the new town of Phoenix and buy some cattle. By this time, most of the good land down along the Salt River was taken up, so he moved out here next to McDowell.

Betsey was just as spunky as Josie Carroll, my good friend from Ft. Moultrie. She was short and a little smaller around than Josie. The best thing about Betsey was her cheerfulness. Her hair was a bright straw-colored, which made her stand out even more. The civilians at the post teased Howard about how pretty she was. She didn't complain about anything, even though they didn't have as much as we did. She seemed happy all the time.

We had a good time together, joking about getting our dairy cattle and their beef cattle mixed up. The dollars we got from our milk and butter and eggs went into our savings account. The Rollins were putting their money into a better house. They didn't have children, but told us that they wanted some. Howard joked about that when he said, "I'm too old to have a family but my little wife needs young 'uns to be with her when I'm gone."

"You're not going anyplace, dear," Betsey said. "You're too tough to let anything get the best o' you."

When we got back to the post that evening, we decided that we needed to get together with them more often. Our older children especially liked Betsey.

News of the massacre of General Custer's troops at the Little Bighorn River in Montana reached us in August. The word spread like wildfire through the camp. One patrol was out in the Superstition Mountain area then and some feared the same thing could happen to them. Now that I look back on it, I realize that things were a lot different here.

It was a sad few days and it was all the men talked about. Some knew men that were in the battle. Pat knew Captain Marcus Reno from the Black Hills days and had seen General Custer's brother, Tom, at Fort Russell. That made him feel tied in to the battle. We didn't get many facts, so there were plenty of rumors and guesses.

CHAPTER 24

ELISHA REAVIS

Keeping a supply of horses and mules for the many patrols was a big part of the job here. On nearly every trip some would play out and have to be destroyed. The Indians would manage to take a few, and others would break their hobbles and take off into the wilderness. It was slow and costly to bring animals in from California and by the time they arrived they'd be worn out. Most Army posts in the West had nearby ranchers who supplied animals to them.

The man who did most of that here was named Elisha Reavis. He had land north of the military reservation and raised pack animals for the Army. He would even take the spent ones and put them out to pasture on grass and hay along the river. Then he'd sell them back later. He had connections all around central Arizona with ranchers. Some said he was good at making "midnight requisitions" of animals from the Indians or other ranchers.

Reavis also worked at the post to help out the regular farrier, Private First Class Gus Armitage. The cavalrymen who had been in the service a long time said this post was rougher on horse and mule shoes than any other. When a large patrol came back from a long trip, there were so many new shoes to put on that Gus would call on Reavis to help. Gus was a mountain of a man and acted like he enjoyed the hard job of farrier. Reavis was older and looked weak, but he wasn't. Pat said Elisha could hold his own when he was working with Gus on a big job.

Reavis was a wild-looking man—-long stringy hair, a dirty beard and a wild look in his eyes. He had two teeth missing in front. He was generally chewing something—tobacco, when he could afford it—and would make a big show of spitting out through the gaps in his teeth.

There was a story that he was captured by the Indians as he was trying to steal some of their ponies. They were about ready to burn him to death in a bonfire when he went crazy. He threw off all his clothes and started shrieking and dancing around wildly. The Indians were afraid of anyone who was mentally unbalanced. They thought these people had supernatural powers. The chiefs decided to let him go after this demonstration. Some of the soldiers said that he acted a little bit like this all the time.

Pat knew him since he was at McDowell a lot. He also raised a few vegetables which he sold to Mr. Smith. When Pat was just a year away from his discharge, Reavis said something to Pat that changed our lives. He made a remark that it was getting too crowded around here, and that he was going to move to the Superstition Mountains, which were about 35 miles southeast of us. No one lived there as far as anybody knew, since they were so rugged.

When Pat asked him what he was going to do with his horses, mules

Elisha Reavis: *Someone in Globe took this picture. It was in the Tempe paper when he died. He was just as messy but much younger when we dealt with him. His beard wasn't this long. I think this one is a fake.* ARIZONA HISTORICAL FOUNDATION

and his land he said, "I'm going to sell 'em all and use the money to start a farm in the Superstitions. I can sell produce to the miners around Globe just as easy as I can here, and I'll be all by myself over there."

While Pat and I were milking that night he couldn't stop talking.

"Annie, this is our chance! His land is right north of here. We can have our farm and stay close to McDowell. This is the best market around."

"But we don't want to buy horses or mules," I said.

"We don't have to. He'll sell those to the Army. He only wants to sell his land."

"Do you know how much he wants?" I asked.

"No, he doesn't even know we're interested. Tell you what I'll do. I'll act like we're interested in buying a horse to pull our milk wagon. I'll get him to take me up there and I'll look over the place."

That's what he did, and when he returned from that visit he was more excited than ever.

"It's good land. His horses have put a lot of manure around the lots. Except for some river rock, the soil's deep and it'll grow things when we put water on it. Every man needs roots, Annie, and I've found mine."

"Does he use the irrigation ditches the Indians built a long time ago?"

"Not much," Pat replied. "Oh, he gets some water down 'em but he's too lazy to clean 'em out after the floods. The one cut into the sandstone river bank is still good, but the surface ditches need to be cleaned out and rebuilt. It's the place for us, Annie. I know it!"

Pat wasn't much for getting worked-up, but he sure was now. He usually would imagine what bad things might happen, but this time he could only see it going our way.

I asked the question that brought him back to earth. "How much does he want for his land?"

"I didn't ask him—didn't want to make it look like we were interested. But I will soon."

Three days later, when Pat was between wagon jobs, he walked up to Reavis' place and asked the question. Reavis told him he'd sell the 160 acres he'd taken for $10 an acre, plus he wanted $500 for the ditches that were on the property. Pat said that he told him that was too much. Doc Wilson had said he should start out that way no matter how much he asked. Reavis just said, "Well, you cain't get better land anywhere in Arizona and there ain't much to be had s' close to an Army post."

For the next week, that's all we talked about when Pat and I were together. We even got Kate and John involved for we knew they'd have to work hard, too, if we did this.

Pat talked to Captain Corliss, who was the commanding officer. He asked if he could be sure of getting his discharge if we bought the land from Reavis. The captain said that he would let Pat go since he had been in service so long and had a good record everywhere he had served.

There was talk around that folks weren't exactly sure where the reservation boundary was. Some said that it should be extended farther north. I told Pat that I thought we should be sure of ourselves before we went any further on buying the Reavis land. I wrote this letter to Captain Corliss, the commanding officer:

143

Capt. A. W. Corliss,

Sir:

We would like to put about forty (40) head of dry cattle on that flat land that is five miles north of the post, the ranch occupied by Reavis. Someone said it might be on the reservation. We do not like to do it without your consent.

Respectfully,
Mr. and Mrs. Patrick White
August 5, 1876

****

Respectfully returned,

I have no control whatsoever over the ranch occupied by Reavis, as it is off the reservation.

Capt. A. W. Corliss
Capt. 8th Inf., Comdg. Post
August 10, 1876

With that settled, Pat and I went up to see Reavis one evening. We agreed to pay $10 an acre for his property, but said we wouldn't pay anything for his ditches. They went with the land, we said, and they needed a lot of work since they didn't always work the way the Indians had built them.

When Reavis saw that we had the money in the bank, he agreed to our offer. As we walked the five miles back to our barracks, Pat was shouting for joy. I never saw him so wound-up. He would yell, "We're ranchers! At last, we're farmers!"

I was thinking more of the change in our lives that would come when we left the Army. We would be on our own. Reavis lived in a dugout in the bank of the river, and his horse pens were flimsy. There would be a house and corrals to build—ditches to clean—and clean again—brush to be cleared and crops to plant and be tended. We had a formidable task ahead but we had two children who would be strong helpers. The others would be good later. At last we had found a place to put down roots. I was as excited as Pat—I just didn't show it like he did.

Pat called on Doc Wilson. "Captain, we want to thank you for suggesting that we offer less. You saved us $500."

"Well, Pat, you helped yourself by having the cash in the bank. I think Reavis wanted out of this country. He seems to want to vanish into the Superstitions."

"We didn't think he acted crazy when we were talking to him. Do you think he really did what they say that time the Indians caught him?"

"No, I don't think he's crazy either—he was just smart to act that way. It was about his last chance to get away, and he managed it."

As Pat was leaving the captain had one last suggestion. "When you can, you should file on that ground to show that you bought it, Pat. You need to do that at the land office in Florence."

From then on, Pat spent almost all of his extra time at our new place. The milking and care of the chickens were done by Kate, John and me. We decided not to get any more chickens until after we moved. We didn't want to build anything else at our lower ranch. We bought one of Reavis' young mares to use as a pony and to pull our produce cart. When we moved here, it would be a little more than five miles to the post, and too far for one of our yearling steers to pull. We named our horse "Daisy."

We had a bad experience with the dairy herd that year. The bull that we got from Mr. Whitlow at Maryville wasn't any good. He didn't settle any cows and with no calves, we had less milk to sell. That year we didn't increase our herd and we didn't add anything back into our savings account. It was low now after buying the Reavis land.

As Pat worked at the new ranch, he concentrated on the irrigation ditches, for we were convinced that our best chance to make good crops would be by getting water on our land. There was another farmer who was irrigating some land below us on the river. His name was John Demarbiex. Most people called him the "Frenchman." We didn't know him very well, since he came there just a few months before we bought the Reavis land. He and Reavis had a falling out over where his land started and stopped.

It turns out that Demarbiex didn't have much frontage on the river, but he did have access to an old Indian ditch. This was a channel cut out of the sandstone in the bank of the river. It carried water from about one mile upstream to our land, where it topped out on the west bank. We both used water from this ditch.

Since John and Kate were busy almost all the time at our lower ranch, it was up to Sally to watch Ned. I took little Willie with me to the laundry and carried him to the lower ranch when I helped with the milking.

Every two weeks the friendly Indians from around the Verde Valley had to come in and be counted by the troops. They'd be given rations to live on for the next period. It was never enough for them to get by, so they still had to harvest desert plants and seeds to supplement what the Army gave them. Some of them grumbled that they had it better before the Army came, but they would be reminded that they were better off than the Apaches who were still hiding in the mountains. They would come down into the valley and raid for horses, guns and ammunition. It was the only way they could survive, for when they had to stay in the mountains they were slowly being starved out.

The children heard us talking about how bad the Apaches were, yet they saw the Indians come in to be counted and get food. "What kind of Indians are those?" Sally asked.

I answered the best I could. "They're mostly Yavapai, dear, but some are friendly Apaches, I think." It was hard for us to tell one tribe from another. They did have a different language but we didn't know enough words to tell them apart. We knew that most of them had a lot of good common sense.

The more industrious Indians would come in with baskets made from the tough grasses that grew near the springs in the mountains and along the river. They might be decorated with native dyes and colors that they found in the desert. It was amazing how they could be artistic with nothing but native plants and their own hands.

They would offer to sell the better baskets to the soldiers or the people in Maryville. Some could be purchased for $2 or even up to $5 for the finest ones. When that happened, the Indian would immediately go to John Smith's store and use the dollars to buy tobacco, flour, salt or candy. There wasn't much conversation among the soldiers and the Indians—just sign language. Only a few months before, they had been bitter enemies with some of them, and the two groups were wary of each other.

Some Indian women would bring rugs and blankets they had woven. No two were the same. Some would have pieces of straw or dried fibers from the cactus plants. Most of the dyes in the baskets or rugs were so good that they could endure the washing with home made lye soap. It seemed like the Indian women worked harder than the men. The soldiers said that most of the gathering of cactus fruit and berries was done by the women. They made most of the pottery, too.

One day, I was carrying Willie from the laundry room back to our barracks home when I saw a frightening event. A large Indian man had brought a beautiful stone axe in to the fort, hoping to sell it. The man came in every two weeks and was so large that the soldiers had picked him out as someone special. He knew no English and didn't try to communicate. The soldiers called him " Big Joe."

His axe had been shaped carefully from dense black stone. The handle was ironwood that had been carved into a slight curve to fit a hand. Rawhide was used in a criss-cross pattern to tie the handle tightly to the stone blade. I had been told that the Indians soaked the rawhide, then wrapped the handle and axe blade together. When the rawhide dried it shrank and bound the two tightly. Even I stopped to look at it when several soldiers were gathered around him. One soldier said, "Geez, I've seen many an axe in the villages, but none as pretty or well balanced as this 'un."

Joe wanted $5 for his axe and one of the corporals was trying to buy it for $2. Another soldier got into the trading with a bid of $3, but Joe kept shaking his head and holding up five fingers. Then something happened just as I was walking away. I could never be sure what it was for I heard three different stories later. Whatever it was, I guess the corporal snatched the axe away from Joe, threw two dollar bills on the ground and started to walk away. Quick as a flash, the Indian was upon the corporal, smashing down on his arm in a spot that made the soldier scream and drop the axe. Joe grabbed it and lifted it high and was just ready to split the corporal's skull. Three of the soldiers clasped the Indian between them and grabbed his arm.

I heard the yelling and the curses as this was happening, but then there was an strange silence. Big Joe was scowling and furious at being overpowered. The corporal was pale as a ghost and realized he was an instant away from death. The other soldiers were looking around to see if other Indians would come to the aid of Joe. There was a stand-off, then someone picked up the two bills and handed them back to the corporal. The soldiers released Joe and pointed to the Mazatzal Mountains to the east. Joe picked up his axe and walked toward the river, and we never saw him in camp again.

The Indians that came in to McDowell were a mixed lot. Some were dignified looking and carried themselves like they were the ones who had conquered the white people. Others were poor physical specimens looking for anything they could find to steal. Doc Wilson said one time that the different tribes fought among themselves as much as they did against the white man.

One of the last big patrols that occurred while Pat was still working there was a 16 day trip south of the Salt River in the Gila Bend area. A band of Indians had robbed the stagecoach between Maricopa Wells and Gila Bend. The soldiers found them camped on the Agua Fria River. A chase followed, which lasted for 30 miles, much of it with horses at a full gallop. Captain Sanford's report said that after 13 consecutive hours in the saddle they tracked them around the south side of the McDowell Mountains. The Indians were on faster, lighter ponies and weren't as loaded with gear. They got away in the mountains on the south side of the Salt River. Captain Sanford was apologetic in his report but said he was surprised that the cavalry horses stood it as well as they did. They had ridden 150 miles in three days.

One time during the count and rationing, an Indian family came in with three children that attracted the attention of Sally and Ned. One boy was maybe just a little older than Ned, but since he hadn't eaten as well, he was smaller. He was a lively one. Sally and Ned were playing with him while his mother and father were standing in line to get their rations. Sally found out that the boy's name was something that sounded like "Da-na-ne" so that's what she and Ned called him when they said goodbye for another month. After that, my two children made it a point to play with Da-na-ne each time they came in. With the innocence of boys that age, Ned soon became better friends with Da-na-ne than any of the soldier's children.

In the fall of 1876, 16 enlisted men and one officer came into Pat's Company C. We were amazed to find out that the officer was Lieutenant John Summerhayes. His wife was Martha, my good friend from Fort Russell. They now had a two-year-old son, Harry. She had sent trunk loads of fine clothes and china on the steamship *Montana* from San Francisco. It was scheduled to come up the Colorado River to Ehrenberg, then overland to McDowell. The *Montana* was destroyed by fire as it lay in port somewhere along the Mexican coast. Everyone said she was really discouraged about it, but I knew that she wasn't much for complaining.

I waited for the right time to greet her. I wasn't sure how much she remembered meeting me at Fort Russell, even though it was an important time for me. During their first week here, Lt. Summerhayes stopped Pat. He remembered Pat because of his experience with the Army wagons at Russell. "It's now Corporal White, isn't it? Congratulations!"

"Yes, lieutenant. It is good to see you again, sir. I'm sorry to hear of the loss of Mrs. Summerhayes' things on the boat."

"She is too, Pat. After you show me around your wheelwright shop here, I will be sure to remind her that you're here. She thinks a lot of that fine wife of yours." When Pat repeated this to me, I was mighty happy, for I valued her friendship.

Just a few days later, the lieutenant called on me and asked me to stop by her home on officers' row. Mrs. Summerhayes greeted me as if we were family. She was even more attractive than I remembered.

I started calling her Mrs. Summerhayes. It was satisfying to hear her again invite me to call her Martha. "Now Annie, are we going to have to do this all over again? Just like at Russell, if it's just you and I, you're to call me Martha." This made me appreciate her even more.

Martha soon asked me to do a lot of sewing for her to start replacing what she had lost. She would order in fabric from Goldwater's in Prescott and have me make dresses, shawls and undergarments. I learned some things from her about making nicer clothes. I did this at night in our quarters by the light of the coal-oil lamps. To have the time to do the sewing, I stopped my job at the post laundry. I was only working there part-time by then, for the chores at the ranch were growing.

Martha's face was like a china doll and her eyes were dark as if she had a Spanish background. Because she was of small stature just like myself she later gave me some of her everyday dresses that she didn't use. We talked about things just like I did with Amanda Egan. She told me that just before she went to bed she allowed herself 20 minutes as her time to write in her diary. She had kept it ever since they were married.

As I spent more time with Martha Summerhayes, my boys, Ned and Willie, would play with Harry. Harry didn't know my boys were just sons of an Army corporal and he didn't care. Some of their play was in sand boxes the men made out of mesquite logs and sand from the river. There was plenty of both. There weren't any purchased toys but we would get old horse and mule shoes and stray pieces of harness. These, along with all kinds of empty tin cans, crates, boxes and worn out kitchen pots, gave them all they needed. On hot days, the afternoons were usually spent along the river with adults there to watch the small children.

Just before Pat's retirement, the Pima Indians stole some of Otero's cattle down below Phoenix. Lt. Henry Kearney and Lt. Summerhayes and fifteen men were sent there to settle the matter and to recover the cattle.

CHAPTER 25

HOME

Pat was discharged in October, 1876. He was proud of his more than 20 years of Army service. Captain Corliss and Lt. Summerhayes took special notice of his retirement and came around on the last day to wish him well. The corporals and sergeants showed up at the wheelwright's shed and had a party for him after retreat.

This attention meant a lot to Pat. He had not felt close to very many of them. They all knew about our buying the Reavis land and that we were going to continue to sell produce to the post trader. Each man shook his hand and wished him well.

On his discharge papers, Captain Corliss wrote, "He has been a good soldier." That made Pat feel that his hard work and attention to his job for these many years was worth the effort.

We received another surprise on the day of his retirement. Lt. Summerhayes asked him if he could stay on for a while as a civilian blacksmith and wheelwright. At first, Pat was going to say "no," but when Captain Corliss told him the salary would be $125 a month, he decided to talk to me about it. I believe he smiled more that night than I can remember. He was proud that they asked him and astonished at the salary they offered. He had trouble understanding why it was so much more than the $19 he was making as a corporal.

As we talked, he began to see that he wasn't going to be furnished food and a place for his family. Then he also said that this would be only until a trained person could be transferred here. Apparently, the officers had settled on getting Pat's replacement assigned here before he left. This person had been injured in a battle with the Indians in Wyoming and that's why they needed to have Pat stay on.

He was flattered that they wanted him. He was excited about earning the extra money. We finally agreed that he would do it for three months if they would let our family continue to live at the post and get our rations during that time.

When Pat came home that night he said that Captain Corliss had Lt. Kearney with him when they talked about these terms. He said that Lt. Kearney argued with the captain. Right in front of Pat, Kearney said, "He milks cows while he's on the government payroll and uses an Army wagon to haul his dammed milk. Now he wants to stay on at civilian wages and get full benefits! That's too much!"

But the captain ruled over him and said it would be the best way for such a short time. We didn't think about it then, but that day probably made things worse with Kearney.

John stopped the half-days of school and started working full-time at our new ranch north of Demarbiex's place. The other children and I kept the lower ranch going until John got the corrals up. We decided to locate them about 75 yards from the west side of the river. Here, the bank was about 15 feet above the regular water level.

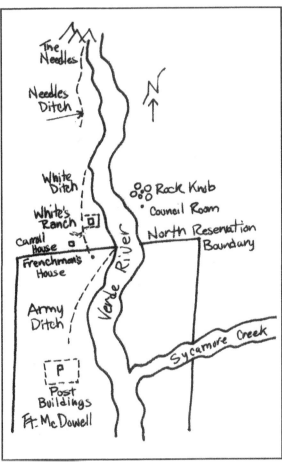

The Home Ranch

John, with Pat's help in the evenings, got enough corrals built in two months for us to move our livestock up there. From then on, the children and I travelled the five and one-half miles each way every day. We had to do this to help John tend the stock and get the produce back and forth to sell at the post.

The next thing to build was our house. I stopped all my sewing, except for Mrs. Summerhayes, so I could help with the building. Pat decided that we should dig down in the ground a little so that the house would be cooler in summer and warmer in winter. John dug down about three feet in an area about 20 feet by 12 feet. Pat helped him roll big river rocks in place to make a foundation for our adobe house.

There were good deposits of clay in several places along the river.

Folks said this was the same clay the prehistoric people used for their pottery. We mixed straw and some grass into the clay mud to give it more strength and then set the bricks out to dry. It was late fall and dry, so they cured in about three days. We put a thick layer of clay on the floor to give us a smooth, hard surface.

Pat's replacement arrived and, after a week of working together, Pat was released from all duty at the post. The last day of work Pat said Lt. Kearney was standing near his wheelwright's shop. He overheard Kearney say to another officer, "The Army's been feeding his whole family while he's been earning big wages just because we were short-handed."

When Pat told me this he said, "That Henry Kearney seems to complain about most everthing I do. Wish I knew why."

We moved into our new home even though the roof wasn't on. Fortunately, there was no rain. Both John and Pat worked long days on the house for it was January and the days were cooler. When we got the walls up about four feet above ground level, the men cut two large mesquite limbs with a "V" on one end. They buried these two with the notch at the top and that was what we used to hold another long mesquite limb that was our ridgepole. From then on they found smaller limbs for the rafters and laid brush across the top of those. The last layer was straw and grass laid down in a way that would generally let the water run down the pitched roof.

Kate only worked a little on the house since she was now staying with children at the fort during the evenings and sometimes in the daytime. When she wasn't doing that she took care of Willie and Sally.

When I was taking in milk and produce one day, John Smith told me that I should go see either Captain Corliss or Doc Wilson. I felt that I knew Doc better so I stopped by the hospital.

"I'm glad you came in, Annie. You folks should know about a new law that has been passed. It's called the Desert Land Act. It will let you claim another 640 acres of land if you want it. Here's the paper that tells about it."

"How can that be, Doc? They don't give land away for nothing, do they?"

"In this case, it could be. This is like the Homestead laws back in the Eastern United States. Except out here they let discharged soldiers claim 640 acres instead of 160."

"What do we have to do?" I asked.

"Just post notices on a one-mile square piece of land. You put the notices on trees saying that it's claimed. Then file on it at Florence. You would probably want to claim right above your Reavis land."

"Yes, I'd think so. Then we could keep control of the water from the river." I thanked Doc and took the paper home with me. I was almost as excited about this as Pat was when we bought the Reavis land.

Pat couldn't believe it could be this easy. "You mean all we have to do is post a notice on a tree."

"That's what it says. Then we can file on it at Florence later. This is only because you're a soldier, dear. It must be another way of the government trying to thank you for being in the Army."

The very next day we stepped off one mile back west from the river and one mile north of our line and posted the notices. We could not imagine our good fortune and agreed that we owed Captain Corliss and Doc Wilson our thanks for telling us about this new law. We started thinking of how we could find a way to get water to this new land.

I was helping at the ranch and doing fancy sewing for the officers' wives. When I finished with an alteration or the making of a dress I would launder it with a good bit of starch. Then I'd iron all the ruffles and fancy crinkles that the wives liked so well. The children teased me about the way I looked as I was holding a dress up high in the wagon so it wouldn't get wrinkled as we drove in to deliver it.

One evening, Kate was staying with Elizabeth Kearney's children. Their five-year-old girl wandered out onto the post's parade grounds and was watching the cavalry practicing maneuvers at sunset. Kate saw that the girl was in danger of being trampled by the horses. She went to get her and immediately returned to the house. While she was gone, the Kearney's three-year-old girl wandered out the back yard. As Kate was returning with the older girl she saw the child taking a few steps into the sagebrush, which was only a few feet from the back of their house.

Suddenly she screamed, and as Kate ran to her she saw a huge rattlesnake coiled to strike again at the little toddler. She snatched her away, carrying her to Doc Wilson's home only three doors away.

Capt. Wilson took the little girl to his office and gave her some medicine for the poison. When Mrs. Kearney heard what had happened she went into a rage. Kate told us that she said, "It's all your fault. You never should have left her alone."

Kate tried to explain that both girls had wandered off in opposite directions and that she thought the older one was in danger from the cavalry horses. Mrs. Kearney wouldn't take any excuses and ordered Kate to go home without paying her anything for that evening's job. Kate arrived home in tears and sobbed out the story to me on the porch of our quarters.

"She'll never want me again, Mother," she wailed. "She'll tell the others that I can't be trusted."

"Now Kate, you did the right thing to go after the girl that was in danger of getting trampled. Did you tell the other girl to stay inside?"

"Yes, but she didn't pay any attention to me."

"Next time, you'll just have to be more strict and scare them into minding you every time. Otherwise, it will be hard to take care of more than one."

As it turned out, Mrs. Kearney didn't say anything more right then. Maybe she calmed down when she saw that her child wasn't seriously hurt by the rattlesnake bite. Probably she just thought about it and decided that it was an easy thing to happen.

We began to see that we needed more help at the ranch. As we built our dairy herd, that took more time to milk and churn butter. We wanted to get more chickens, for the price of eggs at the fort was still 50 cents per dozen. We knew that we could also raise hogs. There was more land to clear and canals to repair.

We celebrated the first Easter by having a special dinner of two ducks that Pat killed with his rifle along the river. He had to shoot them while they were sitting still on the water since he did not have a shotgun. The rest of the meal was our everyday food like milk, eggs, homemade bread, butter and vegetables. Our garden stayed good all year except for a couple of months in the middle of summer.

I felt that our new home was complete when we smoothed and sprinkled the clay floors. After they dried, Pat and John pegged down two layers of the best canvas John Smith had. In some ways I liked this floor better than the drafty wood ones we had at some of our Army barracks.

The first year we found that the canals needed more work than we thought. The river would be at or near flood stage once or twice each year. The place where the water came off the river was called the "head." This part would sometimes have to be rebuilt as the river changed course or cut lower into the ground. The natural desert washes would also dump sand and other debris into the canal. It was almost a full-time job for one man to keep them working properly.

The hot summer of 1877 was a hard time for us. Pat had to do most of the work himself, although John was helping clear the land for grain crops. There was a pile of brush burning every few days. There sure wasn't any problem with firewood during those years. We had all we needed close at hand. Pat did the heavy work but John was good with clearing the small plants. He surprised both Pat and I with his willingness to work at the chores and the light field work.

I helped with extending the first canal around onto some new parts of the Reavis land. We had to be careful to dig it so that the water would flow properly. Too much slope and it would wash out the ditch. Not enough and the water would soak in faster than it would move down the canal. It was slow, frustrating work but we knew it had to be done.

When Pat took the produce and vegetables in one day, he met Howard Rollins. When he returned home, he told me that Howard said he'd like to see our place now that we were settled. I suggested that we invite both he and Betsey up for a Sunday meal some day soon. Then we got busy again and I put it off until it was too late.

While extending the surface canal back from the river, we dug through a mound of rocks and pottery pieces. We had seen them lying on top of the ground but never this many. We thought they were from the Aztecs or Maya Indians. Pat took some of the pieces to McDowell the next time he took produce in. He asked one of the Pima scouts what they were. He said, "Jar—Hohokam."

"Who are they?" Pat asked.

"Gone people—all gone."

We knew they were gone and it must have been a long time ago. Some of the pieces we found were under several inches of soil that had been washed down the hill. When we went across the river to round up our cows, we found remains of rock walls on almost every ridge. We supposed that the same people built them.

We thought a lot about how to get water to our new 640 acres upstream from our first land. Pat rode upriver and spent hours figuring out exactly how the river and the west bank sloped. He knew a sergeant at the post who had been a surveyor's helper before he enlisted in the Army. He had him spend one Sunday with him looking at the "lay of the land," as they called it.

After that, we asked John Smith if he could find someone in Phoenix who had the experience and equipment to do a good job of finding the right place for another canal heading.

About one month later, John had a man named Colonel William Breakenridge out to talk with us at the sutler's store. He and Smith had been friends for several years and they were now getting together in an irrigation project along the Salt River. Colonel Billy, as John called him, had been a surveyor on the Atlantic and Pacific Railroad through northern Arizona. He was now a Deputy Sheriff in Maricopa County. Pat did a lot of explanation and drawing of lines in the sand outside the store. Finally, Colonel Billy agreed to survey for a new heading. He said he would provide the equipment and a helper for three days for $200.

We were shocked at such a high price but John Smith and Colonel Billy said that was the only way to find out where to start. If we didn't, we might do a lot of work to find out that what we dug could not get water to the right places. We told him to go ahead.

This extra land and the additional work convinced us that our own family could not do all of it. Pat didn't want to hire Mexicans or the friendly Indians who were now around the fort. He said we didn't have the money to pay them and we wouldn't know if they could be trusted to stay with us and see the job through to a finish.

When we thought about who we would like to have as partners in our venture, we both thought of the Carrolls. Every time we exchanged letters they talked as if they wanted to have land of their own. James had been discharged from the Army a year before Pat and was working on a farm near Macedonia, Ohio.

"There's no one I'd trust more than James," Pat said when we talked about it. "He's a good worker."

"It would be marvelous to have Josie close to me again. There's a lot we could talk about and we could help each other with the chores," I said.

We wrote them in late 1877 to ask if they would like to come and live near us and share in the profits for our sales to McDowell. Six weeks later we got a letter saying that James was on the way. If it looked like the right thing for them, he'd build a house for Josie and their two children and send for them.

It was March of 1878 when a telegram arrived at McDowell from James saying that he had taken the train to San Francisco and was now back to Yuma. People told him that he couldn't survive by walking here by himself. Either the Indians or lack of water would get him, they said.

Pat talked to Capt. Summerhayes—he had been promoted by then—to ask what would be the best way for him to get here. Capt. Summerhayes said that there were 32 recruits in Yuma who would be walking to McDowell within a week. He told Pat to have James see Captain Ernst at Fort Yuma and he would arrange it. Pat advised James by telegram. James did come with them and said he had never had such a good time as he did on that walk.

Something else good came out of that group of recruits. Martha Summerhayes had been unhappy with the house man that had been assigned to them. She had told me that he was a terrible cook. The day after the recruits arrived a Pvt. Bowen knocked on the Summerhayes' door and announced that he was their new striker. She was thrilled, for he had worked for them before.

Within two months, James and Pat had built an adobe house for Josie and the two girls, and the Carroll family was on its way. The two men also worked with Colonel Breakenridge when he surveyed for a new canal. After his report came back to us, we were discouraged. He said to reach our new land we had to start the canal at the mouth of Camp Creek, which was more than four miles upstream. This was where the "needle rocks" were in the Verde River. He said it could be done and put stakes along the line we should follow as we dug.

The good thing about the report was that it confirmed that we could get 1000 miner's inches of water down the ditch. With this we could irrigate the best 400 acres of our new land.

Pat asked, "What are miner's inches?"

"It's a way of measuring irrigation water," Colonel Billy said. "It's about what this canal will handle if you make the bottom five feet wide."

He also told us that we should claim water from the Verde River as soon as we started building the ditch. He said that the claim had to be posted in writing. One Sunday afternoon, John and Pat printed a notice on paper sacks and nailed them to trees at each corner of our 640 acres.

Josie and her two girls came from Yuma with a wagon train of soldiers in May of 1878. We had a joyous reunion. Pat and James said that Josie and I didn't stop talking for a month! Their house was a little south of us and further back from the river. It was beyond a large arroyo on land that we couldn't reach with the irrigation ditches. Josie and I saw each other almost every day.

The work never ended. The livestock chores were getting more all the time. Sally now started helping and Ned could gather eggs. He was now six years old. He made certain that he went to McDowell when the Indian families came in. He wanted to spend a few hours playing with

Da-na-ne, his favorite friend. Da-na-ne sometimes came to our house.

Since we were close to the river a lot of the children's free time was spent there, throwing rocks, swimming and building little dams along the river's edge. They tried to copy the beavers. Every year we were on the river we saw at least two beaver dams near our ranch and one year there were three. Da-na-ne taught Ned how to sit silently for a long time until the beavers came out to work on their dam. He also showed him how to make food out of the mesquite beans, palo verde seeds and saguaro fruit.

Ned learned a lot about nature and the desert from the friendly boy. He also learned a bit about the people who lived here long ago. When he and Da-na-ne played in the hills across the river, they saw the rock walls on most of the ridges that overlooked the river. There was nothing on our side of the river like that. The soldiers at McDowell who had studied them said that the prehistoric Indians on this side lived mostly underground in what they called pit houses.

Ned said that Da-na-ne explained through sign language and his broken English that some of these ruins east of the river were shelters for lookouts. He pantomimed how Da-na-ne sat on one of the ridges and looked in every direction with his hand shading his eyes. He said that the people who had vanished posted sentries on the hills to watch the river valley, both for animals to be killed for food and for enemies. Most of these walls were now collapsed since they had been abandoned so long ago. There were plenty of rocks on that side of the river, so I can see why they built rock walls instead of pit houses. Da-na-ne said the ancient people used saguaro ribs, branches and grass for their roofs just as the soldiers did at Ft. McDowell when they started the post.

We finally got Da-na-ne to have a meal at our house. Pat asked him what his name was. When he told him, Pat's face lit up and he said, "Da-na-ne! Danny! Why that's a fine Irish name. You'll be our Danny Boy." From then on that's what we all called him and since we smiled every time we said it, he liked it and soon was calling himself by the same name. He learned a lot of English words from us and especially from Ned.

Danny Boy never spent the night with us. He would not tell us where he lived, either. He would just wave his hand toward Four Peaks and say "they," the word he used for "there." Danny Boy taught Ned how to make a bow and arrow, how to weave grasses together to make baskets and how to track animals. He did not come to see us often. He never asked Ned to visit where he lived. In his broken English he would only say, "No time come more. Help they." Then he would gesture toward the mountains across the river. Ned and Pat decided that his band of

Indians probably camped along Sycamore Creek near Sugarloaf Mountain, which was about seven miles southeast of us.

One day in mid-summer Ned insisted that some of us go with him to see a ridge that he and Danny Boy had found. It was almost directly across the river. He said there was something different there. The ridge was just south of the big pile of rocks we all called Rock Knob. We were busy as always working in the fields and canals but I promised him I would go with him to see it the following Sunday. Kate and John went with us after our usual fried chicken dinner. The river was low enough so that we had no trouble wading across.

Ned showed us a set of rock walls that were higher and larger than any I could remember hearing of before. Some of the walls were five feet high and still piled up just as they were originally constructed. The room was much larger than the usual ruins we found. We stepped off about 50 feet the long way and at least 30 feet the other way. There was nothing left to show what kind of limbs or poles were used for a roof support. Kate and I decided that this must have been some kind of a meeting place and that perhaps there wasn't any roof on it—just a big walled-in room. It was way out on the end of the ridge, so it could be seen from a lot of places on the other side of the river. There was even a leveled-off place where we decided they had built large bonfires.

After thinking about this, we felt it must have been where the chiefs or medicine men from the different tribes went to have their councils. We liked that thought, for if they built big fires and had dances or speeches from there, the villagers would have been watching from where our ranch buildings were located. From then on, Kate and I would make up stories to tell the younger children about what might have happened right across the river.

John and Ned used Rock Knob across the river as their playground whenever they had a few hours of spare time. The boys found dozens of caves among the huge boulders and plenty of evidence of the earlier civilization. I warned them about the rocks caving in on them and was always cautioning them to be careful of snakes and scorpions. Providence took care of them for there were no problems. I had to admit that it was a tempting place to explore, especially when they'd bring home pieces of pottery and stone tools that had been shaped by those people long ago.

We talked about how the rocks east of the river changed shapes and colors as the sun moved. One day Pat said, "We can see the bare bones of the Earth here." Then a bit later, "If we can control the water, we'll control this fertile land, Annie." I decided that my Patrick was getting mighty sentimental about this place. We often thought about how different our lives were here compared to the crowded, smelly, smoky conditions in New York. We knew that we were right to go west to the open spaces.

Rock Knob

About this time we got our first family dog. It was probably an Indian dog that strayed away and was found at Ft. McDowell. John Smith asked Pat if he wanted it and from that time on "Patches" was our pet. He had already learned to avoid the many cactus thorns scattered on the desert floor. It was amazing to watch him cleverly step around them even when running at full speed. He was also a fine "ratter," the term the workers at Smith's store used to describe him. He was as efficient as any cat in keeping our house and corral areas free of field mice or pack rats. Until then, they had been a constant problem so Patches became a welcome addition.

Pat started giving Ned field chores. By now the crops were so important to us that Pat wanted all the weeds pulled out of the fields. This was a never-ending job and it was something he could do. It was a backbreaking job, for it required bending over constantly. We only had one hoe and the older men used that to work on the bigger weeds.

Pat and I were sorry that we were not attending mass each Sunday as our parents had taught us. There was no church except in Mesa, Tempe or Phoenix. It was impossible to travel that far. We did insist that the children say their rosary prayers every night.

We still respected the Sabbath by stopping all the heavy work. We did the stock chores and housework that was needed, but work on the canals or in the fields waited. On Sundays we tried to find some time to rest— to enjoy our view of the mountains and to walk along the river banks to see the birds and animals. The trees and shrubs along the river were full of different kinds of birds. Almost every tree had flickers of movement as the birds kept moving in their search for food.

Even with all the shooting by the soldiers, there was still plenty of wildlife to show the children. It was a peaceful, primitive scene. We only wished there was more time to enjoy it.

CHAPTER 26

THE KILLING

In May the next year, Pat came back from McDowell with awful news. Two Indians had killed Betsey Rollins that morning. Howard saw them riding away just as he returned from rounding up his cattle. He had only been gone about an hour but they had stripped her naked, violated her and then killed her by cutting her throat. Howard didn't know anything was wrong until he stepped inside the cabin and saw blood everywhere. She was already unconscious and died soon after.

As soon as Pat told me, we told the children to stay at the house and we walked to the bank of the Verde to be by ourselves. As we stood there watching the quiet scene below, it was hard to imagine that such a terrible thing could happen just a few miles from us. Betsey was such a dear thing—and so excited about her first child that was on the way. She was small—no match for two strong warriors. "What savages would do such a thing?" I wondered.

"No one we know unless it would be that one we called Joe. He was a bad one, I could tell that."

"Will we have to keep our children with us all the time now?"

"I don't know, Annie, the talk at the camp is that they're going to call in the Indians next Monday. They've sent interpreters to the hills. They're going to tell them no more rations unless they come in right now. I'll be there to see what it sounds like." Pat, John Smith, Doc Wilson and Captain Summerhayes formed the burial detail that afternoon.

On Monday, Captain Corliss stood in front of about 200 Indian men, women and children who had gathered on the parade grounds by the flagpole. Interpreters Al Sieber and Tom Horn were on hand to pass along the captain's words to the Yavapai and Apache who had come in as ordered.

"Two of your brothers have killed a white woman," Captain Corliss began. "They did this as cowards. The woman and her husband had done nothing to hurt your people. You must tell us who did this. If you do not, all of you will be punished. If you tell us and bring them in you can still receive food and clothing each month as you have. That is all."

The captain waited until the interpreters had finished, then addressed them again. "Tell them I want to know right now. Tell them we know that they can tell us who did it."

After this exchange, and more chattering with the interpreters, Al Sieber said, "They say they aren't sure who did it but they have some ideas who it might be. They will tell you next time they are to come in."

"I want to know now, not at the next counting time," Corliss said.

After more talk Tom Horn said, "They think it may be Big Joe and his friend. They live in a cave along the Salt River one day's walk from here."

"Tell them to find out. They have ways of making them tell."

After more muttering and nodding of heads the Indians left and Pat came on home. It was an uneasy few days. During that time Pat and I walked over to see Howard Rollins. He was letting his chores go—just sitting in his cabin with no energy to go on. "I've lost everything I cared about. I never should have brought her out to this God-forsaken place."

I tried to console him. "Howard, you know that Betsey loved it here. I remember her saying that she'd never been in a place that made her so happy."

"She was happy, but neither of us knew what was around the corner."

"None of us did, but there's renegade Indians just like there's renegade white men," Pat said. "The Army says they're going to find out who did it and bring them to justice."

"That won't bring back Betsey or our baby," said Howard.

Before the next counting day, two bodies were hanging from a cottonwood tree across from the fort on the east bank of the Verde River. They were out in the open so the frightful scene could be viewed from the west bank. The men who did the killing had been found and brought in as prisoners by the other Indians. One of them was Big Joe. The military court was set to try them the following week. Both were put in the guard house overnight.

During the night the sentry was surprised by six men with hoods over their heads. The sentry was silently tied up and left inside the cell. The two killers were bound and gagged and carried to the river bank where cottonwood limbs made a convenient gallows. It all happened so quickly and quietly that no one in the post knew who did it or how it was carried out. Everyone said it must have been someone else. No one tried very hard to find out who it was.

Howard sold all his cattle to John Smith for meat and moved away. He was heart-broken and nothing any of us could say seemed to console him. We never heard of him again.

The few settlers around the valley breathed a little easier after that. Pat and James went back to working on the canal from the needle rocks and on clearing land. They liked to work on the canals after every rain. That softened the dirt some so they had an easier time digging. Of course, that didn't happen very often. Eventually they got water into the canal to test the amount of fall they had. From then on, the leading edge of the water softened the earth enough so that they moved along faster. One thing led to another, though. After that, they had to build a brush dam at the canal head to avoid having too much water come down the new ditch.

There was usually plenty of water in the old ditch by our house, but in 1879 there was no rain from April to August. The Verde was down to a small flow and our canal heading was getting harder than ever to maintain.

John Demarbiex came to see us. His small house was just south of the military boundary fence and he used water out of the same ditch we did. The Army didn't seem to mind that he was there. John didn't speak English very well. He worked on the post farm for William Hancock and later John Smith when they leased the McDowell land.

We were using almost all the water and John was hurting. The first time he just asked about it in his halting English. The second time he complained and asked for more water. Pat said he would try. Then during the best of the growing season for the barley and wheat, he came again and said he had to have water. This time he and Pat nearly came to fighting about it.

"You's no right to dat water," John shouted.

"It's our water, we cleared the canals, you didn't," Pat returned.

"I's here first, it's mine!" he insisted.

Each man acted like he was going to fight but instead just threw up their hands in disgust and turned away. When Pat told me of the argument that night, I said, "I think I did read that the first one on a canal has the first right to the water"

That meant that the Frenchman did have the first call on the water since he was there before we were. Pat snorted, "Well, let him work to clean out the canals then, like we've been doing. Besides, Reavis was here before the Frenchman and we bought him out." For a while John did come up and help with the canals, but when the water was plentiful later on and he didn't need much, he stopped offering.

When Kate and I took in a load of milk and eggs that fall, people at

McDowell were laughing about John Smith, the post trader. John was well liked around the post. His sutler's store had been used as a polling place and he had made political speeches in the new little town of Phoenix. He had decided to run for the state legislature in 1874, and was defeated just after we arrived in Arizona.

We heard that when he was in Phoenix a couple of months later one of the politicians said to him, "John, you can't expect voters to elect somebody with such a common name as John Smith." Apparently he thought about that and petitioned the courts to legally change his name to John Y. T. Smith. Everyone teased him about it, for his name was still John Smith. But from then on he used his initials every time he wrote his name and even changed the sign on the front of the sutler's store.

We all tried to get him to say what the 'Y. T' stood for. Some said it was for "Yuma Territory" since he once lived there. Others said it was for "Yours Truly." But John never would tell. We all made up words that would fit and Pat said some of them weren't very nice, but because they liked John he never heard them.

CHAPTER 27

THE LETTER

In the fall Pat went to McDowell with a wagon load of eggs, butter, and milk. When he returned, he was waving a paper and his face was etched with anger. "Just look at this!" he shouted as he stepped down off the wagon. "Those Eastern idiots don't know what they're talking about." He handed me a dog-eared copy of the New York Herald dated September 11, 1879. It was folded to an editorial that someone had circled.

SETTLERS MURDER INDIANS

It has come to our attention that there are still white settlers in the West who think they can take justice in their hands. Recently members of the noble red tribes have been murdered without even so much as a trial. We have taken their lands and their food sources without compensation. Now we take their lives without due course. We have it on good authority that this has happened twice in New Mexico and three times in Arizona just in the last three months. On one occasion two redmen were lynched from a military guard house and hung without a trial.

It is easy for us in the big cities of the East to be comfortable. But how can we be when our blood-thirsty colonists in the West murder peaceful Indians who are rapidly being turned into wards of the government without any hopes of a future?

For centuries they have been living peacefully on the bounty of this land. Now we are taking away their land, their buffalo and their water. It is time to give these lands back to the red man and prevent more needless slaughter. I say we should take the red man by the hand and guide him gently, kindly toward a better life and the hope of salvation hereafter.

Dudley Freeman, Editor

When I finished reading it, I said, "He should have known Betsey Rollins. He wouldn't look at it that way."

"That really makes me mad," Pat fumed. "I'm going to give him a lacing he won't soon forget."

"What do you mean?"

"I'm going to write him a letter and burn his ears. I'll tell him just how it is out here."

He did. The next week when he took produce to the fort he told me that he got that editor "told off." That letter probably made our troubles worse. I couldn't have guessed it at the time.

We sold 52 tons of hay to McDowell in 1879. We also sold 150 bushels of barley and 175 bushels of wheat. The crops were good, even with the stretch of dry weather. We threshed our grain by hand, in a way that wasn't much different than long ago in Ireland. Because of the dry weather here, we just cleared and swept an area on the ground. Then we'd walk around on the heads of grain until we shelled out the grain. Then we'd separate the grain and the chaff with a screen. The post trader would supply us with bags for the grain. This was another job where we were glad we had so many children.

The canal was keeping our gardens alive. We took vegetables most weeks along with the milk and eggs. By now we were building up money in our savings account again. We were working hard, but were happy and could see that we had made the right choice in coming here.

James and Pat announced one evening that they now had 200 acres of land cleared. Most of it was on the Reavis land, but some was on the land we claimed under the Desert Land Act. The needles ditch, as we were calling it, was progressing. It was down about two miles. The first part had been very difficult but they were in better soil now and they were making good progress.

Another baby was on the way. We decided that we needed to build another room onto our adobe house. The lean-to shed on the north side was working fine as a kitchen but we didn't have enough space for everyone to sleep. The next addition was on the south side. Pat and James worked for two weeks making adobe bricks from the clay beds east of the river. We had plenty of straw from the grain crops to mix in with them. Since the weather was dry the bricks cured in a few days.

John and Kate cut mesquite branches and grass for the roof and we soon had another room that would shelter the three boys. If the next one was a boy, he could sleep out there, too, when he got old enough.

One day when Danny Boy was with Ned, they went for a ride on one of our horses. They often rode on the same horse with no saddle, just a bridle. Danny Boy didn't have his own pony but he let us know that some in his band of Indians did have horses. They splashed across the Verde, as it was low at the time. East of the river was their favorite place to ride since the canyons and ridges made it more exciting for them. Late in the afternooon, Danny Boy limped back to our house, exhausted and bleeding from his head and shoulder.

He was in bad shape. After drinking water, he was able to tell us in his crude English that there had been an accident. "Come—Ned hurt." That was about all we could get out of him.

Kate and I patched Danny Boy a bit and gave him some jerky and a dried corn cake. He had to go with us to show us where Ned was. Pat and James were away working on the needles ditch.

We filled water canteens. John bridled another horse and took Danny Boy. I rode my pony, Daisy. In less than an hour we were a couple of miles up Agua Chiquita wash and on the ridgeline beyond. Danny Boy took us straight to Ned.

We arrived there just before dark. He was caught in between boulders where he had been thrown. They had been riding too fast down a slope and the horse stumbled. Danny Boy landed in the loose gravel and rolled free. As the horse fell, he had dislodged big rocks and then rolled on top of them. The horse was on top of the boulders and both the horse and Ned had their legs pinned underneath. The pain was awful for him at first but by then he had lost feeling. He was crazed for water since the boys had none with them.

We were able to move the horse off the boulder. He would have to be destroyed, for his leg was broken. John found a palo verde limb that was sturdy enough for us to pry the boulder off Ned's leg. Danny Boy insisted that he had to go on home and hobbled off toward Sugarloaf Mountain. Ned rode with me and John went on ahead to tell the family what had happened.

By the time I arrived, Pat was shouting at the children and blaming Danny Boy for the accident He acted like he had when John was hurt in Cheyenne. I knew that I should take Ned to Doc Wilson right away.

John and Pat went back to destroy the poor horse. Kate and I made a bed in the wagon and took Ned to Doc Wilson as fast as we could. It was a bad break and Doc said he hoped he wouldn't lose part of his leg. When I heard that, I was in a cold sweat.

"Oh, no, Doc!" I moaned.

"Well, he's young and there's some circulation coming back in his foot. If we're lucky he may only lose some of the joint action."

That's what happened. Ned had to stay at the post hospital five days until the swelling went down and Doc could put a cast on his lower leg. Pat and I were mighty put out with him for being foolish with the horse. Pat finally agreed with me that we couldn't put the blame on Danny Boy. Now we had a doctor bill, Ned wasn't going to be able to help in the fields for a while and we had lost a horse. We tried to look on the good side of it. We were thankful that Danny Boy was with him and not also trapped. If he could not have come for help, we would not have found either of them in time.

We kept adding corrals to keep the hogs and cattle penned up at night. Mountain lions had killed two newborn calves across the river this last summer. We couldn't keep the cattle in the corrals all the time since there was so much good grass along the river. However, once they got east of the river it was so rough that we had trouble finding them. We decided to let the non-milking cows graze over there but when they were close to having their calves, we'd keep them in the corrals.

We had a few more grown cattle slashed by mountain lions but never as bad as the first incident down at the lower ranch. The patrols and sol-diers on their time off had done a good job of cleaning out most of the predators by now. Pat said they'd shoot at anything—even the birds. We had skunks and ringtail cats nosing around the corrals almost every night. The coyotes and bobcats were still numerous but we didn't worry about them damaging anything except a newborn calf or the chickens. We kept our 300 chickens penned up all the time as we did on the lower ranch.

We now had five barns for keeping our 50 milk cows safe at night and as shelter for the 65 hogs. Each of these had a pen or corral attached to it. Another shed and pen housed our six horses. After Ned's accident we were down to five. Just keeping all these in good repair was getting to be a big job. Luckily, John was good at this. Pat and James would work around the corrals, too, when the weather was too rainy or too hot to dig or repair canals.

We were lucky to have lots of mesquite trees along the river. It was the best for the corral fences. We could find good limbs that were seven to 10 feet long. The small branches were trimmed for firewood. We used that for our cooking and to keep warm in the winter. We had a good iron stove that we bought from Benjamin Velasco for $10 when we bought his cows.

I went in to the post hospital for my delivery. Doc Wilson took good care of me. Our baby girl was a jewel. She was the largest of my girl babies. He said the reason she was so big and healthy was because I had been eating fresh vegetables and working hard on the farm. He said that I was in better physical condition now than when I first came to McDowell in 1874. I did feel stronger.

We named our new one Veronica. She had black hair and it was curly from the day she was born. With six children in the house, we were crowded but since the weather was usually nice, we were seldom all inside at once, except to sleep. In the summer, the older boys wanted to sleep outside and we would let them as long as they were up on cots to avoid rattlesnakes.

It would have been hard for me but Kate was always good with the younger children. She took care of them while I helped with the livestock and farm work. She was just as busy as I and almost never complained. She was even good with the cooking.

Kate often went with me to McDowell as we delivered produce or grain. One day John Y. T. Smith asked a soldier to help store some of the bags of barley that we had delivered. He was a bright, young man named Albert. As he worked with us, he and Kate exchanged a few words, and each time I'd notice that Kate would blush. On the way home I asked her if she liked him. She blushed even more and said, "I don't know, but I think he's nice looking." I didn't think any more about it but after the next sitting job she had at the post, she said that Albert had come by and sat with her for a while on the porch of the Kearney's house. This time she volunteered, "He knows about a lot of things. I think I do like him."

Late one Sunday afternoon, Albert came riding up the road that connected our ranch with the post. He very politely greeted us and removed his hat. The children were down by the river playing while Kate, Pat and I were sitting under one of our ramadas to take advantage of the shade. He asked if Kate would like to walk down to the river with him. When they came back, we invited him to have supper with us. Just as we were finishing, a full moon started rising over the Mazatzal Mountains to the east. Kate said to him, "Let's go to the river bank and watch the moon reflect in the water."

They didn't return until after dark. Then Albert said goodbye to us and rode back to the fort. At 17 years old, Kate was naturally excited about the first boy to really pay attention to her. "Oh Mother," she said, "he's so nice to me. He even asked to hold my hand." I was glad for her to have something else to think about for a change.

After two months, Doc Wilson removed Ned's cast. It was a long time before he could put his entire weight on his leg—he still has a limp.

After the one serious talk we had with him about what he did, the accident was never mentioned again. He was back in the fields by early 1880.

CHAPTER 28

CAPTAIN ADNA CHAFFEE

When Captain Chaffee came to McDowell, things changed. Chaffee had been a decorated officer in the Civil War, we found out. Then, after fighting Indians in the Midwest, he was sent to Arizona. Just before coming here he was the Indian agent at San Carlos, where there had been a lot of trouble. He did a good job, they said, so he got the head job at this post, replacing Captain Corliss. We hated to see Corliss leave.

The talk around the trader's store was that Chaffee was a stickler for detail and a strict military man in every way. The captain's orderly was an enlisted man and loved to brag about him. He said the captain had been injured three times in battle. Once he had refused to be exchanged as a prisoner of war unless they also exchanged his enlisted men. That made him a real hero all around the Army circles.

While commanding a company of infantry troops in Texas, they were surrounded by Indians. He supposedly yelled, "Forward, men, if anyone is killed, I'll make him a corporal!" Another time he got angry

Adna Romanza Chaffee: *The Captain was severe looking every time I saw him. Maybe that's why he was so tough on the enemy.*

ARIZONA HISTORICAL FOUNDATION

because his men weren't shooting at Indians when they showed themselves above the rocks. He shouted, "Shoot, dammit! What do you think your bullets are for—to eat?"

Pat found out that Captain Chaffee had been in the battle of Antietam, where Pat had been captured. The next time he saw the captain, Pat started to ask him about it. Pat said later that his dark eyes looked a hole right through him and he just grunted, "I was there." That was all. Pat said his bushy mustache and eyebrows made him look so fierce that he was afraid to say anything more. It was obvious that Captain Chaffee wasn't interested in talking about Antietam with a former corporal.

Pat got to know Tom Horn well. He was Al Sieber's assistant interpreter and helped Al with the control of the Pima and Maricopa scouts. When Tom heard that Chaffee was coming here, he said he had been with him at San Carlos.

Chaffee's House: *Only the Commanding Officer had a home this nice*
ARIZONA HISTORICAL FOUNDATION

Tom told Pat, "In a fight, Chaffee can beat any man swearing that I ever heard. He swears by ear, and by note in the commonest way and by everything else in an educated way."

For the next few months the discipline at McDowell was more strict than ever before. When we took produce in, some of the soldiers that Pat knew would talk about it. Robert Egan also mentioned it one day when Pat and I went in together. Pat later said, "I'm lucky that I got out when I did. I don't think the new captain is easy on the men."

After a full day with the children, Kate would often ride our pony, Daisy, down to the fort to spend the evening sitting with the children of the Wilsons, the Kearneys and sometimes with little Harry Summer-hayes. One fateful night Kate was involved in an event that may have changed our lives. Thinking back, this was probably one of the triggers for our later problems.

Mrs. Wilson had asked her for that Saturday night since there was a dance to be held at Maryville. As soon as she got there, she took the Wilson's children out on the porch so their parents could finish getting ready. In a few minutes, Mrs. Kearney saw her. They lived just two houses away. She shouted for Kate to come on over. When Kate told her she was supposed to be at the Wilson's, Mrs. Kearney started yelling and screaming at Kate. "You were going to be here! Not there. You idiot girl! Can't you get anything right? First your Dad writes crazy letters and now you try to leave me without a sitter!"

Kate said she tried to explain that she was to be at the Kearney's the following night but Mrs. Kearney wouldn't listen. Finally Mrs. Wilson came out to see what the noise was about. She and Doc finally helped Kate by telling her that she could bring the Kearney's three children over to their house for the evening. Mrs. Kearney yelled back, "Not over there, my children are staying in their own house."

Mrs. Wilson then said to Kate, "Take ours over there then, dear. It will be alright. I'm sorry for this."

When the Kearneys came home at nearly midnight, Mrs. Kearney brushed in past Kate and said, "There'll be no pay for you tonight, nor any other night."

Kate was bewildered and took the Wilson children home where Mrs. Wilson paid her the usual 50 cents and again apologized for the mix-up. "I think Mrs. Kearney has received a letter from a friend out East that has made her angry at your folks. Don't ask me why but it's too bad, dear. It really isn't your fault." Kate was in tears when she arrived home that night. When she told me what Grace Wilson had said, a deep feeling of worry began gnawing inside me.

A few weeks later, John Demarbiex hailed James Carroll as he was walking to our house to help with chores. "Ya' hogs in my crops last night. Get 'em out." James said he would. He and John went down and rounded up five small ones that had found a hole in the mesquite rail corral fence. James later said they had made tracks in the Frenchman's garden and rooted around but not much damage was done.

On our next trip to the trader, there was a letter from Captain Chaffee.

Mr. Patrick White,

Lieutenant Kearney reports to me that there have been complaints about your hogs damaging the property of your neighbor. The officers at this post cannot be bothered by claims such as this that occupy the time of military personnel.

I will expect you to see to it that your animals do not continue to inflict grievance on others nearby.

Respectfully,
Adna Romanza Chaffee
Captain, Commanding Officer
Sixth Cavalry
Fort McDowell, Arizona Territory
June 4, 1880

When Pat saw this letter he wanted to go in to the fort and argue it out with Chaffee. James and I talked him out of it. We convinced him that it might make matters worse.

CHAPTER 29

RUMORS

The next sign of trouble was what John Y. T. Smith said one day when we were there with milk and eggs. "There's a crazy story going about, Annie. It can't be true, but they're saying you run a house of ill repute out there."

I thought he was joking so I said, "That would be a lot more exciting and more profitable that the boarding house for children that we're running!"

His only response was, "I told 'em you couldn't be doing that, but I heard it for the truth."

I just brushed it off with a "Hmpf," and got in the wagon to go home. More anxiety ate at my insides. Too many accusations were swirling around us to be a coincidence.

A few Sundays later, the Egans rode out to the ranch to fish in the Verde with us and have a meal. When Bob and Pat were sitting together and a little apart from the rest of us, Bob said, "Lt. Kearney is telling a story about you folks that I don't like. Have you heard anything of it?"

Pat said, "No." That was true, since I hadn't thought to say anything to him about what John Smith had told me.

Bob told him about the story of our running a bawdy house and wondered how such a thing could come up. Pat brushed it off and said they must be hard up for rumors to put any stock in something that crazy.

It was strange to see Bob Egan again the next Sunday. He rode out to our house by himself. Without the usual talking about general things, Bob asked Pat, "Do you know a man back East named Freeman?"

"No," Pat replied.

"He must know you. Doc Wilson was telling me somebody with that name had a banker friend who is the brother of Mrs. Kearney. This banker wrote Mrs. Kearney a letter saying she had better be careful because there's a madman named Patrick White living at Ft. McDowell. He told her that this man, White, was trying to get all the Indians killed."

Pat groaned, "Oh, now I know who Freeman is. He's the editor of the New York Herald. Right after Betsey Rollins was murdered, I wrote him a letter blasting him for wanting to give the land back to the Indians."

"Well, that explains part of why Mrs. Kearney has it in for you and your family. Doc Wilson feels real bad about what happened between Kate and Mrs. Kearney."

"Kate feels bad, too," Pat said. "Now I can tell her the reason why. I don't know what I can do about it, though."

"I don't either, Pat. By the way, Doc Wilson doesn't want you to mention his name. He only told me as a friend of yours. Please don't tell anyone at the fort that I came out here today."

When Pat told me I was numb. It was no good to scold him for writing the letter. I knew how he felt after seeing Betsey and helping to bury her. No telling how the story got twisted between the editor and Mrs. Kearney, but the damage was done. I remembered what Elizabeth Kearney said to Kate. Maybe it's just as well if Kate doesn't work there anymore, I thought.

One day in July of 1880, Kate and I did the delivery of produce to John Y. T. Smith. After unloading at the sutler's store we drove up to officers' row to deliver things to Martha Summerhayes. I had some dresses and petticoats that I'd made for her. I didn't have much spare time but when I did I spent it making things for her.

Martha was glad to get the clothes and paid me more than I had expected. When I thanked her several times, she then said, "Annie, I probably shouldn't say anything, but would you mind if I asked you something personal?"

"No, of course not."

"Well, it's really none of my business, but I just wondered. Did you and Pat ever record your purchase of the Reavis land and the other section you claimed?"

"I don't think so. Doc Wilson said that sometime we should go to Florence and do it but we've just been too busy."

"I hear that there have been some inquiries made about it," Martha said. "That's all I know and I just thought you should be aware of it."

"Thank you," I said.

As Kate and I drove back home, we talked about it. I said, "I'll talk to your father and one of these days we will get over there to get our names on the record."

CHAPTER 30

ULTIMATUM

The crops in 1880 were good. We had more water coming down the original ditch. Pat and James had cleared extra land. The vegetable garden was beautiful since the worst of the summer heat had held back during May and June.

Pat and James and one Mexican helper kept working on the needles ditch. They had the water down about two and one-half miles. It looked like the fall would be just right to bring it to the upper part of our land. The men also built two more sheds to give our cattle and hogs shelter.

One morning in July, John Demarbiex arrived at our house just at daylight and he was very angry. "Ya' hogs. They mess up my ditch. Thees bad—plenty bad, no good."

He was so excited that we could hardly understand even his broken English. We could see that one rail fence was broken down and one pen of hogs was gone. Pat, John and Kate went down to his land and rounded up the hogs. With a couple of hours of running and shouting they were back in the pen. The Frenchman kept saying something about his ditch but Pat said he didn't see anyplace where it was damaged. The hogs had wallowed in the water during the night and walked over the sides, but that was all.

We forgot the incident until that earthshaking day when a courier from the fort rode up to our house and handed us a letter. I'll never forget the date—July 20, 1880—or the letter. I have it on my lap now.

Patrick White, Esq.,

  Sir:

    A few days ago I directed that you take care that your hogs do no further damage to the ditch passing your present place of abode. You have failed to comply with those instructions. You are now directed to remove your hogs off the reservation and keep them off.

    Further, you are informed that between this date and the 31st day of August, next, you must move your family off the reservation. A stake has been set by the side of the ditch which marks the northern boundary of this military reserve.

We were astounded. We weren't on the reservation. Everyone knew that. Capt. Corliss said we weren't when we asked him if we could put our cattle up here. But now Corliss was gone and Chaffee was in charge.

We knew someone had sent a soldier out to check on our hogs the first time they got into the Frenchman's ditch, but he just rode around for 10 minutes and left without saying anything. Now we could see that they had placed a marker on the other side of the big wash just north of our house. Now they were claiming that was the reservation line.

The first thing Pat did was walk down to Demarbiex's place. He was going to find out if he was the one who complained. When he came back he said the Frenchman wasn't all that upset. He told Pat that he had complained to Lt. Kearney the last time he was at the post. Pat pressed him about how our hogs had damaged his ditch but he just shrugged his shoulders and acted like it was nothing.

The next thing we did was to drive in that night to see the Egans. Corporal Egan said to us, "The word is around that they're trying to get you to move. There's some rumors that we don't think are right but we can't say much. It's the officers who run things, you know."

I remembered what John Y. T. Smith said to me. "Is one of the rumors that we are running a bad house out there?"

Amanda Egan blushed, "Worse than that, Annie. Some are saying that soldiers are spending the night out there with Kate."

Pat leaped out of his seat and, for a second, I thought he was going to attack Amanda. Both Bob Egan and I stopped him and I said, "Pat, this isn't Amanda's fault. All we can do is tell people it isn't true. It's a mean trick and I wish I knew who's doing it."

Pat yelled, "I'll bet it's that crazy Kearney woman. She's gotten mad at Kate twice and now she's making up tales to smear our poor girl."

I began to see how this started. It must have been Pat's letter that got back to Elizabeth Kearney from the editor's friend. Then she had two run-ins with Kate that really weren't Kate's fault. But Mrs. Kearney made them out to be and now she had apparently gotten to Capt. Chaffee.

"Is there anything you can do, Bob?"

"Not a thing, Annie, except to tell any of the enlisted men that I know of nothing you folks have done to deserve this. But I don't dare bring up the subject with Kearney or Chaffee."

"I know that, Bob," Pat said. "Do you think we could talk to Doc Wilson about this?"

"I don't know," Bob replied. "Guess it wouldn't hurt to try."

We went up to officers' row and knocked on the Wilson's door. When the captain came out he didn't invite us in but asked us to sit on the porch. He didn't ask Mrs. Wilson to come out, either, and I noticed that immediately. He looked very serious and I think he knew why we were there.

"Captain Wilson," I began, "we got a terrible letter in the mail today."

"I heard that you did, Mrs. White," he said rather formally.

"But it's not right, we're not on the reservation!" I think I must have almost yelled.

"That's not for me to say, Annie. I know there's some problems you folks have with some of the officers here. It's been said that you only bought water rights from old man Reavis, not his land. It's not for me to decide, I'm afraid."

"But what can we do?" I asked.

"I don't suppose you can stop the rumors. But you probably should try to prove that it's your land and that it's not on the reservation."

"We have the bill of sale from Reavis," Pat said.

"Pat, Annie, I can't really talk about this with you. I'm sorry, but the officers in charge are putting a lot of things on you and I'm afraid you'll have to answer to them unless you can prove them wrong."

I could see that we couldn't push Doc any longer. I stood up. The drive back home was slow and grim. Our world had just tumbled on us and we didn't know what to do. Pat was so angry that his thinking became rambling and mixed up. He was convinced that Chaffee was wrong on everything and that we could just ignore it. I didn't agree, for the letter was so strong.

The next day, I went in to the post and found out from John Y. T. Smith how to write Florence to put our name on this land. I did that and sent along a handwritten copy of the bill of sale that we received from Reavis. John said it would take about three weeks for an answer since the mail only went from here to that part of the territory once a week.

I studied in my mind how to stop the rumors about Kate and about Pat's letter to the editor back East. I thought about talking to Martha Summerhayes but decided she would have to tell me the same thing as Doc Wilson did.

By the next delivery trip to John Smith, I was getting desperate. I knew that something had to be done before August 31st; I just didn't know what it was. I didn't have anything finished for Martha, but I took along a dress that was partially finished. I made up a question about it to give me an excuse to drive to her house.

After I'd gotten an answer to my phony question, I asked her, "Have you heard anything else about us having to move?"

"Yes, Annie, and it makes me sick to think of you leaving. But, you know, selling liquor to the Indians is something that is illegal here."

"I know it is. What does that have to do with us?" I asked.

"Oh dear, you really don't know, do you?" When I looked blankly at her she went on. "Annie, they're saying that Pat has been doing that for a long time. I hate to be the one to tell you, as you've been such a good friend."

I was stunned. "But he doesn't, Martha-uh, I mean, Mrs. Summerhayes!" Suddenly I felt a separation from her. Here was an officer's wife telling me things she shouldn't. I saw myself trying to explain my husband's actions to an officer's wife. It was almost too much. But I had to try and tell her the truth.

"I know Pat takes a nip once in awhile but not often. But to sell it to Indians—he would never do that. He has never thought of it, I know." As I finished, I got more excited and I think she believed me.

She said, "I shouldn't have said anything, but I have heard that story and you did ask, Annie. There's a case against you and I find it hard to believe. I have to be quiet and not get Captain Summerhayes in trouble. Gook luck, Annie."

I knew I must go. All I could muster was a feeble "thank you" as I walked to my wagon. Doc Wilson was on his way to the post hospital as I slowly drove back toward the road to our place. As I passed him I decided that at this point I had not much to lose by talking to him again. "I did write to Florence like you said to do, Doctor Wilson."

He smiled and replied, "Hello, Annie. That's good. I've also heard that Prescott is a good place to go to plead your case if you think something isn't being done right. That's the territory capitol, you know."

"Thank you," I said and drove on.

On the 11th day of August I decided that I must go to Prescott to see John Fremont, the Territorial Governor. I would take the letter from Capt. Corliss that said our ranch wasn't on the reservation. That copy was folded on my lap along with the one Chaffee wrote. Those two letters seemed to frame our problems and surely if someone saw them they could straighten things out for us.

On the morning of August 12th, I left for Prescott with high hopes. Pat and James went to work on the ditch. The younger children were in Kate's care and the older ones were weeding the vegetables.

CHAPTER 31

THE BURNING

My pony, Daisy, was plodding up the wash. The loose sand sucked at her feet with every step. We would both be glad when we reached higher ground and the trail would become firm and rocky. Our chores were done in the dim light before dawn. I left as the morning sun began to rise over Four Peaks, the mountain that dominated our landscape.

On the low banks of this desert waterway my eyes focused on the next saguaro ahead. Long ago I had learned this was a good way to relieve the routine of a long ride in the desert. Each sagebrush, mesquite, and palo verde tree looked much like the others but every majestic saguaro is different.

I would imagine what each plant looked like. Sometimes it would be a cowboy with his arms out to the side or perhaps an outlaw in a "hands up" position. Some of them looked like a telephone pole with a bird clinging to one side. Then I'd see "granddaddy" saguaros that people said were maybe 200 years old. Those would have bird nest holes along their tall stems and some would have drooping arms.

We were now learning how to adapt to this strange, dry place that really didn't look like a desert. There were plants of all kinds in our valley. We didn't know what they were called so we made up names. Even though I had lived here for six years, I never tired of the variety of wildlife that depended on them for food and shelter.

This was an urgent journey that could mean everything to Pat and our children. Only eleven days earlier we had received the crucial letter from Captain Chaffee. I knew it would be up to me to set things straight. Pat was a good man—had always been—but he was obsessed now with his ranch. From dawn 'til dark, he and James Carroll slaved on the land. If he wasn't clearing brush or chopping weeds, he was working on the second canal that he said would bring lots more water to our acres. He would get too angry if he were to talk to the officials.

We both knew it wouldn't do any good to talk with the main officers at McDowell. We got along well with most of them, but for some reason the top two had it in for us. There was no time to try and make that right. Something drastic was needed. Prescott, the Territorial Capitol, was where I had to start.

Daisy and I were a couple of miles up the long slope towards Cave Creek when I heard shouting behind me. It was John. He was riding one of our best horses and yelling all the time. When I heard his voice I stopped. As he got closer I could hear "FIRE! FIRE! Mother, our house is on fire!"

We both turned around and headed back down the sandy wash toward the Verde River. John fell back for his horse was winded but I kicked Daisy on as fast as she could run. Now I could see the smoke but I couldn't imagine what could have happened. As we got closer, I saw our livestock and chickens running loose. They represented a large part of the stake that Pat and I were building on our desert homestead.

Daisy was tiring from her fast pace through the sandy ditch. She lunged up the rocky banks of the wash close to our house. I was terrified by the sight. Our adobe and brush house was engulfed by flames. No children in sight—only pigs and chickens running around. I saw a glimpse of soldiers riding south toward McDowell. I recognized only one—it was Lt. Kearney.

My children!! Where were they? How could this happen? The roof of our house collapsed, sending sparks high in the sky. Daisy reared up in fright. I must have screamed. I only remember seeing the ghastly sight, the hopelessness and Daisy rearing away from the flames. Blackness took over.

CHAPTER 32

NIGHTMARES

From a great distance, I heard a voice. "She hit her head on a rock when she fell." As I tried to say that I could hear, someone else said, "You'd think they would at least have taken better care of the children."

The anguish I felt must have jerked my body for I felt like I was falling off my horse. I heard someone say, "She's wakening. Shall we tell her about the children?"

Weakly, I opened my eyes again and saw a ceiling. Just then Doc Wilson's face appeared over me. He had a worried look on his face. "Annie, can you hear me?"

"Mm..m..m."

"You have a bad bruise on your head. Do you remember falling?"

"Wh...where am I?"

Then Josie Carroll was beside the doctor. She said, "Don't worry, Annie, the children are all with me and everything will work out."

"Why did I fall?"

Josie looked at Doc Wilson and he nodded a bit and said to her, "Go ahead, she needs to know."

"Your house was on fire, Annie. Do you remember that?"

"Oh no! How did that happen? The children? Where's Pat?"

"Easy now, Annie." Doc Wilson placed cool cloths on my forehead and my wrists. "The best thing you can do is rest and get your strength back. Not too many questions now."

"The children are alright. James and I will take care of them for you."

"That's too much Josie, Pat can do it 'til I'm home."

Josie and Doc Wilson exchanged glances again and I could tell there was something they weren't telling me.

"What's wrong?" Fear swept over me and I tried to sit up. A wave of sickness and dizziness hit and I fell backwards with a groan.

I tried to protest that I couldn't get hurt, the children needed me and I had to get to Prescott. But the words didn't make sense and I was so-o-o tired. This time when I eased back on the cot, I began to understand that

I was in a hospital. But where? Are we at Fort Russell? Will Martha Jane Canary come to help me?

"I'm going to give you some medicine now," Doc said.

I gulped it and forced my eyes wide saying, "What about Pat. Why isn't he here?"

Josie took a big breath and said, "Well, Pat is gone. No one is sure where he is but he does know about the fire and he's probably just fine."

"But where did he go?" I whispered now, for fatigue was gripping me.

"Maybe just to think, Annie. Maybe just to decide what to do. We're not sure, but the men are out looking for him."

"Annie, take some more medicine. You must rest." Doc Wilson was again pressing a spoon to my lips. I was so faint that I couldn't say more. I swallowed and lay back on the pillow with my eyes closed. There were many more questions but both the doctor and Josie were gone. Before the medicine took hold of me, I had some thinking to do.

So many hard things have happened. Why this, when Pat and I finally had things coming our way? I told myself that I musn't lose hope. Mother always said, "Th' race is not always to th' swift, but 'tis to those who endure." Why would I think of that? Dear Mother and her proverbs. How patient and enduring she was. It was comforting to remember Mother and how she cared for me in New York. I drifted back into a deep sleep.

My eyes slowly opened. The room was dim but I saw light through the blinds. My head felt better. Dreams of New York faded and roughly plastered walls swam into my view.

I didn't try to go back to sleep. Oh, Mother, dear Mother. You did so much for me. What would you do now? How would you handle this? I opened my eyes to see a ceiling and I was in a room that was white-washed.

Someone was bending over me and I knew her. It was Josie again. My throat was parched and my head was whirling again. I was having trouble getting myself roused. Faintly she said, "Patrick has been found and he...."

As my eyes focused, I interrupted, "What about Pat?"

"He's having trouble speaking, Annie. He got cactus thorns in his mouth."

"How? Is he alright?" I mumbled.

"Well, he isn't feeling very well, Annie," Josie said.

"How did he get cactus in his mouth?"

"We don't know, he can't talk much. We'll have to wait a few days until he can. I must go now, Annie. I wanted to wait 'til you were awake. With your six and my two, there's a powerful lot of cooking and washing to do. Doc Wilson says in a day or two you can come home with me." Doc was there.

"It's late afternoon, Annie. Time for some more medicine and another good sleep." That's all I wanted to do. I was so exhausted that I couldn't bear to lift my head from the pillow.

Before sleep claimed me, I tried to think what could have happened to Pat. He was dependable and he knew all about cactus. How could he get cactus thorns in his mouth?

I thought of our six children. Josie said they were all at the Carrolls' house. It wasn't any larger than ours and we were crowded. How could they manage? Of course, Josie needed help. Dear Josie, what a good friend she has been. I thought, or dreamed, of the time we met and the good days at Fort Moultrie.

Now as I look back on the incident, I believe I must have been delirious for part of this time. I'm not even sure I recall it correctly. Maybe I was just having dreams because of the blow on my head and the shock of seeing our house burning.

I awakened just as the sun was coming up over Four Peaks. It had been my best sleep since the accident. Doc Wilson told me he would decide at noon if I could leave. As I lay there thinking of Pat, I thought about how many times our lives had been changed by events that we couldn't control. There were times during the Civil War when I was as worried as I was now. I remembered my stay in Baltimore and all the doubts I had while Pat was in Libby Prison.

My memories of the distant past seem so clear. Why can't I remember yesterday or what happened the day of the burning. I think I fell asleep, or dreamed again. As I again became aware of my headache, I heard a voice.

"Doctor, do you think we could take care of her?" It sounded like Josie again.

I raised up and said something like, "Don't burn it! What's happening?"

189

This time I heard Doc Wilson. His strong voice cut through the fog in my head. "Annie, you are talking in your sleep. Wake up!"

I jerked and opened my eyes to see Doc and both of the Carrolls standing over me.

"Am I sick?" I asked.

Doc spoke again. "You've been in a deep sleep for two days now, Annie. It's time to wake up and let us try and get you back on your feet."

Josie added, "We have your children at our house, Annie. We want you to come back to us."

"Where have I been?"

"You've been right here in the post hospital," Doc said. "Ever since your house burned."

The ghastly sight came back to me vividly. "Oh, yes, oh dear God, what happened to the children?"

"They're with us." Josie said "and they're alright."

I still couldn't quite understand. "Why did the house burn? Where was Pat?"

"He was working on the ditches," Josie replied. "He is...well, he is...uh.. going to be OK one of these days."

"Going to be? Oh yes, the cactus?" I was finally awake and could remember something about Pat and cactus thorns. I had to get home to take care of things. I could tell that I was better—the pounding in my head was less now.

"Dr. Wilson says that you can come home with us if you feel up to it," Josie beamed at me.

"I'll help you walk out to the wagon. There's a bed all fixed for you there." James was anxious to help.

Josie said again, "The children and Pat are at our house and there's a place for you there, too."

"I want to see them."

Doc helped me out of bed and watched me take a few steps on my own. He said I could go if I felt like it. I was ready.

The trip home was not easy, but after a mile or so lying down in the wagon, I wanted to sit up so I could look around. For some reason I didn't ask questions about what had happened and the Carrolls didn't offer any answers. They just talked about our crops that were in the field.

When we arrived at their house I had a joyful reunion with all six children. Pat was sitting on the Carrolls' front porch and waited until the children and I had hugged and kissed each other. Then I turned to him and he got up.

Pat's face was puffy and his lips were covered with sores. There were scratches on his arms. "How did this happen to you, dear?" I said.

"Fire," he mumbled. "Got lost, thirsty, hungry."

James tried to help Pat tell me, for it was obvious that he was in pain. "He wandered for three days before we found him. When we did, he was way up in the mountains. He tried to get water out of a barrel cactus. He was nearly gone, Annie."

"Why did he do that?" I asked.

"No one knows," James said. "When John left on his pony to find you, the soldiers who burned your house took the children upriver and told them to stay. But Kate came up where we were working and told us what had happened. Pat and I got them and took them all back to our house."

Josie picked up the story. "I had gone over to your ranch to see what was causing the smoke. I got there soon after you fell and brought you over here in a wagon. When James and Pat came with your children, I took you to the post hospital."

James said, "Pat was beside himself with anger. He went over to see what was left of your ranch. Then he just disappeared into the desert."

While he was telling me this Pat just sat there gazing into the distance. He didn't offer any response. Josie saw me look at him for an explanation.

"I think it's best if both of you just take it easy for a few more days. Pat needs to heal and you must be tired from the trip out here."

I was exhausted. The excitement of seeing the children and the shock at seeing Pat was overwhelming. I let Josie lead me into their back lean-to room where she had a pallet ready for me. She said, "James and Kate and John will take the other children and work in the fields the rest of the day."

I took a nap. Later in the afternoon, I awakened and went back to the porch and sat gazing east toward the mountains. Pat was not around the house but Josie was working in the kitchen. What would become of us now? Would Pat give up on our ranch? I wanted to think of how happy we were when he was discharged. The thoughts that kept crowding in, however, were the horrible scenes of our house burning and our stock scattering through the desert.

As I was thinking about this, Josie came out and sat with me. She didn't say a thing, bless her heart. She knew that I needed time to sort out my thoughts. For some reason, I didn't think there was anything more to ask about Pat. His condition was too painful for me to discuss. I knew they didn't know all that had happened to him, either.

So I broke the silence by asking, "Why did they attack us and not the Frenchman?"

"We don't know, Annie. But they have told him he has to move—that he is on their land, too."

"Poor man, now he's getting punished just because of us."

"Maybe so, Annie, but remember, he was complaining about your pigs in his ditch and that was one of the excuses they used for destroying all your property."

"What happened to our cows and our pigs and chickens?"

Josie sat there a long time before answering. "That part hurts James and I almost as much as the burning of your house. Those scoundrels broke down all the mesquite rail fences in your corrals and let your stock just run out in the desert. They opened the gate on your chicken pen and they scattered, too."

"Can we get them back?"

"I hate to be the one that has to tell you all this bad news, Annie. Do you really want to know?"

"Yes."

"Well, the fire and shooting and commotion scared all the stock so they ran in all directions. James tried to round them up but there was no place to keep them if he could. As it was, he only got Daisy and another one of your horses and three milk cows to stand still long enough to get a rope on them. One by one, he led those five back here. They're tied to trees out back and we're taking care of them."

"What happened to the rest?"

"Ah, that's the pity. The soldiers used them for target practice and so did the Indians. Both of them butchered some for meat and lots have just been left for the vultures or the lions and coyotes. The chickens were all lost to the varmints in the first two days. Annie, I'm sorry to be telling you this but it's the way it happened."

My only thought was, "Why?" I voiced it out loud, I guess, for Josie replied.

"We can't figure it out. We know most of the men at McDowell liked you and we don't think anyone had anything against us. James and I have decided that they must have been ordered to destroy everything you had built just to prove that you were wrong to be living on the military reservation. Once the stock was loose—well, you know how the soldiers are, they like to shoot at a live target."

"Oh, Josie, it makes me sick to think of all we'd built up—and now it's gone." Tears started to come to my eyes and I could say no more. I buried my head in my hands and my body shook with the realization of our gigantic loss.

Josie knew my torment and said no more. She just reached over and squeezed my hand. It was the kindest thing that she could have done at that point. And it helped. Nothing was said as I tried to think about our situation and decide what we should do now.

We couldn't stay with Josie and James. With Pat in a half-dazed condition, I didn't know if he would be able to rebuild and work the canals. I must talk with James to get his opinion. I still need to go to Prescott to get them to reverse this terrible thing the soldiers have done. We must then get repaid for our losses. I will try and get a court martial for Chaffee and Kearney. They are the ones who caused this evil thing to happen. I wondered how a civilian went about doing that.

As my thoughts swirled in several directions, I almost felt faint again as I had for those days in the post hospital. "I can't let myself be sick," I thought. I must have said it out loud for Josie was by my side and briefly held my hand again.

"I'll help keep you from being sick, Annie. You will have to be strong, for I fear the whole family is yours to care for—at least now."

"Do you think Pat will get well?" I asked.

"We asked Doc Wilson that when we took him in to get some of the thorns out of his hands and tongue. Pat hardly knew who Doc was. After Doc did what he could, we asked him that same question."

"And what did he say?'

"He said he thought Pat had a severe shock from seeing the house and that you were hurt. Probably something like a heart attack, though nothing was wrong with his heart. Then he had bad sunstroke and dehydration when he got lost in the desert."

I shrank back a bit and I guess I started getting tears in my eyes. "Does that mean Doc thinks he gone ah..off..uh....out of ...uh.....does Doc think he's gone crazy?" I could hardly say the word.

"He didn't say that, Annie. He did say it might be a long time before he could do much work and that we would have to watch him closely to be sure he didn't hurt himself again somehow."

I couldn't respond. All I could do was gaze at the ribbon of cottonwoods along the river—at Four Peaks on the horizon, at the irrigation ditch and the new field of barley that I could see from the Carrolls front porch. This had been such a dream come true for us. Our future was so bright—and now all is shattered.

I could see the Frenchman's house off to the south. Was it all his fault? No, I decided. We could have worked that out between us. It had to be Mrs. Kearney and that friend back East. Captain Chaffee may be a Civil War hero but he has done a dastardly deed that must be punished. Pat can't do it. I must and I will.

After working these thoughts through my mind, I actually felt stronger. The period of contemplation had helped me see things more clearly. I knew what I must do. I made up my mind that I wasn't going to let anything stop me from getting back what we had lost.

CHAPTER 33

RECOVERY

I had to find a place for the family to stay. I must get to Prescott and start legal action against Chaffee and Kearney. I must get an answer from Florence that our names are square on this land to prove our title.

All our possessions were burned in the house. Three days later Corporal Bob Egan and a private that used to work with Pat came out with a wagon partly filled with cast off clothing from the post. Bob Egan was apologetic. "I'm sorry about what has happened, Annie. The men want you folks to have these things to tide you over. If you need anything else special let me know. Beyond that, there's not much else we can do."

Josie was there to help unload the clothes. At the botton of the wagon was a quarter of beef and some choice cuts of pork. "Oh thank you, corporal," Josie said. "This will really help all of us."

"I know you have a lot of mouths to feed now, Mrs. Carroll. These came out of John Smith's cooler. It might make up a little for some of the stock you folks have lost."

There was enough meat for two weeks of eating for both families. It was a kind thing for Bob Egan and the men at the post to do. As Bob was leaving he said, "Amanda and I can't see you much anymore, Annie. If I can get another load together, I will, but the word is that we at the post aren't to take sides in this matter. We both wish you well. Goodbye."

As he drove off, I wondered if that message meant that we weren't welcome at the post now. It was all so unfair! We haven't done anything wrong! I have to set things right! It's going to be up to me and I will get it done somehow.

The vegetable garden had a crop about ready to take to the fort. I decided that we had to test the situation. John and Kate finished picking the beans, squash and melons that were ready. Two days later, Kate and I drove the load to John Smith's store.

His greeting to me was "Mrs. White." It had always been "Hello, Annie."

"Here's our produce, John," I said. "We'll have some more next week but Pat isn't feeling up to planting a winter garden now."

"Uh, um, uh." John cleared his throat and tried again. "Maybe it would be best if you didn't bring any more for awhile, Mrs. White."

"Why?" I said.

"Well, I hear you have to move off the reservation. I guess that land is really part of the post now. Uh, Mrs. White, I don't want to get into any of the politics around here but I have to follow the orders I get from the military, you know that."

I couldn't believe what I was hearing. We always thought John was one of our best friends. He had always treated us straight and trusted us. I couldn't bear to argue with him. After he paid me, I walked out with my head held high and said, "Goodbye, Mr. Smith."

He came to the door. "Annie, I'm sorry. It's just the way it is, that's all. I'm really sorry."

He probably was sorry—and I was sorrier, but I was also getting mad. Someone was going to pay for this!

We were going to have to use our savings to tide us over until we could get clear title to our land and until Pat got well. The next day Kate and I asked James Carroll to drive us all the way in to Tempe. It was a little village that had started between Mesa and Phoenix. It had been Hayden's Ferry until last year when the name was changed.

We knew George Arnold, a former soldier from McDowell, who lived there. After his enlistment was up, he had married a Mesa woman and they had gone into the grocery business. Pat and he were good friends but I didn't know them well. At this point, I didn't have a choice. They were the only people I knew in Tempe and, as Catholics, we didn't think we would be welcome in Mesa. I decided that we would see if they could help us find a place to rent for awhile until our affairs were in order.

I also needed to visit a bank. Our savings account book was burned in the fire. I knew that we had almost $2000 saved but I couldn't draw against that until I could prove it. James took Kate and I to the Union Cattlemen's Bank and explained to them what had happened. They agreed to wire our bank in New York for a replacement book and to confirm our balance. Pat had wanted to change our account to the Cattlemen's Bank a year before but I felt more comfortable staying with the one my mother used in downtown New York City.

The Arnolds did tell us about a house on West 3rd Street that was for rent. Kate and I took a look and thought it would be alright for us. Actually, it was larger and a lot nicer than what we had at the ranch. We asked if there was something cheaper but there wasn't. It was owned by

John Sadmore. He lived near the corner of Mill and 3rd Street where he also had a restaurant and operated the Post Office. It was only four blocks from Our Lady of Mount Carmel Catholic church. That was a mission church out of Florence built by the Mexicans that lived in San Pablo, right south of the Hayden Buttes. This became our first church home since coming to Arizona. That night Kate and I slept with the Armolds and James made a bed in the wagon.

On the way back to the ranch, I began to think what I needed to do first. James and Josie said they would finish harvesting the grain and vegetables. They thought they could get John Smith to do business with them, and if not they would haul them in to Mesa or Tempe. I needed a pony to travel to Prescott and, if necessary, to Florence. I would let John, Sally, Ned and Willie go to school. Kate would take care of Pat and Veronica, and on days when I wasn't away, she could go to school, too.

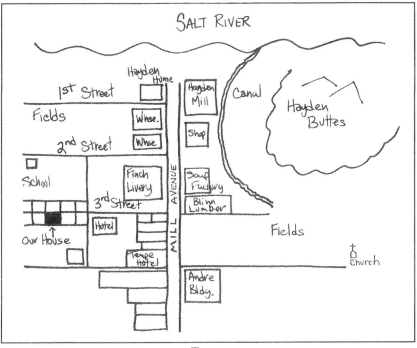

Tempe

Close to us was a one-room adobe school building. John Sadmore said it had been built in 1873. William Hancock's sister, Carrie, was the first teacher and was there until just before we moved to town. I wished she was still there since we knew Mr. Hancock at Fort McDowell.

There was a corral in back of the place we rented where I could keep Daisy so we took her with us when we moved. I gave the other horse and the three cows to the Carrolls for milk and butter for their family. They offered to pay for them but I couldn't think of it after all they'd done to help us during our tragedy.

We were a pitiful sight when all of us trudged to Tempe on the old wagon road from McDowell to Phoenix. The youngest girls and Willie rode part of the way and James and I took turns driving. Kate and I traded off riding Daisy. We sure didn't have much to take with us. Just the salvage things the soldiers had sent out with Bob Egan.

Pat walked the whole way without saying much. When I told him of the plans I'd made he mostly just stared but when I'd ask him something he would answer. He just said "Mmmm." Or he would nod his head. The only objection he made was when I said to the Carrolls that we wouldn't be back out there for awhile. Pat shook his head and whispered, "Yes. You need help." In recent years his thick red hair had gotten sandy colored and thin. Now, for the first time, I noticed it was graying. He had aged 10 years in two weeks.

As soon as our savings book came, I withdrew some money to pay rent on our house and for my trip to Prescott. This trip was discouraging. John Fremont, who was called the great Pathfinder of the West, was the governor. It took me two days to get an appointment with him. I was frightened when I finally got in see him for he was the most well-known man in the west at that time. He had been an explorer and a candidate for President.

I knew he was a famous person but I wasn't prepared for such an impressive figure. He was tall, with a full beard and a dominating personality. It was easy to see how he could have been a mountain man and a guide for expeditions. He owned a lot of land in California and was married to the daughter of a senator. Looking back now, I must say that I was afraid of him.

He listened to my story. Although he had been governor for two years, he didn't seem to know very many people in Arizona. To help things along, he suggested that I talk to several other men in the territorial government. That's how I spent the next two days. Everyone I talked to was sorry, but said there was nothing they could do to help. They'd blame the Army or the regulations or the paperwork or someone else. I was told that they would follow up on my request. This trip took six days, counting my travel, but Kate kept things going at home.

A few days later I rode to Florence. They told me there that they had no record of our ownership of the Reavis land but they had sent some forms to us a month before. They were lost now and I tried to fill them out while I was in the office. Some facts I didn't know and after I did all this, they told me that the Army had already written them that this section of land was on the McDowell reservation. They wouldn't even accept my application! All they would tell me was the same thing they said at Prescott: "Get an attorney." I knew that cost lots of money and I wasn't willing to do it. This was a three-day trip and nothing to show for it, except to visit our mother church while I was there.

I saw the French priest, Father Edouard Gerard. He was the one who sometimes came to Mount Carmel to say mass. He made a trip to our church and to St. Mary's in Phoenix at least once every three months. After telling him of my distress he gave me sympathy and said a prayer with me. This helped a bit but despair soon gripped me again.

I returned to Tempe feeling beaten into the ground. The one bright spot was that Pat was feeling and acting better. Some more of the thorns had festered and Kate had been able to pick them out. He could talk better now and was eating more like he did. When I told him what I had learned, he didn't seem to mind. He said, "I better find a job so you won't have to keep taking money out of savings."

"Do you think you're ready?"

"If it's close. We'll just have to start over, Annie."

"Pat, even if you get a job, we still have to prove to those Army crooks that the land is ours. They can't kick us off like that. We have to get paid back for all the stock and things we lost in our house."

"Maybe." Pat said.

I couldn't imagine that he would let it go like that. But then, I thought, it may be better than if he's real angry. At least he is feeling better and if he would rather work here in Tempe for a while, I shouldn't argue with him. I will have to carry the fight.

He found a job on his own. It was as a repair man at the Hayden Flour Mill, just three blocks away on the south bank of the Salt River. Mr. Hayden had one of the largest mills in the territory. Part of the year he could use waterpower from the river to turn the mill wheels. He had diverted part of the Salt River into a canal around the butte. When there was water he had a 25 foot waterfall to turn the mill wheels. When dry spells came, he used steam engines. We could hear them from our house.

199

Hayden Flour Mill: *The original mill. I saved this from the Tempe paper.*   ARIZONA STATE ARCHIVES

We didn't hear much from the Carrolls. We knew they were busy trying to keep the crops alive. They did tell us that they had found two of our hogs up the river. The Carrolls didn't have time to butcher the hogs so they sold them to John Smith and gave us the money. I took that, as our savings had gone down.

Pat's job earned enough to pay our rent and buy groceries but there was nothing added to savings. The five oldest children were all in school now. My time was spent in caring for Veronica and writing letters to Prescott and Florence. I kept trying to get someone to admit that there had been a horrible mistake. Every time I wrote to Fort McDowell, the letter was unanswered. I even rode out there one day, with Veronica strapped on my back, to see Captain Chaffee but he was already transferred someplace and Lt. Kearney wouldn't see me.

I saw Doc Wilson but all he would say was, "Annie, there's no use. I can't do a thing. I'm sorry but I must get back to work."

I stopped by the Egans. I asked her if she had heard anything more about our house burning and she said that there were some who thought it was right and others who didn't. I said, "How could anyone think it was right?"

Amanda just shrugged her shoulders. After that there wasn't much more to say.

The next week, as the children were getting home from school, the Carrolls drove to our house in their wagon. They looked tired and angry as they stepped down. "Annie, now they've done it to us, too!" Josie cried.

"What?"

"They burned us out, Annie, just like they did to you and Pat," James said.

"Oh, dear God!" It was all I could think to say.

We stared at each other. Finally I asked, "Why you? You didn't write the letter. It wasn't your daughter that got Mrs. Kearney mad."

"We don't know," said James.

"I'm so sorry, Josie. We never thought it would come to this. We shouldn't have invited you out here. We thought the Army would treat us right after all Pat did for them. Oh, I'm so sorry." I collapsed into a chair, sobbing.

When Pat came home from work and the Carrolls told him, he was totally changed from the placid, spiritless man he had been in recent weeks. He yelled and screamed against the officers that did it. I tried to hush him. I told him he shouldn't do that around the children. He ran out of the house in a rage and disappeared down the street.

James jumped up to go after him. Two hours later he was back. "I lost him. I'm worried, Annie. This is like he acted at the ranch after your burning. He might do something to hurt himself or others." James went back out to look again while Josie and I wondered what would happen now. James returned about midnight without him. The Carrolls and their children stayed the night with us. It was now our turn to crowd them in with us just as they had done at the ranch.

The next morning Pat walked in as if nothing had happened. He was confused. He stared ahead and, except for short answers to direct questions, he had nothing to say. I was terribly frightened. It was like the first few days at the Carrolls after I came home from the hospital. James went to Hayden's Flour Mill to tell them Pat was sick and wouldn't be in for the rest of the week.

The Carrolls were defeated. They made one more trip back to the ranch to harvest the vegetables that were left. After selling them to John Smith, they came back to stay one more night with us, then left for Ohio. I wanted them to stay but they were now afraid of Arizona and the rough ways of both the Indians and what they had seen of the Army. In many ways, I couldn't blame them. I knew they had to do what they thought was best for their family. Our farewell was tearful and wrenching for all of us.

Mr. Hayden had added a soap factory next to his mill and told James that he might try Pat there as a foreman. As more people had moved to Tempe and Phoenix they were finding that they no longer had access to the ingredients for making their own soap as they had in rural areas. We all made our own when we butchered animals and had plenty of wood ashes. Now Mr. Hayden bought fat from the butchering plants and instead of using ashes, he got other chemicals to finish the process.

Pat did return to work but he couldn't do the job as foreman. He was never the same. Charles Hayden was a good man and tried to find a place for him. He put Pat on in his blacksmith shop. Mr. Hayden was still big in the freighting business so Pat had wagons to work on again. I thought that might shake him out of his depression. Pat worked with Julio Marron and Sam Jarvis in the shop and I know they tried hard to help.

It was not to be. The second burning opened all the old wounds and apparently inflicted deeper ones. It was the beginning of the end for him. Three months later he was laid off. They said business wasn't very good and they didn't need him any more. I knew the real reason.

That October, there was a big gunfight in Tombstone. Three lawmen, the Earp brothers, and a friend, Doc Holliday, were involved. *The Tombstone Epitaph* said that they killed three cattlemen in 25 seconds.

CHAPTER 34

DESPAIR

The months drifted by. We had used most of our savings. Pat had reduced himself to almost a statue. He would sit on our porch and stare. Nothing that the children or I could say seemed to make a difference to him. He was dead but not buried. The children stayed in school. I started working in a laundry in Tempe and took in sewing jobs that I could work on at home in the evenings. We were able to pay our bills and nothing more.

In 1885, Pat stopped eating and spent most of the days in bed. A week later he died with only a few words to me in his last days. It was almost unbearable to see someone who had been so good at his job, so in love with his land, lose his desire to live. He withered away and all because of the dastardly deed that was done just for spite. I promised myself that I would spend the rest of my days proving to my family and to Pat in Heaven that we were right.

Later that summer, Tempe was shocked by the news of the death of Charles Hayden's young daughter. She ate too many green apples, they thought, and died of what was called indigestion.

At that time Mr. Hayden was one of the most prominent men in both Tempe and Phoenix. The daughter's name was Annie. Maybe that gave me more reason to grieve or perhaps because she was only seven years old, not much older than Veronica. I suppose I wanted to express my sympathy because Mr. Hayden had been so good to us in giving Pat a job and then taking him back when he was not well.

The best kind of pie I could make was pumpkin, and they were in season. Two weeks after the funeral I took two pies to his home and left them with their maid. I also wrote a sympathy note on the best letter paper I could find.

A few days later, a messenger from the Hayden Flour Mill called at my home one evening to ask if I could stop by Mr. Hayden's office the following day. Of course, I did. Mr. Hayden greeted me and said, "Mrs. White, that was thoughtful of you to bring us your special pies and the nice note. Thank you."

"You were kind to my Patrick when he was sick and needed a job. I'm very sorry about your little Anna, Mr. Hayden."

"Yes, we both know what it's like to have a tragedy in our family, don't we? I know about your loss on your ranch near Fort McDowell. Then my foreman told me of Pat's death last summer. I'm sorry for you, Mrs. White. He and I had some good conversations."

"Pat told me that you understood wagons. That made you a good man in his mind."

"I was a wagon master once. Had my own string of wagons carrying goods from Kansas City to Santa Fe. Then later from Tucson to the Army forts in Arizona. My men knew of Pat's wagons from the time he was a wheelwright at McDowell."

"I'm still hopeful that something will come of all my letters to Prescott, Mr. Hayden."

"If not, I'll be glad to help out in any way I can, Mrs. White." I thanked him and left feeling that I had an important person on my side.

Charles Hayden: *Carl Hayden gave me this after his father died.*

That fall the papers were full of the news about Geronimo. Although the Indians in this part of the territory were now confined to reservations, Geronimo and Natchez and their tribes in Southeast Arizona had still been giving the Army and the Mexicans a bad time. Finally, after General Crook had them worn down, General Miles got them to surrender at a place called Skeleton Canyon. The papers said it was the mirrors on top of mountains that finally scared them into giving up. Others said they were just tired of running and decided this was the only way. After this, there weren't any more organized groups of Indians fighting the Army out here.

At last I received a letter that gave me some hope. It was from the new Arizona Territorial Governor Conrad Zulick. It was a result of my many letters to Prescott. He said that he would be in Tempe visiting the Haydens in February of 1886 and would meet with me in Mr. Hayden's office. At that time I found out that Mr. Hayden had suggested the meeting. Governor Zulick promised to appoint an investigator to look into our claim.

We waited for the report which Governor Zulick said would be within a few months. The investigator turned out to be a Colonel Bevans, a retired Army officer living near Prescott. I found out later that Colonel Bevans was a land agent for the Arizona Territory. He inquired of citizens residing around the post and also interviewed John Y. T. Smith.

His report to Governor Zulick was:

"I have found the houses of Patrick White and James Carroll to be, in fact, off the military reservation of Fort McDowell. The burning and subsequent abandonment of their children in the desert was an outrageous act without basis in fact."

Colonel Arnold J. Bevans
November 18, 1887

Now we thought the matter would be resolved and our compensation paid. We could return to the ranch. Governor Zulick wrote me that the report had been referred to the Army. Later that year he wrote saying that all the Army denied doing anything wrong. He said he would forward the report to Washington but it would probably take several months to get a reply.

There was a big piece of news in 1886, I think it was, when George Wilson gave five acres for the building of a higher school in Tempe. I heard that Charles Hayden helped on that, too. It was decided to call it the Territorial Normal School. The second year, Kate enrolled. You can imagine how proud I was about that.

In May of 1887, we were shaken by what we thought was a big explosion. In a few hours, the telegraph office heard from Tucson that it was an earthquake and there was a lot of damage there. No property here was affected but it gave us a lot to talk about for a few days.

It was hard to believe, but we heard nothing about our claim for three years. I was getting affidavits from people I knew that were aware of what we had lost. I would include copies of these when I wrote to Prescott. I tried to get them to tell me who to write to in Washington. They would always say that it had to go through Prescott and they would take care of it.

My efforts even made the papers. I kept this clipping from the *Phoenix Daily Herald* of January 5, 1888:

Mrs. Annie White, formerly of Ft. McDowell and now residing in Tempe, has just returned from Prescott. Her claim for damages is still pending in both Prescott and in Washington, but she has possession of the land adjoining the reservation. She has sold a one-third interest to a Prescott gentleman for $1,000 on the contingency that a clear claim to her irrigating ditch can be obtained.

Nothing came of that since I never got any action on my claim. That was another wasted trip to Prescott but I had to try everything possible.

The seasons passed. John enrolled in the Normal School. It was hard to find the $20 for him and Kate twice each school year but they worked in the summers and helped with the fees.

I tried to think of things other than our loss. There was a big fire on Mill Avenue where the Coon-Burtis and Lon Forsee's stores were badly damaged. Later in the year the Tempe Daily News said, "The building boom here is still on the rampage. Houses are being built in all directions."

The younger children were in a new school that had been built at 8th and Mill Avenue. It had grown so much that it was now a two-story building. I worked full-time in the laundry. My sewing now provided a big part of our income for it was well known that I knew how to do it properly. When Kate graduated from the two years at the Normal school she found a job in Phoenix and moved into a room of her own close to work. John also graduated and went to work at the Hayden Flour Mill. He stayed at home and helped me around the house.

To save money, I decided to sell Daisy. She was getting old, I didn't need her for transportation and the three dollars a month for her corral and feed was more than I could justify.

I went to see Charles Hayden again. He complimented me by saying that John was a good worker. We talked again about Pat and their common interest in wagons. When I showed him Colonel Bevans report, he thought it was outrageous that everyone had stalled me for so long. He said we had enough to try another time for a settlement. He said if I could go to Prescott again, he would arrange for me to have a personal visit with Governor Zulick.

My trip was paid for by my savings from my sewing jobs. I had seven new affidavits with me that I thought should help my case. I still have copies of two of them:

E. B. Powell, being first duly sworn and deported says:

That he is over the age of twenty-one years and a resident of Maricopa County, Arizona Territory; that he is acquainted with one Annie White and has known her since 1875; that he has read the affidavit made by said Annie White and noted the statements therein made; that he was first duty sergeant of Company C, of 6th U.S. Cavalry commanded by Captain Chaffee and stationed at Fort McDowell during the years of 1875 to 1882; that during all of said time he was well acquainted with Annie White and has known her to be a hard-working woman; that she has always borne a good moral character; that on or about the 12th day of August 1880 that said Annie White was in the actual occupation of 640 acres of land or more, about five miles north-east of Fort McDowell on the Verde River, and had been there for three years or more prior thereto; that she and her husband, the late Patrick White, had erected a house on said land and for the purpose of irrigating said land had constructed a ditch or canal two and one half miles in length, leading from the Verde River to said land, and had on said land a number of horses, a large number of cattle, hogs and chickens; also a portion of said land under cultivation; that during said time the Whites were furnishing the troops, stationed at Fort McDowell, and citizens residing there with butter, eggs and milk, and was in a way to earn a large sum of money by so doing; that a detail was made from Co. C of 6th Cavalry, by order of Captain Chaffee, to burn the property of said Annie White on August 12th, 1880; that at the time said house was burned Annie White was on her way to Prescott, Arizona and her husband was away working at the upper canal; that their six children were left homeless and that the other soldiers sent blankets and food up to them until the Carroll family could help them; that the soldiers at the fort stated they had never witnessed anything like it.

(s) Edwin R. Powell

Sgt. Co. I, 6th Cavalry

Subscribed and sworn to before me this 13th day of March 1889

(s) James M. Gray

Notary Public

In addition to Sergeant Powell's statement, I had one from Benjamin Velasco who had the land below the post where we had our first milk cows while Patrick was still in the Army. John Y. T. Smith even gave me one but he had to be careful what he said. Though he wasn't the post trader now, he was still doing business in the area. He mostly testified to the good character of Pat and I. Others did, too. I got three that told about how Pat could never have sold liquor to the Indians and how I never had a house of ill repute.

This one from William Thomas talks about the value of our property at the time of the burning:

Territory of Arizona

County of Maricopa

Personally appeared before me, a Notary Public in and for the County aforesaid, William Thomas to me well known, who being duly sworn, deposes and says; that he is a resident of said County and has been for the past twenty-six years;

that he was well acquainted with Patrick White and Wife, in 1880, when they were living on their Ranch located some half mile or more North of the North boundary of the Fort McDowell Military Reservation, Arizona Territory, and of which they were dispossessed and their house and out buildings burned by the soldiers acting under orders based on the mistaken assumption that the White ranch was on the Military Reservation of Fort McDowell, Ariz.; that the house probably cost $250; that the corral which was destroyed, was a large one capable of holding some 200 cattle or more; that the Whites at that time owned about 150 head of cattle, about 70 of which were milch-cows, as I recollect it, for they sold milk at the Post and had to have good milch-cows; that the value of their herd I could not positively state, but think that it was around $12,000; that they had a large drove of hogs (60 or 70) worth about $400; that they had a lot of fowls; that they had some six or eight horses and two or three burros which were worth about $500; an Irrigation Ditch some three miles or so long, which I suppose cost them in the neighborhood of $8,000; with flumes and dams, and was in working order; that they had some 200 or more acres of the section of land they were on, under cultivation; that the expense per acre for clearing said land was at least five dollars per acre; that to the best of my belief the loss of the water-right for five years would be at least $10,000, as water rents for $2.55 per inch per year, since I understand they had a recorded right for 1,000 miner's inches of water.

(S) William Thomas
Subscribed and sworn to before me,
this 25th day of March, AD, 1889

(s) J. C. Phillips
Notary Public

I was told that I should knock down some of the rumors that the Kearneys, or someone, had spread about Pat and I. There was one person who I felt would do the job. It was Pat's former commanding officer, Captain Corliss. He had been transferred to Fort Whipple, on the edge of Prescott. Before I went to my meeting with Governor Zulick, I got an appointment with the Captain. I took a copy of Pat's discharge and told him what had happened.

Captain Corliss had heard about it. He said to me, "Annie, there must have been something powerful to cause all this trouble. I can't imagine what it was and I don't dare try to get involved in it. It is not in my control any longer."

"But Captain," I begged, "can't you help me somehow?" Captain Corliss sat still for a long time. Finally he took a piece of paper and wrote out these words that I have kept until this day:

To Whom It May Concern,

I knew Corporal Patrick White at Fort McDowell, Arizona Territory as an intelligent man beyond the ordinary and always a perfect gentleman.

Captain Augustus Corliss
Adjutant, Fort Whipple
Prescott, Arizona Territory
April 16, 1889

As the captain handed it to me he said, "Annie, we go back a long way. If I could, I would say more but this will have to do. I wish you the best." He had a pained look on his face as he said goodbye.

Governor Zulick acted sympathetic. He said, "I can see how you feel wronged. Captain Chaffee said you were on the reservation and Colonel Bevans tells me that you weren't. You certainly have a good case."

I asked, "Can't you just say that to the Army or to the government in Washington and get them to restore our land and pay for our losses?"

"My dear Mrs. White, I wish it were that easy. I tried to do that right after Colonel Bevans' report. But we are only a territory and no one in Washington worries too much about citizen's rights out here. I don't think the Army is going to admit they made a mistake."

"But what can I do, Governor?"

"I can only think of one other thing. I'm a good friend of Congressman Newlands of Nevada. He's a good man who knows the value of water in this part of the country. He will appreciate the value of your canals. I will send him this file and ask him if he would help you in Washington during this next session of Congress."

"Please do that. I'll travel there if it will help our case."

"You will be hearing from me, Mrs. White. Good day."

I returned home feeling that I had someone in authority that was on my side. Governor Zulick made it clear that it depended on his friendship with Mr. Newlands. I wished now that we were a state and that I had an Arizona Congressman to ask for help.

I had almost given up hope of hearing anything when a letter copy arrived.

Representative Francis G. Newlands
House Office Building
Washington, D. C.

Dear Congressman Newlands,   *July 11, 1890*

Pursuant to our exchange of letters in April of this year, I am acknowledging your agreement to aid a Territory citizen, Mrs. Anna White of Tempe, Arizona. By copy of this letter I am advising her that you will schedule an appointment for her with you and your staff in Washington sometime this fall.

It is my belief that Mrs. White's claim has merit and that it should be pushed forward in Congress by a respected member such as yourself.

Thanking you in advance, I am,

Yours truly,
Former Arizona Territorial Governor Conrad. M. Zulick

cc: Mrs. Anna White,
     157 West Third Street
     Tempe, Arizona Territory

The waiting continued. In December I received a letter from Representative Newlands suggesting that I come to Washington in February. I lost that letter so I can't include it here. But I did make my plans and withdrew $300 from our savings account to pay my expenses.

I called on Charles Hayden to tell him of my trip. I was lucky that he took the time to see me for his mill had been destroyed by fire just a few weeks before. It was another example of what a fine man he was.

He knew of Mr. Newlands and thought he would be a good one to push my case through Congress. Mr. Hayden also suggested a hotel in

Washington that was clean, safe and reasonably priced. Not only did Charles Hayden help Pat and I, he was an honest man with good character. All who knew him said that he didn't use tobacco, drink any alcohol and never used cuss words. You couldn't say that about very many men in those days.

My trip to Washington was long and tiring. The city was big and construction jobs were going on everywhere. It was dusty and windy and cold. I was glad that the carriage driver knew how to find the hotel Mr. Hayden had recommended.

My first meeting with Mr. Newlands was formal but pleasant. I was surprised at how young he was. He told me that he was just elected as a representative two years before. He had already seen my documents and thought it was worth pressing ahead. To gain support, he suggested that I visit several other offices to show them the strong evidence I had.

That next week in Washington was filled with frustration as I was pushed from one office to another. I had no idea that there were so many departments. Even though Representative Newlands' office had set up appointments, most of them would tell me that I needed to see someone else. Then at the next office I would be told that I should go some other place. I had all my affidavits and letters from respected people in my black sewing satchel that I had used for years. Some of the office people that saw me many times that week started kidding me about it since it never left my side.

I was all by myself and I was frightened. Washington was then much larger than Baltimore had been when I was there. It was more confusing than New York. I spent very little money on food for I knew I was using our savings. This gave me an urgency about getting my business accomplished. Still, the days became a blur of one waiting room, then another. Many people told me I should hire an attorney but I didn't want to spend the money.

At a meeting on my last day, Mr. Newlands promised that he would introduce a bill into Congress to repay us for our losses. He said it would be called House Bill #1205. When he told me that, it was a glorious moment. He cautioned that, as a new member of the House, he didn't yet have a lot of power. Since he felt we had a good claim, he was willing to do it as a favor to his friend, former Governor Zulick.

He gave me a copy of the bill. I still have it. It looked so official that I was certain we were to at last receive what we were due. Here is the language they used:

THE HOUSE OF REPRESENTATIVES
OF THE UNITED STATES

A BILL

H. R. 1205

For the relief of Annie D. White and the heirs of Patrick White.

Be it enacted by the Senate and House of Representatives of the United States of America in Congress assembled, That the Secretary of the Treasury is hereby directed to pay out of any moneys in the treasury of the United States not otherwise appropriated, to Annie D. White, widow of Patrick White, deceased, thirty-eight thousand dollars, as full compensation for the wrongful and illegal ejectment of said Annie D. White and Patrick White from lands held by them in the county of Maricopa, in the Territory of Arizona, and for the loss of personal property, and for the violation of any rights of said Annie D. White and Patrick White by the officers or soldiers in the military service of the United States in the year eighteen hundred and eighty.

I thanked Mr. Newlands as much as I could and immediately left for Arizona on the next train. I memorized #1205 for I thought that we were finally getting repayment for Pat's loyalty to the Army for those 20 years. At last we would recover at least part of our losses.

In Tempe, I told our family the good news. We even thought that we might take the money and go back to our ranch. We could start over. Kate and John were old enough to do most of the farm work. We could hire someone to help. Both of them had been steady and dependable workers.

Again the routine of school for the children, laundry work and sewing began. John had found a room of his own and a short time later he was married and moving to Bisbee to work in the copper mines. Later he became the sheriff of Cochise County where Tombstone is located.

Sally, our third child, had never wanted to work on the ranch and didn't seem to mourn its loss. She remained a shy, sensitive person who was more interested in drawing pictures of the desert and the beautiful flowers that brightened our small yard in Tempe. Sally didn't want to move away after graduating from high school. I didn't mind since the house now seemed large for our reduced family. She stayed on and worked in a book store just a few blocks from us near the Territorial Normal School. She attended the school and graduated two years later, married David McCarthy and settled in Phoenix.

All of us in Tempe had a real scare when the Salt River had its biggest flood in history. It came up into the basement of the new Hayden's Mill and within a few feet of our house. A few squatter's houses closer to the river were swept away. Some lost their lives. The big bridge across the river that had replaced the ferry was washed away and so was the railroad bridge. In a few days the river went back down as fast as it rose, and the cleaning began.

Tempe was getting winter visitors who had lots of money and were looking for a warm place to spend the winter. One Kansas man was so impressed with our irrigation ditches that he wrote back to the newspaper, "The Salt River valley is a place where every man can be his own rain maker." The paper said that our little town had 2,000 people now.

We had some big excitement in Tempe in the middle of the summer of 1892. One of the last men in the Graham family was murdered right on West Broadway just as he was leaving town. People thought he was killed by one of the Tewksburys since the two families had been fighting each other for several years. It was a part of what was called the Pleasant Valley War out beyond the Mazatzal Mountains. I believe they did convict the Tewksbury man after a trial.

The next year and a half passed with no word from Washington. Although Representative Newlands had told me that it might take a long time, I was expecting to hear any day that House Bill 1205 had passed. I thought of the many ways we could use the money we would receive. I finally got too impatient for an answer and wrote Representative Newlands' office in Washington. The reply, three months later, put me into my deepest despair since Pat's death.

Mrs. Anna White,
157 West Third St.
Tempe
Arizona Territory   *May 16, 1894*

Dear Mrs. White,

I have been advised by Representative Newlands that House Bill 1205, that he had proposed to settle the destruction of your property in Arizona Territory, has failed to receive sufficient support to reach the floor of the House.

Representative Newlands asks me to convey to you his sincere regrets that he was unable to secure some recompense for your grievous inconvenience in the summer of 1880.

Sincerely yours,
Edward M. Strater
Assistant to Representative Newlands
Washington, D. C.

Veronica found me in tears as I held the letter in my hand. "Darling, I don't know what else to do." My sweet cherub daughter leaned her head against my shoulder and tried to comfort me. "Mom, you've tried everything. Those rascals are all alike. I think they just protect each other."

"Dear, I can't believe they would do that. Mr. Newlands seemed like he was concerned about what had happened. He said he would try to get us paid back."

"But see what they do now!" Veronica was angry. "Just give it up, Mother, and let's get on with our lives as best we can."

I tried to do that but every night, my thoughts before going to sleep were of the burning, the livestock scattering in the desert and the soldiers riding away. It was so unfair. It haunted me.

My life settled into a routine as I watched Tempe grow. We got a telephone in our house for the first time in 1895. That same year Mr. Hayden sold his blacksmith shop, the last place Pat worked, to Joseph Ford. Later that year it was destroyed by fire.

The Tempe News reported that Elisha Reavis was found dead along a trail south of his ranch in the Superstition Mountains. Although Pat never said much against him, I felt that he wasn't truthful with us. He made out like he owned the land north of McDowell free and clear. We apparently just bought the water rights.

Ned couldn't wait to get on his own. I had to talk hard to keep him in school until he finished the 12th grade. He was a gifted poet and won honors in his English and literature classes. Ned started working at the Congress Mine near Wickenburg as soon as he graduated. It wasn't long before he was being called the "Miner's Poet." He later moved to Bisbee and became known as the "Bard of Brewery Gulch."

Ned wrote lots of poems but the one I appreciated most was the one he named "The Silent Trail" in honor of his father, my Pat. As a reminder, here are the first and last verses of that one:

> Onward, Westward toward the sunset
> Over prairie, hill and vale,
> He has passed and gone forever
> Down the lonely, silent trail.
>
> ******
>
> Yes, they are gone, the old frontiersmen
> With the legends of the West,
> They are sleeping on God's mesas
> In His twilight shores of rest.

Willie followed John to southeast Arizona. He worked in the mines at Bisbee and later was a Deputy Sheriff along with Ned. They both worked for John who was still sheriff in Tombstone, the county seat of Cochise County.

Veronica, my talented seamstress was still here. She was also my happy companion and often kept me from falling into a deep depression.

As I look back on those times, I wonder how we managed to get by. I think it was because all of my children were doing well. I believe that our experiences on the lower ranch and on the Reavis place made an indelible mark on us. Even with the hardships, I think it was for the best. We sure learned that hard work would pay off and it was working out just fine until that awful day when the Army betrayed us.

CHAPTER 35

ONE MORE VISIT

A longing for the ranch still burned within me. One part of me hated what had happened but another part reminded me how much I loved that river and the two ranch sites where we had realized our dreams.

One day the wound was opened again when I heard two men discussing the news at the grocery store. They were talking about the war in Cuba where Teddy Roosevelt and his Rough Riders from Arizona were fighting the Spanish. One man said, "I hear that Colonel Chaffee was a hero when we took San Juan Hill. That's the man who was in charge of Fort McDowell about 20 years ago."

The reply was, "That's going to make heroes of all of our Arizona Rough Riders, too."

I wanted to shout out to both of them that Chaffee had ruined my family and that he couldn't be a hero. Instead I just turned away and went home feeling low again.

I had to keep trying. I got a horse from Finch's Livery Barn and rode out to McDowell without telling anyone. It had been eight years since the post was closed in 1890. The north line fence was right where it always had been—at least a half-mile below our house. Demarbiex's hut was in ruins. They never burned his house as they did ours and the Carrolls.

All that was left at our home site were the foundation rocks and the hole in the ground where Pat and John had dug down to set the rocks and get us sheltered a bit by the earth. I could still see lots of wire around and some nails. The rains and wind were covering up the traces of what had once been a busy and profitable ranch.

The canals were still there but filling in with weeds and trash. After we were burned out no one tried to do anything with them. The sage and creosote bushes were already growing back on the fields we had cleared. It was a painful trip and I told myself that I'd never do it again. I still had trouble believing that the burning had happened the way it did.

On the way back to Tempe I rode down the irrigation ditches the Army had once used to bring water to the post farm. Several small shacks were now located near the big ditch. They were using the water to irrigate some vegetable gardens. Below the post I crossed to the east bank of the river and saw our lower ranch site. Only a few pieces of wire wrapped around trees remained. Most had been washed away by a big flood that spread out over the east side three years ago. There were also cattle grazing along the river. They belonged to Pancho Monroy. His ranch buildings were farther downstream on the Verde. I remembered that one of his boys was at Cuba School with Kate and John. It was dusk when I returned to Tempe.

My job at the laundry was just as hard as ever but I did get two raises in pay and was earning enough to pay all my bills. All my sewing money went back into savings and now it was growing again.

Veronica had a good job as a dress maker. She actually was better than I and she earned more money at it than I ever did. She still lived with me and I was glad for that. Later she married Gerald Wood and moved to Bisbee where he worked in the mines.

Now that there were no children at home to care for, I again turned my attention to getting repaid for the burning. Every time the children would tell me that I should forget it, I would remember all that we had lost. The injustice of it caused me to become bitter against any form of government and especially the Army. Each letter of rejection and each referral to some other office reinforced and drove my resentment deeper. I wrote to Representative Newlands once to ask for another hearing but one of his staff wrote back saying that since the bill had failed, the Congressman didn't feel he could bring it up again without any new facts. I didn't have any new ones—just the same old ones that should have been good enough a long time ago!

Later that year, I heard that Charles Hayden had suddenly taken ill and had died. At his funeral I met his son, Carl, who came back from Stanford University for the funeral. I told him of his father's kindness to me after our loss. To my surprise, he said, "I've heard about it, Mrs. White. My father talked about the wagons your husband made and how he came to work at the mill after the burning."

"I'm surprised that you know about that, Mr. Hayden. I have been to Prescott and to Washington to plead my case but so far no one will give us our due."

"My father said he arranged for you to see Governor Zulick."

"Yes, and the governor set me up to see Representative Newlands in Washington. He tried to help but the bill didn't get passed."

"Dad always thought that you received a bad deal out there on the river."

"We did, Mr. Hayden. Your father was a fine man and he did try to improve our chances."

"I'm sure he did, Mrs. White. I'll be coming back here to work in the business. If I can be of any assistance, please call on me." Soon after that, I heard that Carl Hayden was elected to the Tempe Town Council.

Two more years passed with no response from my letters. Territorial Governors came and went, with none of them taking an interest in my affairs even though I wrote to all of them.

The Tempe newspaper began following the big news story of 1903—the search for more water for irrigation. Each year, during the two rainy seasons, the Salt River would be full of water—sometimes too much. Then the rest of the year it was dry and there was no water available for the crops. The local canals were no good when the Salt was dry. It was obvious that a dam was needed to store the extra water but no one had the money to build it.

I read that Carl Hayden was planning to travel to Washington to testify in hearings on that subject. I saw that the person in charge of the hearings was Senator Newlands. That was the first time I knew that he was now a senator. When Mr. Hayden returned from Washington, I got an appointment to see him at the Tempe city government offices.

He remembered that I had visited Mr. Newlands in Washington several years earlier. He also told me that when he was reviewing the status of the Salt and Verde Rivers, Senator Newlands remembered the Verde River since my claim was for land that was on the Verde. The Senator had said that he was sorry he could not get something done. I told Mr. Hayden of my ride out to our ranch and that the reservation fence was still where it always had been—one-half mile south of our house.

"Mrs. White, you're a Tempe resident and I'm on the Town Council. I'm supposed to be helping our citizens in any way I can and I wish I could find a way to help you on this."

"I think you could help me. I would like to have you see the lay of the land and the exact situation we had there when the burning happened. Then I'd like to show you where that boundary fence is—just like it was 23 years ago."

He sat there a few seconds, then sat up straight, pounded his fist on the desk, and said, "I'll do it! I owe it to you and Mr. White—and to my father who liked your husband a lot." He quickly consulted his calendar and asked, "How about next Thursday? I have an open day."

"That's fine, Mr. Hayden. I appreciate this."

"Just one thing, Mrs. White. You will have to stop this 'Mr. Hayden' business. I haven't done anything to deserve that kind of formality. If I'm to spend the day with you on a long ride like this, you must call me Carl. That's what I would prefer. Please."

"Yes, sir, Mr. Hay...uh..., Carl. It may be warm and it will be a long day—let's get an early start."

"How about six o'clock at the mill? I'll arrange two horses for us."

Carl was at the mill as promised. We walked to Finch's Livery for our horses and then rode to the wagon road up along the Salt River.

Just before we got to Red Mountain we passed the old ruins of Maryville off to the right by the river. I showed him where the village was when we lived at McDowell. I told him about the big parties that were attended by the officers and wives from the post. Several nice stores and businesses had once been there. Now most of the buildings had been torn down by the Mormons. They used the lumber in starting their town of Lehi on the south bank of the Salt.

After Maryville the road turned up the canyon to the ridge overlooking the Verde Valley. Even though he was a native of Arizona, he admitted that he hadn't spent much time in the open desert around Tempe and Phoenix. I was liking him better all the time. Even though he was an elected town official, he didn't act snobbish or put on airs with me.

At one point he said, "You and Mr. White were born in Ireland, weren't you?"

"Yes, we were."

"Maybe that's another good reason for my trying to help you. My fiance, Nan, was also born in Ireland. I met her at Stanford."

I learned that she was from County Cork in a little town not far from the city of Cobh, where Mother and Father and I departed for America so long ago.

As we rode I told him what had happened at Fort McDowell. I told about our lower ranch and the killing of Betsey Rollins and Pat's letter. He was polite and made some notes in a little book he had with him. He wasn't used to riding and several times had to get off and walk around to get the cramps out of his legs. By the time we got to the old McDowell grounds he had loosened up a bit and was able to laugh at himself and his lack of experience on a horse. I felt like I was a pretty sturdy woman and let him know how I'd worked and how many miles I could ride without rest. I wanted him to know that I'd seen some rough times and knew what hard work was.

The ride past the old buildings at McDowell was sad. Like Maryville, many of them had been torn down for the boards. The first walls had been adobe and the first roofs just brush and mud, but later logs and even some sawed boards had been shipped in from Ft. Whipple. Some of the officers' houses were made out of good lumber. The squatters that came in after the post was abandoned made good use of these to build their shacks. The stables and barracks that were always adobe were melting down into the ground. There were just ridges where each wall had been. Anything of value had been scavenged long ago.

Carl told me that he heard in Washington that there was talk of making this a government reservation again. This time it might be used for Indians, he said. I told him that a lot of the Indians in the territory knew all about McDowell because they used to come in every two weeks for rations and to be counted.

More people were living along the irrigation ditches than when I'd been out here 5 years before. Some had built lean-to sheds beside their one-room shacks. I told Carl that's what we did when the children kept coming along. Most of the shacks looked like they didn't expect to live there very long. Either that, or they didn't have money to build something better. I showed him where the Frenchman lived. Not much was left to mark the place.

By noon we arrived at the old north line of the post. Most of the wires were down but I could still show him where the fence line and the road to our place was located. I showed him the Carroll ruins and then we walked toward the river to the place where we had lived. We looked at the fence posts from the chicken yard—some of the tangled wire was still there. I pointed out the old hog pens and the cattle corrals. Then I showed him where we kept our horses. There was enough variation in the posts and wire so that he could tell the difference. He was making notes furiously in his notebook.

As we walked to the edge of the depression where our house had been I started to tell him what we had there. I only got a few words out and, without any warning, my voice choked and tears came. He didn't know how to react. He tried to offer me his handkerchief, then halfway opened his arms to me.

"Please, Mrs. White," he said. "Please don't."

At first I was embarrassed. Here was a man younger than my John, and I was acting like a school girl in front of him. As I tried to compose myself and explain about our house, I completely broke down. I turned away and leaned against a mesquite limb. The memories overwhelmed me and I could not speak. I could not look up. I was suffocated by what had been—and by the desolation here now.

I had not expected to display my feelings in this way. All day I had tried to convince this man that I was tough and disciplined and capable of taking care of whatever I faced. Now my show was over. He would see that I was a pretender. He will brush me off as just a foolish woman without any business sense. But I didn't care. It was how I felt and nothing could be done about it. I put my head on my arms and let my body shudder with the sobs that couldn't be buried any longer.

Since the burning I had not allowed this to happen in front of others. It was my job to stay strong for Pat and the family. For some reason, when I rode out here before, these emotions didn't take over like they did today in front of this young stranger.

My whole being trembled with what might have been. I felt as if I would be sick to my stomach. But then the wave passed. I cleared my throat and wiped my eyes. I composed myself. I told Carl that I was sorry for that display but that I just couldn't help it.

"Mrs. White," he said, "you surely don't need to apologize. I can imagine what you must have gone through."

With that, I resumed my listing of the property we lost and how Pat was affected by it. Although our time there was getting short, I rode with him to the river and showed him the canal that was carved out of the sandstone river banks. He didn't know that it was made by the Indians many hundred years before. Then I traced the path of the canal where it was irrigating our fields around the house.

We rode upriver a bit so I could show him the rocks that we called the "needles." We talked about the two and a half miles of canal Pat and James had finished before the burning and how much it was worth. I told him about our claim for 1000 miner's inches of water and what it would have meant to us. Carl made notes as fast as he could write.

On the way back to town we didn't talk much. I had said all I had to say and Carl seemed deep in thought. Once he said, "I had no idea there was this much going on out here so many years ago. Dad used to talk about Fort McDowell. Now I can imagine what it was like. I thought the only real civilization around here was in Phoenix and Tempe."

We left our horses at the livery barn and Carl walked me home. As we parted, I think he was too timid to shake my hand. He took off his hat and partly bowed, "Mrs. White, I want to say that this has been a great learning experience for me. My father taught me to help those who have suffered misfortune or injustice. I'l try to help you with my report to Senator Newlands."

"Thank you, and good day, Carl," I said.

As I thought of our trip, I was reminded of how the burning changed the lives of the children. In spite of the tragedy, all of them were doing just fine with their lives. I was determined to stay focused on my

Carl Hayden: *I asked for this after he started helping me. He said it was taken the last year he was at Stanford.* ARIZONA STATE UNIVERSITY ARCHIVES

one mission—to set things right with the Army. I couldn't have known what a turning point that day's trip would become.

CHAPTER 36

REVIVAL

In late 1903, I received a letter from Carl Hayden saying that Senator Newlands was to be in Phoenix and Tempe the next month. He asked me to meet with he and the senator at his Tempe Town Council office on the first Monday of February. I took a half-day off from my job and met them there.

Carl greeted me in a very friendly manner. I was pleased for I thought he might have taken me for a foolish old lady after my breakdown at the ranch that day. "Mrs. White," he said, "we're fortunate that the senator is visiting us. Besides working on our irrigation problems, the senator was interested in my report after our trip to your ranch site on the Verde."

"I'm glad," I said.

Senator Newlands remembered my visit to Washington. "Mrs. White," he began, "Carl surely agreed with your contention that you weren't on the military post when your house was burned and your livestock destroyed."

"Of course we weren't, Senator. That's what we've said all along."

"I know, and I tried to get something through Congress a long time ago, as you know, but there were powerful forces against me." The Senator paused and took out a small stack of papers from his case.

"This is a bill that passed the last session of Congress. President Roosevelt has signed it. There are 37 pages here but the important thing that affects your claim is that the old Fort McDowell post is going to become an Indian reservation."

"I don't see how that makes any difference," I said.

"It may make a lot of difference, Mrs. White," he said. "Another provision in this bill is that all persons who have lived on the former military property will be paid a fee to vacate the land. The amount they will be paid depends on how many improvements they made on the military property."

"But we weren't on the Army's land!" Then I began to see what the senator was getting at. "You mean...?"

"Yes, Mrs. White, there is nothing in here that says when the improvements had to have been made or even if they are still usable. Carl and I have read it very carefully in thinking about your case and we think you can apply for restitution under this bill."

"Even if it has been over 23 years since our property was burned?"

"Yes, there are no time limits and we can prove from the post records and newspaper clippings what actually happened." The senator seemed to be getting excited for me as he outlined the plan he and Carl had made.

"What do I need to do now?"

"You will have to hire an attorney," Carl said. "We can't prepare your actual entry for being included in the payment. There is an application form and it must be accompanied by a statement that the attorney should prepare in the proper manner. I have a copy of the application. Send the whole thing to Senator Newlands' office in Washington as soon as you complete it."

The senator stood up. He cautioned me that we couldn't claim any of the profits we could have made in the 23 years since the burning. We could only include just what our property and livestock was worth at the time. He said that we shouldn't say anything about the burning since the bill didn't ask for dates. I could tell that it was time to go. "Thank you, Senator Newlands. If this works out, my family and I will bless you with our prayers."

Carl ushered me out and gave me names of three attorneys in Tempe. He said any one of them could do the job.

As I walked back to my house, I found myself humming aloud for the first time in months. At last I had important people on my side and they seemed to want to help. Even though I knew we weren't on the Army's land, if I could get paid this way it would finally justify what Pat and I did so long ago.

The attorney charged me $20 but I didn't care. I attached Blumer Brashear's affidavit saying he thought our property was worth $38,000. Then I put in William Thomas' statement that he thought the value was $37,250. Also Frank Sheridan's sworn statement that he put everything at $43,000. I didn't include any of the ones that talked about the burning or what the increased number of livestock would have been worth over the years. After sending in the forms and statements, I tried to forget it for I knew it would take a long time for any action. But every day I found myself thinking of something else I should have included in our list of lost property.

In 1903, John Y. T. Smith died at his home on Adams Street in Phoenix. I was sorry to hear it for I had good memories of our business dealings with him at Fort McDowell.

Summer and fall passed and no word. Then a letter came from Washington that again broke my heart. I had promised myself that I wouldn't get my hopes too high—but I had. The Senator and Carl Hayden had been so sure this would do it. The letter was short:

Mrs. Anna White
157 West Third Street
Tempe
Arizona Territory   *January 8, 1904*

Dear Mrs. White,

   Re: House Bill #257—Appropriations and Restitution Act for the Fort McDowell, Arizona Territory property scheduled to become Yavapai Indian Reservation.

   This is to advise you that your claim for your dwellings, irrigation ditches and corrals located on what was formerly the Fort McDowell Military Reservation has been denied.

   A careful survey was taken prior to turning this property over to the Bureau of Indian Affairs. The legal description of your property as shown in your application is clearly not a part of the land that was the military reservation and therefore not subject to the restitution provisions of this bill.

   Sincerely yours,
   Captain Ernest L. Perkins
   Adjutant, Joint Congressional Committee
   U.S. Army/Bureau of Indian Affairs
   Washington, D. C.

cc: Senator Francis G. Newlands
    Senate Office Building
    Washington, D. C.

I sat on my porch with the letter in my hand. Hot waves of nausea began to sweep over me. The senator had seemed so sure that this would be the answer. Another blow. How many more could I stand? Why try again?

Strangely, though, after the initial shock of another rejection, I was more calm and composed than I had been for months. I sat in a state of detachment, observing myself from afar. After all, I had tried—the

227

Senator had tried. I couldn't have asked for more cooperation from him and from Carl Hayden. We did our best. "Let it go, Annie," I told myself.

My thoughts drifted.

Patrick, I tried to do this for you—for all the hard work you and James and I did out there. I've fought all the fights I can handle. It must be time to give up.

Then I re-read the letter. "Your property...is clearly not a part of the land that was the military reservation." I read it again. "That's it!" I exclaimed out loud.

I could barely contain my enthusiasm for what I now saw as the answer to the dilemma that had tormented us for 23 years. My pen scratched furiously that night. I kept this copy of my letter:

Senator Francis G. Newlands
Senate Office Building
Washington, D. C.   *January 19, 1904*

Dear Senator Newlands,

I have received the letter from Captain Perkins dated Jan. 8, 1904. This made me feel bad that they won't pay us as we thought but I want to call your attention to their statement that our land was not on the military reservation.

That is what we have been saying for 23 years and now the Army has admitted it. Can't we use this letter as the reason for paying us as they should have a long time ago? Please take this to the Army and maybe you can get it straightened out at last.

Sincerely yours,
Mrs. Anna White
157 West Third Street
Tempe
Arizona Territory
copy to Mr. Carl Hayden

I took Carl's copy over to the mill since we lived so close. I knew that he spent about half of his time there. A few days later he had one of his office men deliver me a note that I've since misplaced. It said that he thought I raised a good point but since we had made the point many years ago perhaps it was best not to get my hopes raised too high.

The waiting began again. My correspondence with the children living in Tombstone and Bisbee occupied my time when I wasn't sewing. The job at the laundry was a little easier, for I now supervised three younger women who did the hardest work. I even got to sit at a desk for part of the day.

Carl Hayden was so well regarded that he was elected Treasurer of Maricopa County. This was an important job and made him very well known all around these parts. He was still very involved in the irrigation projects. Senator Newlands' name was mentioned a lot in our papers because he promoted a bill that made it possible for a dam to be started upstream on the Salt River. The businessmen said it would hold enough water to irrigate all the farms in the valley.

My evenings and weekends of sewing were more difficult because my eyesight was not as good as it used to be. Instead of one lamp, I now used two to give me enough light and even then, on the smaller stitches, I could tell that I wasn't making them as even and fine as I once did. My customers never complained but somewhere around this time I started turning down the jobs that involved fancier work.

One of the highlights of this time of my life was this article in *The Tombstone Epitaph* in its September 12th issue in 1904.

> The appearance of the three White brothers, John, Bill and Ned, gives confidence to the citizens who believe in keeping the laws, and their eyes of cold steel keep the unruly from taking chances. These three tall men, always in business suits, ride with easy grace on their horses and are courteous under every circumstance. But let a lawless man cross their path and their response is quick and effective. Tombstone is safer with the White brothers on the watch for trouble.

That's enough to make a mother proud! Here I had three boys working together as lawmen in Tombstone, just 13 years after the famous Earp brothers.

Ned also got recognized in a book about him and poems. It was called "The Bard of Brewery Gultch." Carl Hayden was even more well-known then and he wrote a nice statement for the front of the book. This is how it read:

A TRIBUTE
by CARL HAYDEN

I am glad to know that a book is to be published containing the poems of Ned White, with whom I was well acquainted.

I first met him when he came with his father and mother

229

John F. White: *Taken when he was Sheriff of Cochise County in* *Tombstone.*

from Fort McDowell to Tempe, where his father was employed by my father in connection with our flour-milling business. His sister and I graduated in the same class from the Arizona Territorial Normal School in 1896. I am sure that the book will be of great interest to many people in Arizona

During the summer, I received a letter from Senator Newlands' office. I couldn't find that one, either, but it said that the senator was hopeful that something could be done about my claim and that he was still working on it.

Then this letter arrived:

Mrs. Anna White
157 West Third Street
Tempe
Arizona Territory   *December 11, 1904*

Dear Mrs. White,

  This is to request your presence in my office in Washington during the second week of January of next year. It appears that the Senate will be able to hear testimony on your claim at that time. The points you have raised about the Army's reversal of opinion on the location of your ranch will be the subject of our inquiry. It would be most helpful if you could be here.

  Please advise me if you can travel to Washington at that time.

Sincerely,
Francis G. Newlands, Senator
U. S. Congress
Washington, D. C.
cc: Carl Hayden
   Hayden Flour Mill
   Tempe, Arizona Territory

My answer was quick. I told the senator that I would be there. My savings account was raided again. I was really encouraged this time. I had promised myself that I would not again get excited about my prospects. Even so, I must admit that my pulse quickened a bit when I thought of this trip.

I put all my affidavits and letters in my little black bag and took the train to Maricopa Wells, where I boarded the main line train for the East.

This time I knew where to go—I wasn't afraid. Senator Newlands made me feel welcome and seemed very happy about something. After I was seated in his office, he pressed a buzzer and a secretary opened his door.

"Now you can bring him in, Eleanor," the senator said.

I turned to see who was coming and there was Carl Hayden! He had a big smile on his face and quickly gave me a hug just as if I was his own mother. You can imagine how welcome I felt.

"Mrs. White," Carl said, "this has been our little secret. When the senator was able to arrange this hearing on your claim, he scheduled it during the same week I was to be here to testify on the irrigation project back home.

Senator Newlands added, "Mrs. White, Carl Hayden is becoming one of the experts that the Senate is depending on to get my new bill working in Arizona. You picked a good man to help your cause along back here."

"He's too modest," Carl said. "He's the one who knows how to get things done. He learned the ropes in the House and he knows the water needs in the west. Now that he's a senator, he has the force to help us in many ways."

"We don't have a lot of time today, Mrs. White. I've made appointments for you and Carl to meet with some of the other senators on the committee. Then one week from today, please be here at 9 o'clock and we will spend a few minutes before the hearing convenes at 9:30. I'm optimistic, Mrs. White."

Now they said we could talk about the burning. "Everything," Senator Newlands said as I left their office.

My case was to be heard before a Joint Senate Committee of the Army and Bureau of Indian Affairs. They didn't meet often and weren't anxious to hear what I had to say anyway, according to the senator.

Carl went with me to meet with five members of the committee. He said we shouldn't try to tell the whole story to each one but just make one point if we could. So with one, he would get me to tell about losing all our livestock and chickens when the corrals were torn down. With another, he would have me describe how Pat reacted to the burning and how he was never "right" again. With some, we talked about what Elisha Reavis had told us and how we tried to file our claim under the Desert Land Act.

With one senator from Colorado, I explained about filing our claim for 1000 miner's inches of water from the Verde and how we had posted the notice on trees near there. This man knew how valuable water was.

He seemed real impressed that we had done two and one-half miles of work on the new canal and that the burning had destroyed any chance to use the water. I showed him some of the affidavits about the canal value.

I was on my own for a few half-days because Carl had other business there. He was also preparing for his own testimony. I reflected on what had happened since the burning. Our family had been devasted by those acts of violence but I felt satisfied that my actions were within the law and not destructive.

When we both met with the senator on the morning of our hearing, Carl reported the results of our visits to Senator Newlands. The senator said that he was encouraged by what he had heard so far.

Carl very gently said, "Mrs. White, I would like to urge you to try not to show too much emotion as you testify. It's not that you shouldn't show your disappointment but it's better if you don't lose your temper or something like that." I knew he was afraid I would break down as I had done at the ranch site with him.

I said, "I'll try hard but if they press me too much, I don't know what might happen."

Senator Newlands patted my shoulder and said, "You just tell them what you've told us and you'll be just fine."

With that we went into a room that was larger than the entire laundry building where I worked. I was trembling but both men ushered me into one of the seats facing 14 men sitting behind a long table. There was gold paint decorating the front of the table and gold figures around the room on moldings just below the ceiling. I had never seen such a fancy place.

The chairman started by saying, "I see we have the woman with the black bag with us today." Some others smiled, then the chairman also smiled and said, "Welcome, Mrs. White, you have made quite a name for yourself with your black bag full of papers."

I didn't know if they were making fun of me so I just said, "Yes, sir."

Most of them were friendly. The questions were about things I had already told when Carl and I met with some of them earlier. A few questions were about the claims Lt. Kearney had made against Pat. I started to pull the affidavits out of my bag but Senator Newlands rose and very carefully said, "Senator, if you will please refer to Exhibits E and F you will see a number of affidavits from respected individuals that rebut each and every one of these charges."

One senator asked if it was true that Pat had written a wild letter to the

While I waited in Senator Newlands' office, I asked his secretary if she had any pictures of him. I wanted to show my children how young-looking he was. This was his campaign picture when he was elected to the Senate in 1903.   SALT RIVER PROJECT

editor of the New York Herald. This time I looked at Senator Newlands before I answered. He nodded his head to tell me to answer the question myself. I took a deep breath and began: "Senator Davis, I never saw the letter that my husband wrote but I do know that he wrote after he saw a story praising the Indians and saying we should give the land back to them. This editor's column said that the Army should not be protecting civilians in Arizona Territory." Then I went on to tell about Betsey and Howard Rollins and how much Pat and I had liked them. I described Betsey and how pretty and lively she was. Then I went through what Howard had told us about how she had been abused before she was murdered—and that she was with child when all this happened.

By the end of the story, I was raising my voice. I think the senator was afraid I would lose my composure. He started to stand but before he could speak, I felt that I had to say something else. I will always remember how it came out for it was the last testimony I gave.

"Gentlemen, maybe my Pat shouldn't have written that letter but the government says they want settlers out in the West. Don't they need to be protected just like people everywhere? All Indians aren't good, just like all white men aren't good. Pat's letter was no reason for our being burned out. Now even the Army says we weren't on the reservation. So there wasn't any reason at all for the burning. It ruined our lives and I think my family and I and the Carrolls should be repaid for our loss."

By this time I was getting heated. Senator Newlands stood and said, "Gentlemen, we have taken a lot of your time. If there are no further questions of Mrs. White, I would like to close with this statement. It is clear to me that an injustice has been done in a territory that is adjacent to my state. The White's property was either on the reservation or it was not. Either way they are due restitution for their losses and I will outline to all of you in a letter exactly the form I believe that restitution should take." He paused for a few seconds and then said, "Thank you, gentlemen," and turned and motioned Carl and I to follow.

Back in his office, Senator Newlands said, "Mrs. White, you handled that in just the right way. You helped your cause. I will write that letter to the committee this afternoon. Is there anything more you want to suggest?"

"Yes, Senator," I said. "More than anything, we want an apology from the Army. Then the money claims should be honored, too. But for the sake of my children, I want the Army to admit that they were wrong."

"Well, I don't know that we can get all that but I will make some suggestions and press for a positive answer for you, Mrs. White. Thank you for coming. My office will keep you advised."

The trip home was a happy one. I was encouraged by what had happened. The thought of both men spending those hours trying to help me satisfied a lot of past heartaches. I spent the hours studying the landscape. The railroad line branched north and for two days we were on the same rail line that Pat and I had taken from New York to Camp Russell at Cheyenne so long before.

There had been many events in our lives since and so many changes along this route. In 1872 there were not many settler's homes west of the Mississippi River. Now there were roads and houses in sight almost all the way. They were not all built of logs, either. The homes had painted boards for the outside and tin sheets or wood shingles on the roof. Windmills and fences could be seen almost every mile. Almost none had been there when we went to Cheyenne.

Upon arriving home, I wrote the children about the trip but cautioned against getting too optimistic. As I put it, "We musn't get too excited for we have been disappointed before. However, Senator Newlands and Carl Hayden have done everything they can to get something done for us. I think we have to accept whatever happens now. We'll wait again."

CHAPTER 37

RESTITUTION

This time the wait wasn't as long. Much to my surprise, just after I returned home from work one evening in May, there was a knock on the door. It was a Western Union messenger with a telegram for me. I had never seen one before.

```
Washington, D.C.                    MAY 16, 1905

Mrs. ANNA WHITE
157 WEST THIRD STREET
TEMPE, ARIZONA TERRITORY

   YOUR CLAIM APPROVED    STOP    ARMY  WILL
PROVIDE RESTITUTION AT YOUR RANCH SITE ON
DATE OF OCTOBER 18, 1905    STOP    PLEASE
CONFIRM BY WIRE THAT YOU CAN ATTEND THIS
DATE   STOP
                  CONGRATULATIONS
         SENATOR   FRANCIS G. NEWLANDS
```

My joy was so complete that I uttered a yell that startled the Western Union boy as he was starting to ride away on his bicycle. "Is everything alright, ma'am?" he called to me.

"Oh yes," I yelled back. "Everything's just fine. Thank you! Thank you!"

Chapter 38

THE CEREMONY

After receiving the telegram I wrote the children immediately, asking them to be here on October 18th. The Carrolls came from Ohio and stayed with me. The others stayed with school friends or at the Tempe Hotel. It was glorious—a time of rejoicing for us all, though we weren't sure what to expect.

Carl Hayden came to our house first on the morning of the 18th. With him were an Army captain and two corporals. Carl didn't tell me what was going to happen but he said he thought we would be pleased.

What a caravan we were as we went out the old wagon road! Three wagons and four buggies. Six of us had horses to ride and the three soldiers were also mounted. We rode up along the Salt, past the old Maryville ruins until we were almost to Red Mountain. Then we turned up the old canyon road past McDowell, which was now full of activity again. Yavapai huts and a trading post were in existence where the Army barracks and stables had been located. It was now the Ft. McDowell Indian Reservation.

The Carrolls and I rode in one buggy and talked over old times. They were now farming in Ohio and almost ready to buy some of their own land. They didn't expect to be involved in any settlement but made the trip after I told them what the telegram said. They wanted to see all of the children and visit with me again.

Carl had arranged a picnic lunch for the entire group and brought it along in his buggy. As we approched the north end of the new Indian reservation we stopped along the river and ate. At this point we had a chance to get to know Captain Gregg and the two corporals who were with him. One had a flag wrapped tightly around a staff and the other was a bugler.

I remember that Willie asked the captain what they were going to do. He smiled and said, "Well, young man, we have a little ceremony to perform and then we'll be on our way back to Fort Whipple."

"You came down all the way from Fort Whipple?" I asked.

"Yes, ma'am. Those were our orders from Army headquarters in Washington."

As we ate, we enjoyed seeing the hundreds of birds of many species that were present along the river. We must have seen a dozen of the great blue herons that nest in the big cottonwoods along the river. They are such huge, graceful birds. Kate and John had small children by then and none of them had seen how the herons stalk along the shore searching for minnows to eat. They would stand for so long on one leg and so still that it seemed they were frozen. Then, quicker than the eye could follow, they would thrust their huge bill in the water to grab a small fish.

Even the two Army corporals joined the younger children in the fun of throwing rocks in the river and watching the birds. As for me, I was so anxious to see what was going to happen that I could barely wait. The Carrolls also felt that way. We knew that the ceremony was to be where our house had been. As we finished eating, the Carrolls walked on over to where their house had been burned. They wanted a few minutes alone with their memories which I could understand.

We rode on up to our ranch site, where the Carrolls joined us. Carl suggested that we all stand or sit on the foundation rocks that were still scattered around where the house had been.

After we had settled, Captain Gregg took a rolled-up document from his saddlebag and nodded to the bugler. He played a stirring call that I remembered hearing before. I think it was the "call-to-arms" signal the Army used to tell the troops to move out. As the bugler played, the flag-bearer unfurled his flag and stood at attention with the flagstaff at a 45-degree angle, and pointed toward the captain who began to read as the bugle call ended:

Be it hereby determined that;

The United States Army, in recognition of their error in burning the houses of Mr. and Mrs. Patrick White and Mr. and Mrs. James Carroll in August of 1880, do hereby acknowledge the damage that was done to the White and Carroll properties and present a check in the amount of $45,000 to Mrs. Anna White and a check in the amount of $5,000 to Mr. and Mrs. James Carroll.

Furthermore, the United States Army apologizes for the unnecessary hardship and sorrow caused to the Whites, the Carrolls and their families.

This presentation to be made at the site of the former White Ranch, five and one-half miles north of the old Fort McDowell Military Reservation flagpole, October 18, 1905

Respectfully Yours,
General Adna Romanza Chaffee
Chief of Staff, United States Army
Washington, D.C.

As Captain Gregg read the dollar amounts of the checks we were to receive, an immense sense of gratification swept over me. Tears came to my eyes as Kate, Josie and I embraced. Nothing was said for we were hanging on his every word, wanting this moment to last a lifetime. The captain slowed down and emphasized every word when he came to the part about the apology and the hardship caused. That was the most rewarding of all. That's what I wanted to hear and what I wanted my family to hear.

When the captain read the name of the person who signed the document, I gasped. Carl was watching me closely with a smile on his face. Josie and I stared at each other in disbelief. How could it be?

As he finished reading the official presentation, he very carefully said, "General Chaffee sends his personal regrets and his wishes that this will erase some of the bad memories."

We dared not speak for the bugler was now playing again. It was "retreat" a cadence that they used to play at the forts as the flag was being taken down at sunset.

Then the flagbearer folded the American flag and presented it to me as Captain Gregg gave each of us our checks and copies of the official document. He then said, "The ceremony is over folks, we will be returning now to Ft. Whipple." As he looked at me, he said, "Good day, ma'am." After handshakes around with the adults, the three men rode off toward the Stoneman Military Road.

As Carl watched, our family fell into each other's arms with joy. Josie said "At last, Annie, you got what you wanted." All the children were celebrating. I know they will never forget that moment—and neither will I.

I turned to Carl and asked, "How can it be that Captain Chaffee signed that?"

"Mrs. White, you'll notice it's not "Captain" anymore. He's now a general—the top man in the whole Army—the Chief of Staff. As you may remember he was a decorated hero of the Civil War and he got many more medals after he was here."

"But why would he be the one who signed this apology?"

By this time all the children and the Carrolls were listening to our conversation.

"That was another surprise from Senator Newlands. When he saw how solid your claim was and how you had been mistreated, he decided to pursue your case right to the top. As it turned out, he and General Chaffee became close friends after the Spanish-American War when the

General was promoted to Washington. He couldn't imagine General Chaffee doing anything like this"

"Did he admit it?"

"He remembered it, Mrs. White. He knew that Lieutenant Kearney and another officer disliked Mr. White for some reason. He also remembered that Lieutenant Kearney's wife heard from some influential man out East that wanted Mr. White to be punished."

"But Pat wasn't even in the Army at that time."

"We know that, and that made the Senator follow up even harder for he felt that there was no excuse for what they did, no matter what Mr. White might have said in his letter."

"How did he get Chaffee to agree to sign this?"

"General Chaffee admitted that he was tired of hearing his two top officers complaining about your husband and just told them to do whatever they thought was best. He never imagined that they would resort to such drastic action."

"So he knew it wasn't right all along," I said.

"Perhaps, but we can't be sure. You will remember that he was just coming in from a hard time at San Carlos and only two weeks after the burning, he was transferred out to pursue Geronimo in Southeast Arizona. In two months, he was transferred again—out of Arizona. It's not surprising that he never heard of it again until Senator Newlands brought the whole matter to his attention."

James Carroll spoke to say, "I guess he and the Army are trying to put it right now. Annie, thank you for staying with this and Mr. Hayden, please thank Senator Newlands for Mrs. Carroll and myself."

I heard myself saying, "Oh, Carl, how can I ever thank you enough! You have been so very good to help us. Our family blesses you, my dear man, and please thank the senator from the bottom of our hearts!"

Carl beamed and shook hands all around. Then he said, "I'll be heading back to town now. In case you want to stay awhile, that's fine. You need not go with me."

I gathered all the family around me while the Carrolls walked back to the ruins of their house for one last look. "My dears, after all this time, it's their way of saying that we weren't wrong. Remember this day. It's a gift from your father and me to all of you."

EPILOGUE

This is a story based on fact. Annie Dowling and Patrick White *were* born in County Kerry, Ireland. They *did* meet for the first time in New York City. Patrick *was* at Ft. Bliss, Texas, in South Carolina, at Libby Prison and at Fort Russell, Wyoming. Their first child *was* lost as described. Calamity Jane *was* the Godmother of their son, Edward.

Pat *was* a wheelwright and Annie a hospital matron, laundress and seamstress. They *were* friends of the Summerhayes family. The Whites *did* supply milk, butter, eggs and grain to Ft. McDowell and *did* purchase Elisha Reavis' water rights. They *did* claim 1000 miner's inches of water from the Verde. They *did* use the prehistoric Hohokam canals.

A rancher's wife *was* killed and Pat *did* write a letter to an Eastern editor. Their house *was* burned and their livestock scattered by the Army. After the burning Pat *did* get lost in the desert and was never "right" again.

Annie White *was* known as the "Woman With the Black Bag" in Washington as she tirelessly fought for her rights.

Adna Romanza Chaffee, the commander of Ft. McDowell at the time of the burning, *was* a military hero and was the Army Chief of Staff from 1904 to 1906.

Carl Hayden of Arizona and Francis Newlands of Nevada *did* hold the offices named. Hayden represented Arizona in Congress for 57 years.

White's Home Ranch in Ruins: *The author at the site of the ranch house as it looks in late 1999.* Bob Fedden

Anna White died in May 1919 and is buried in Greenwood Cemetery in Phoenix, Arizona.

This story is based on the above facts, and many others as documented by family records provided by John Micek, great-grandson of Patrick and Annie. Other events and locations have been created by the author to develop an integral narrative.

The Whites are a fitting representation of the hundreds of thousands of hardy souls who fought in the Civil War and who, as pioneers, worked, suffered and persevered to cause the development of the Western United States.